GOOD HANDS

KELLY JAMIESON

This book is a work of fiction. The names, characters, places, and incidents are products of the writer's imagination or have been used fictitiously and are not to be construed as real. Any resemblance to persons, living or dead, actual events, locale or organizations is entirely coincidental.

Good Hands © 2021 by Kelly Jamieson
Cover by Dar Albert, Wicked Smart Designs
Editing by Kristi Yanta

BRANDON

"You must be the guy who's going to buy me a drink."

I turn to see a pretty blonde smiling at me. I smile lazily back at her. Hell yeah, I'll buy her a drink. I'll buy her a drink all night long. "Cute line."

"Thanks." Her smile broadens. "I have lots."

I laugh. "You go around getting guys to buy you drinks a lot?"

"Only the ones who remind me of a magnet."

I tilt my head and lift an eyebrow.

"You remind me of a magnet because you're attracting me to you."

I laugh again. "Nice. What would you like to drink?"

"I'd love another Ariba." She holds up an empty glass, which I take from her.

"When in Aruba," I say. "I'll be right back, beautiful."

I head to the bar. My friends and I are hanging at this spot on the beach in Oranjested, having just finished dinner. We're here in Aruba for a week of sun, sand, and sex. At least, I'm *hoping* for the sex. As one of only two single guys with the group, that wasn't a given. On the other hand, women usually find me attractive…and tonight is now looking promising.

Women approach me all the time, so this isn't unusual, but her cheeky lines and saucy attitude, not to mention her flirty smile, are damn appealing. I mentally rub my hands together as I order the cocktail and another beer for myself. Then I cross the wooden deck and step back onto the sand where she's waiting for me.

The sun has set, but the air is still warm and sultry. White lights twinkle all around us and the sound of ocean waves is a faint backdrop to the music and voices here at the beachside bar. It's tropical and magical and seductive.

I hand her the drink.

"Thank you. I'm Lola."

"Hi, Lola. Nice to meet you. I'm Brandon."

She sips her fruit-garnished drink through the straw, her shoulder length pale hair stirring in the breeze off the ocean. The lights strung above us illuminate her face, and yeah, she's beautiful, with amazing, clear turquoise eyes. Her loose, button-down white shirt has the cuffs folded back, and is partially tucked into cut-off denim shorts that leave a sweet length of tanned leg visible. The combination of pale hair, light eyes, and tanned skin is incredibly sexy.

She's checking me out, too. Fair. *Check away, Lola.*

"So you're here on vacation, too?"

"Yep. With some friends." I wave a hand in the general direction of the group, gathered around a picnic table on the sand. Lola's part of another group we met up with, discovering some of them are also from New York. "Are you from New York, too?"

"Yep."

"Awesome. How long are you here for?"

"Tonight's our last night," she says with a regretful sigh.

"Damn."

"I know, right? I love it here."

"She says that now." A woman passing by pauses to interject. "We had to drag her by her hair to get her here."

Lola shakes her head and huffs. "Sure, Kaylee."

The woman grins and continues on her path toward the bar.

I smile. "Your friend?"

"Cousin. And best friend."

"Why didn't you want to come to Aruba?"

"I did…but I'm super busy at work and taking a vacation is hard." She looks briefly troubled, then shrugs. "But I did it and it's been super fun."

"Is it your first time in Aruba?"

"Yeah. How about you?"

"Same. Tell me some things I should make sure to do while I'm here."

We start chatting about the activities Lola and her friends have done—snorkeling, sailing, horseback riding. "And we did the cave jump thing," she says. "That was fun!"

"What is that?"

She describes driving ATVs along the coast, seeing the rock formations and caves, and jumping into a natural pool.

"I'll have to check with our cruise director to see if that's part of our itinerary," I say.

She blinks. "You're on a cruise?"

"I'm kidding. We call my friend Nadia the cruise director because she likes to plan everything." I grin. "Tomorrow we're going snorkeling."

"Oh, that sounds amazing. One night we did a bar hopping tour on a party bus. That was fun, too."

Sipping our drinks, we drift away from the group and our conversation turns more personal. "What do you do for a living, Lola?"

"I'm a change manager." She makes a face. "I know it doesn't sound exciting, but I love it."

"Well, that's what's important. But you have to tell me what a change manager does. I assume you manage change."

She laughs. "You got it! I work for Synoptic Global Services."

I'm sure I look blank, but I nod.

"We're an international insurance consultancy. We provide independent insurance due diligence, insurance program review, and financial solutions to the mergers and acquisitions business."

"Ah. That explains it." I'm still totally lost.

"Basically, my job is helping the client manage the changes that the merger or acquisition will bring about. Working with the people of the organization to prepare them and help them adjust."

"I assume you're talking about really big businesses."

"Yeah." She nods. "Right now, my job is working on a project for one of our clients who just bought another company. I work with our project manager and the client's senior leadership to manage the changes that will result from the new programs. I make sure everyone's engaged and on board. I deal with resistance to change and handle communications. I also do training for management and supervisors so they can do the same with their teams." She shrugs. "There's more, but that's basically it."

"Holy shit. That sounds impressive."

"Eh. Most people's eyes glaze over when I talk about it. Thank you for listening." She tilts her head, eyes shining. "I love my job. I just wish..."

"What?"

"Well, this particular job is a term. A one-year contract. I've been doing contract work with Synoptic for eight years." She sighs. "It would be nice if they'd actually hire me."

"Ah."

"My boss, the VP of our division, is retiring this summer. I'm really hoping if I do well with this project they'll consider me for his position." She holds up two crossed fingers and a big toothy smile.

"Vice president. That would be also impressive."

She gives her shoulders a little shimmy. "I've been working toward that my whole career."

"Well, you sound like superwoman. I'm sure you've got this in the bag."

"Superwoman." She laughs. "Okay. Thanks for the vote of confidence."

I watch her pretty lips close on her straw and feel a stirring in my southern region. Her lips are sexy, but her intelligence and confidence are even hotter.

"I just play a game for a living," I say.

"What?"

"I play hockey."

"Ohhhh." Her eyes widen. She slides her gaze over to my friends, then back to me. "Ohhhhh."

I laugh. "You didn't know? We all play for the Bears."

"I didn't realize." She makes a face. "Sorry."

"Don't apologize. I don't mind not being recognized. Really."

"Are you a hockey superstar?"

"Ha. No. But lots of people know who I am. Not here, though. And actually it's easier in New York."

"Compared to…?"

"I played a couple of years in Montreal. You can't hide from anyone in that city. They're hockey crazy." I smile. "It's cool, if a little terrifying."

"Hockey's pretty popular in New York."

"Yeah, it is. We're gearing up for a playoff run after this break."

"You'll be all rested up and raring to go."

I'm raring to go all right. The way she looks at me, the way she listens to everything I say, attentive and curious, is a huge fucking turn on.

We talk about New York. She's lived there her whole life. She's cautiously vague about where she lives, saying only Hudson Yard, which isn't that far from me in Lincoln Square. I don't mind that she's careful; women have to be.

"It's a tiny condo," she says. "A studio. But I had a bad experience living with a crazy roommate and I wanted to live alone."

"Yeah, me too. I did the roommate thing for a few years when I started playing, and when I moved here. I'm too old for that now."

"Ha. How old are you?"

"Almost thirty."

"Hey, me too. My birthday's in September."

I grin. "So is mine. What day?"

"September twelfth."

"I'm the eleventh!" I laugh. "I'm a whole day older than you."

"I've always liked older men." She flutters her eyelashes at me.

Our eyes keep meeting and heat pulses between us. The sound of the ocean waves on the nearby sand are a rhythmic push-pull that mirrors the pulsations around us and my quickening heartbeat. The sultry tropical breeze brushes over us and I feel like it's her fingers on my skin. I want her fingers on my skin. Or *my* fingers on *her* skin. That would work, too.

The breeze teases the opening of her shirt, giving me a glimpse of pink lace. Jesus.

"Yeah?" I reach out to push a strand of hair off her face. "You're fucking gorgeous."

Her gaze hangs on mine, her lips curved. "Thank you. Did I mention that I find you attractive, too?"

"Like a magnet," I say, studying her face, the small, slightly pointy chin, narrow nose, high cheekbones.

She laughs softly, shifting closer to me in the shadows, the lights of the bar now behind us. "Yeah. A really strong magnet."

Her scent reaches my nose—a combination of coconut and tropical flowers and sunshine. And warm woman. Heady.

"Magnets can also be repulsive," I murmur, my nose nearing her hair.

"You are definitely not repulsive."

"Good to know." I pause, our noses almost touching, our eyes heavy lidded. Our breath mingles.

"Just so you know, my lips won't kiss themselves," she whispers.

I choke on a laugh and briefly rest my forehead against hers. "Thanks." And I brush my mouth over hers.

Her lips are as soft as they look. I kiss her softly again, slow and lingering, then I open my mouth and lick over her lower lip.

She makes a soft noise in her throat and I'm instantly hard as a goddamn hockey puck. Opening to me, her tongue slides against mine. She tastes as sweet as she looks—agave and fruit—with the spice of island rum.

Jesus. I could kiss her forever.

Her hand lands on my waist, first gentle, then fingers tightening as she sighs into my mouth.

"Oh yeah," I whisper, licking again. I turn her and press her back against the wooden railing we're standing next to, and she softens against me. I groan at the pleasure of it, my veins running hot. I cup the back of her head and deepen the kiss even more, tongues and lips gliding, lips nipping and sucking. We're both making needy sounds of pleasure and yearning as heat builds inside me, massing in my groin.

We're away from the group, but it's still a public place. I lift my head and flick a sideways glance at my friends. A bust of laughter fills the night air. Nobody's paying any attention to us.

I peer down into eyes like the ocean, her pupils huge. "Wow."

"Yeah. Wow." Her fingers grip my shirt and her long eyelashes flutter rapidly. "You know what?"

"What?"

"I think I could fall madly in bed with you."

Amusement warms my blood even more but I'm too aroused to laugh. "Your place or mine?"

"Um…where are you staying?"

We exchange resort names.

"Mine's closer," she says. "We can walk. Let's go."

"This way." I lead her through the soft sand in the opposite direction of our friends, around the bar and onto the boulevard. This is perfect. She's gorgeous, sexy, funny, and she's leaving tomorrow. A perfect one-night stand.

2

LOLA

I spotted him the moment he and his friends arrived at the beach bar. He's good looking, sure, tall and muscled, light brown hair that looks thick and soft, a strong jaw. But there's more than that. There's something about him—he has a kind of glamor, with a wide, charming smile, and dancing eyes. I watched him talk to his friends, enjoying the way he leaned in to listen to what they said, how he threw his head back to laugh with genuine enjoyment, the way he clapped a hand onto a friend's shoulder.

Kaylee caught me watching him. She followed my gaze over the sand. "Which one?"

"Him. The good looking one."

"Um. They're all good looking."

"The guy in the crazy shirt." He's wearing a loose shirt with bright pink flamingos and yellow pineapples on a turquoise background.

"Ah. Yes, I see the appeal. He doesn't seem to be with anyone."

"I don't think so." I smiled.

"It's your last night." She nudged me. "Last chance for hot vacation sex."

Kaylee, Isla, and Sadie have been teasing me about hot vacation sex since we got here. Up until tonight, I haven't indulged. I haven't met anyone I was attracted to enough to sleep with. But now...

I'm leaving with Brandon.

I can't explain the attraction, but wow, it's sizzling hot. Even more so after talking to him for a while.

I don't have time for dating or relationships, much to the disappointment of my parents, but I'm not opposed to the occasional hook up. Here in Aruba it feels perfect and right and hot.

"Which hotel is yours?" Brandon asks as we walk.

"The Pacifica. Right there." I point. We can see the big white building already.

"Nice."

"It's lovely."

We approach the front entrance, the trunks of palm trees on either side of us wrapped with white lights. We enter the lobby and I pause. "Can you show me your drivers' license?"

"What?" He gives me a blank look.

"I just want to take a picture of it and send it to my friend. Then if they find my body in the morning they'll know who to start with." I give him a cheeky grin because even though I'm dead serious, I also don't want to ruin the mood.

Laughing, he pulls out his wallet and shows me the license. I snap a pic and send it to Kaylee, then lead the way down the hall on our right to a bank of elevators. We ride up to the sixth floor, then I let us into the room I'm sharing with Kaylee.

It's nearly dark, with just a lamp in the corner on. Sliding doors lead onto a balcony and I walk over and open the doors. "At night you can't see as much of the view," I say. "But the ocean is there, past the trees. It's so beautiful."

Swaying palm trees are silhouetted against the sky and the turquoise glow of the pool can be seen through them.

"You're beautiful." He moves closer and sets his hands on my waist. "Your eyes are just like the Caribbean."

"Thank you." I gaze up at him, enjoying the feel of his big hands on me, firm and steady. I slide my hands up his chest and onto his shoulders. Then I trace an eyebrow. "I like your eyes, too." They're a mossy green with tiny flecks of amber. "And your eyebrows."

His lips quirk. "Thank you."

I can't stop my own smile. I brush my fingertips over the layer of stubble on his jaw. "Kiss me again. You're a good kisser."

"I can definitely do that." He bends his head and his mouth meets mine.

He undid me with his kisses earlier, and he's doing it again. His mouth is perfect—firm, warm, not too wet, not too aggressive. Bold, confident, but also gentle and generous. Am I rhapsodizing over this man's mouth?

Yes. Yes, I am.

And then I stop thinking, because I'm lost in the feel of it all, his hands moving over me, his tongue in my mouth, his hard body against mine. I love how he smells, so clean and crisp and warm, and he tastes slightly bitter, like hops.

I was melting earlier and I am again now, the sheer physical heat of him sliding through me, making me wet. My heart races and my breath catches, and my hips cant longingly toward him. I'm aching for him.

It's like we're already fucking, his tongue sliding in and out, slowly sucking on mine, and I'm drowning, floating, hanging onto his shoulders so I don't drift away. He turns me like he did on the beach, pushing me up against the wall with his big body, which oh my God, I want to see naked. He presses into me and I'm dissolving.

I groan into his mouth and I feel him smile. His mouth moves over my jaw, laying a trail of soft kisses in front of my ear, then down the side of my neck. My head falls to the side, eyes closed, my skin hot everywhere.

He sucks so gently then licks me, sliding his tongue over my collarbone. He inhales like he's smelling me, and I smile too at that because I know the feeling—I'd like to inhale him endlessly, taking his scent inside me, letting it turn me on.

This is crazy, *so* crazy, so intoxicating, so erotic.

"You feel amazing," he murmurs, his fingers on a button of my shirt. I don't stop him and in a moment he tugs the white cotton free of my shorts and tenderly parts it. He studies me in the dim light, tracing a finger over the scalloped edge of my lace bralette. "Pretty."

I make a little moany noise and his fingers slip under the edge of the lace, closer to my nipple but not touching it. My nipples are already hard, and they pull even tighter, my breasts swelling with need.

Brandon's breathing is ragged. Heat radiates off his body and he's pressing an impressive erection against me. I rub against it and he groans, and I love how turned on he is. By *me*. He wants *me*. A thrill runs through me, heightening my own arousal.

I run my hands through his thick hair, tugging gently on the longer strands on top, and he shudders.

"Jesus, Lola." His voice is thick.

His hands on me are big and strong, his body powerful, and yet I feel safe. He presses a kiss between my breasts, a hand sliding down over my hip to my ass. He gives me a firm squeeze that makes me gasp, then slips his hand to my thigh and lifts it. With my leg against his hip, I can feel his hard on right against my pussy, and God, it feels so good.

He pushes my shirt back over my shoulders and I wriggle to get free of it. Then he picks me up, both hands under my butt, and starts walking farther into the room.

"You're just a little thing," he murmurs. "A sexy little thing."

"Oh God. I'm dying, Brandon."

"Good." He kisses my mouth and then we both fall onto the bed. He rolls me under him and I part my legs accommodatingly as we make out with long, wet, consuming kisses. Our hands roam everywhere. I find bare skin under his T-shirt, warm and sleek. He caresses my arms and shoulders and then finally cups my breast. I push into his palm with embarrassing neediness.

"Sweet," he whispers. "Perfect."

"You have something, right? Protection?"

"Yeah." He shifts, tugging down my bralette and kissing the top of my breast. My breath stalls and then he kisses my nipple and gently tugs it into his mouth.

"Oh God!" Sensation pulls from my nipple to my womb, and my body jolts with pleasure.

"Like that?"

"Love that. More. Please."

He smiles and sucks on me again, harder, and I'm blissed out. I lose my mind as he plays with my tits, sucking, squeezing, delicately pinching both nipples at the same time.

"Still aching?" he murmurs.

"Oh yeah."

"Want me to do something about that?"

"I do." I groan, my hips lifting.

"Let's get you out of these sexy little shorts." He flicks open the button, tugs the zipper, then works the denim over my hips. I bend and lift my legs to help him and he draws them down over my calves and feet. He's left on my panties and he covers the front of them with his palm and rubs a tiny circle.

The friction is exciting, electrifying. Not quite enough. My clit pulses and aches and my body burns for more.

"You're wet," he says.

"I know." I bite my lip. "I was wet back at the beach when we were kissing."

"I was hard." He bends and presses a soft, open-mouthed kiss to my lower belly.

"You're still dressed."

He smiles and rises onto his knees, unbuttoning his crazy shirt. I stare at his torso, a goddamn work of art—sculpted muscles, smooth skin, ridged abs. He's perfect. I stretch out a hand to touch him. His abs twitch when I drag my fingertips over them.

He pulls out a condom and tosses it onto the bed, then rolls over to divest himself of his jeans. I watch in helpless fascination. It's like my own private porn movie, he's just so beautiful, his leg muscles heavy, his hips lean and carved. And when he faces me...sweet Jesus, his cock is amazing, lifting proudly, thick and hard.

I swallow. "Dear God," I choke out.

He strokes himself and my inner muscles clench hard on a bite of arousal. I whimper.

"Let's see if you're ready." He hooks his fingers into my thong and slides it off me, too. Then he's the one staring. He parts my legs with his hands on my inner thighs, his lips separated, eyes dark and heavy lidded. "Beautiful. Look at you." He traces a finger through my slit. "Ready. Wet. Perfect."

Heat burns over my skin. His gaze moves from between my legs up over my stomach and breasts, then to my face. Our eyes meet and desire simmers low inside me.

I reach for him. "Fuck me."

3

BRANDON

I'm not sure if I'm still alive. I just came so hard I think I blacked out. I slowly become aware that I'm breathing. And yeah, my heart is thudding, so that's a good sign. "Jesus Christ."

"I know." Lola gives a soft, satisfied sigh next to me in the bed. "Wow."

"That was good, huh?"

"Freakin' phenomenal."

"Gretzky isn't the only great one."

After a startled beat, she starts laughing. And so do I. We roll toward each other, still limp and dazed, but giggling like teenagers. Her body shakes with laughter in my arms, her face pressed to my neck.

This is fun.

Not only is she hot as fuck, I like her.

"You're not the only one with lines," I say. "Do you play hockey? 'Cause I wouldn't mind poke-checking you."

"Oh my God." She laughs more. "That's terrible."

"Hockey players have good hands." I hold up my hands and wiggle them. "In fact, I'm known for my good hands."

"You're going to have to prove that to me."

"Ah. A challenge. I'm up for that." I glance meaningfully toward my groin.

"Already?"

"Oh yeah. Here's another hockey line...I promise I'm good for more than just a one-timer. I even have another condom."

"I guess athletes do have good stamina."

"Damn right. I'll be right back." I slide out of bed and hit the bathroom to ditch the rubber. Climbing back onto the bed with her feels good. "Okay, I might need a couple more minutes. You wore me out, superwoman."

"Oh, come on. That only took, like, two minutes."

"Hey!"

"I'm not complaining! I came fast, too."

"Yeah, you did." I loved making her come so hard, so fast. I slip my arm under her shoulders and pull her close. Soft. Warm. Skin like velvet and hair like silk. And she still smells so damn good. This is heaven, here in this luxurious hotel room bed. "Why do you think hotel sex is so hot?"

"You think it's the hotel room?"

I choke-laugh. "No, that's not what I mean. But you have to admit there's something about hotel sex..."

"Yeah. I don't know...maybe it feels...illicit. Or hedonistic, when you're in a posh room like this."

"Yeah. And kind of...private. Separate from the rest of the world."

"Yes! Like it's not real life and you don't have to worry about buying groceries and cleaning up and whether you forgot to send that email." She kisses my shoulder. "You can just enjoy the experience."

"Mmm. I'm definitely enjoying it."

"Me too." She shifts in the bed and kisses my chest. "How many condoms do you have?"

"Only one more."

"That's okay. I have some." She kisses her way lower, grazing my nipple with her teeth, heat jolting through me. My dick stirs, still half hard.

"Good, good." Anticipation heats my blood as she heads south, kissing my abs, pushing the covers back then taking my cock in her hands. "Christ…"

"This is beautiful." She admires me and my heart damn near bursts out of my chest, blood rushing to my groin, thickening my dick. "Oh yeah." She strokes up and down.

Sensation surges through me, my vision darkening. "Suck me, Lo."

She rubs the head over her bottom lip, her lips parted. My skin prickles everywhere until it's too hot, too tight. I lift my hips, and when she opens her mouth and closes it over me, a ragged groan tears from my lips. My eyes fall closed as white-hot sparks whip through my veins. "Jesus."

Her little tongue explores the head of my cock while her lips wrap around it and she sucks greedily. I can't stop from thrusting deeper into her mouth, but then force myself to stop. *Easy, boy.* I open my eyes, eager to see the visual, to see her pretty lips on my swollen dick. I reach shaky hands out to draw her hair back from her face, loving the look of rapture. At that moment she looks up at me, lashes framing her luminous eyes like starbursts, and I feel like I just got slammed into the boards, all my breath leaving me.

My balls grow tighter at the root of my cock, her mouth consuming me, sensation building at the base of my spine. "Sweet Christ." I watch her suck me with a look of such intense pleasure on her face I almost blow.

Her hands and mouth work in tandem, stroking and sucking me as pleasure builds. My thighs quake, my ass clenches, and my balls draw up tight, tension rippling up my spine.

"Lola…I'm coming…" I want to give her a chance to stop if she wants. I'm past stopping now. She doesn't move, though, drawing on my cock with hungry pulls of her mouth and my orgasm slams into me, pleasure pumping through my veins.

She rests her cheek on my thigh, breathing fast. Once again, I'm not sure if *I'm* breathing. I love blow jobs, but that was outstanding. She loved every minute of it too, and that made it extra hot.

Her hand squeezes my quadriceps and she murmurs, "Your thighs are amazing."

"Thick."

She huffs a little laugh. "Yeah. I like it."

"The thicker the thighs the sweeter the prize."

She chokes. "I see that."

I laugh.

"I want to squeeze your butt, too."

I smile, my eyes closed. "What a coincidence. I'd like to squeeze yours."

She rises up on her knees, stretches, and I have to crack my eyes open to watch. She's lithe and slender and toned.

"Holy shit," I croak. "Your tan lines…" A tiny pale bikini is outlined on her golden skin.

"I have 'em," she agrees, lying down beside me again.

"I want to see that bikini. I mean, I want to see you in that bikini. What the fuck am I saying? Seeing you *out* of the bikini is the best."

She laughs.

I sit up and move between her legs, parting them. "This pretty pussy needs some attention."

"Not gonna argue with that." She settles herself into the mattress as I study her. Again, perfect. Beautiful. Pink, plump lips are the softest skin I've ever touched—like rose petals. She bites her lip as I stroke her there, first with my fingertips, then cupping her with my palm. She throbs warmly against me.

"I want to give you a good tongue fucking," I say hoarsely.

"Oh God." She shudders.

I caress her inner thighs, studying her, then exploring her with my fingers. I slick her moisture all around, parting her, exposing her clit. I gently circle it and she twitches and moans.

"So sensitive."

I rub my whole palm over her pussy, slowly sliding up and down. The sight of my big hand between her legs, smoothing over glistening pink flesh, is so erotic, I'm burning up.

She groans.

I use my fingers again, pinching her plump tissues, squeezing her clit so gently. Her every exhale comes out as a soft grunt.

"Need to taste you." I shift my weight and lean forward to press my face right there. It's fucking heaven, sweet and warm. I kiss her over and over, soft suckling kisses. I don't care about the filthy noises I'm making, slurping and sucking.

Her body trembles, her fingers sliding into my hair and tugging. I smile.

I use my fingers to hold her open and probe with my tongue, my nose pressed against her mound. Her taste is seductive, the feel of her voluptuous.

"Brandon."

"Hmmm."

She shivers. "I love this."

"Me too. Damn. I could stay here all night."

Face between her thighs, I caress her hip and ass and push her leg higher. She rests her foot on my shoulder and lifts her hips to my mouth. I lick her again, all over, in long wet strokes. Her noises get louder, her fingers tightening in my hair.

"I'm coming," she gasps. "There..."

I focus on her clit, lashing it with my tongue, and she comes apart in long, rolling shudders, crying out. I drink it all in, loving it, then I slowly rub my hand all over her wet pussy in soothing strokes as she recuperates.

"God," she says between pants. "That was intense. Sorry if I yanked your hair out."

I smile and move up next to her. "I can spare a few strands."

"Too bad you're leaving tomorrow," I say lazily, a while later. "We could have had a lot of fun."

"It's probably for the best. But this was a fantastic way to end my vacation." She stretches sensuously beneath the covers.

"Yeah, you're right." Although I do feel a twinge of regret that we can't spend the rest of my vacation fucking. "So, what do you do for fun in New York?"

"Well, I work a lot."

"You must do something else." I tickle my fingers over her belly and she shivers.

"Okay, yeah. Lately I've been taking flower arranging classes."

"Huh."

"I love plants and flowers. I have a ton of plants. Taking care of them is very relaxing."

"Cool."

"And I belong to the Professional Women's Networking Association. I'm secretary this year."

I frown. "You call that a hobby? That sounds more like work."

She purses her lips. "You're right. It is. But it's fun, too. I've made friends there. What do you do to relax?"

The word "fuck" comes immediately to mind. As cool as Lola is, that doesn't seem appropriate when we're in bed together. "I don't have that much time during the season. I work out a lot. And I like hanging out with the guys, playing pool, or video games. When I go home in the summer I actually like to garden, too."

"Really? Where's home?"

"I'm from Grand Rapids. I have a place on Lake Michigan where I spend my summers."

"Nice."

"I like all kinds of sports. In the summer, I bike on the trails around the lake. Golf. Swim."

"Did you play other sports besides hockey as a kid?"

"Yeah. I played everything. Baseball. Basketball. Even football. But hockey was what I really loved."

She gazes at me. "You have to be dedicated to play professional sports."

"Eh. I guess. It's a game. It's fun."

Her eyes flicker as she nods.

"You sound like you're pretty dedicated to your job."

"I am." Her soft mouth tightens.

"You look scary." I smile and keep my tone teasing.

"I *am* scary." She flicks hair back off her shoulder. "Anyone who works for me better be on top of their game."

"Stop. You're turning me on again."

She laughs, the tension easing from her face. "You want to be bossed around?"

"Usually I like to do the bossing, but I'm not opposed to switching things up."

Our eyes meet in shared humor and heat.

And she jumps me, straddling me and pushing me flat on my back.

I grin. "Sticks and stones may break my bones, but girl on top excites me."

"Don't make me laugh. I'm trying to be dominant."

"Keep trying, little girl."

"Oooh now you're in trouble."

I bite back a smile. She's a feisty little thing but the only way she can dominate me physically is if I let her.

So I do.

4

LOLA

I'm back in the real world after my magical beach vacation in Aruba. After two days back at the office, it felt like I'd never had that damn vacation. I really do work a lot.

Kaylee was right. I needed a break. I was antsy the first couple of days but then I gave in to the indulgence of spending days lying poolside or on the beach, soaking up sun and rum. I love my friends and we had so much fun.

Now, three weeks later, my temples throb, my shoulders feel like rocks, and I've forgotten the bliss of sun, surf, and sand.

And sex. Okay, I haven't forgotten the sex.

That last night...meeting Brandon...taking him back to my room...and holy wow.

I can't stop thinking about him and his big, hard body. His charismatic smile and charming humor. His hands.

They're good, all right.

I may have to check out a Bears game or two. Just out of mild curiosity.

I sit in my office, looking out my twenty-ninth-floor window at the cityscape, instead of focusing on the training materials one of my team members revised. The February sky is gray, a few icy snowflakes falling from the slate-colored clouds.

It was only one night, and Brandon and I were on the same page about that. We didn't exchange phone numbers or addresses. We're both back in New York with no plans to ever see each other again.

Dammit.

No, no. I'm too busy for boyfriends, dating, relationships, whatever. I don't mind doing the horizontal greased-weasel tango from time to time. But...why do I have this feeling no other guy's ever going to measure up to Brandon?

That's just depressing.

I shake my head and return my gaze to my computer. We've used these training materials in the past but they needed to be updated and customized to our current client. I assigned this task to Zayn. Biting my lip, I spot a few things that could be better. I should give it back to him to fix...but it's faster to just do it myself, so I make a few minor changes.

There's more I want to get done before leaving tonight, but I have to get out of here. Tonight I'm receiving an award at a dinner held by the Professional Women's Networking Association. I'm proud of that, so I'm not going to miss it, no matter how much I have to do.

I check the time. I better get going. I need to make a stop in the ladies' room and touch up my face. My little black dress worked fine for the office with a jacket over it, but I can lose the jacket for the dinner and add the statement necklace I tucked into my bag this morning, a chunky gold piece.

I also need to pop some Advil. I don't think I can handle this dinner with the headache I've got going on right now.

Soon I'm out in the jagged canyon of Madison Avenue, dodging pedestrians heading home from work, skirting traffic that's blocking the crosswalk at 56th Street. I cross over to Fifth Avenue to hail a cab. One sails past me in the traffic, then another, and another. I pull the collar of my red wool coat higher as I sigh with frustration. At last, one pulls up to the curb. I jump in and give the driver the name of the upscale Midtown hotel I'm going to.

Finally I arrive and find the room where our function is being held, at the back of the busy bar.

"There she is!" Wendy greets me and we hug and air kiss. "The guest of honor."

"Hi!" Wendy and I have gotten to be friends through our work with the PWNA. She's a little older than me and does project management for a big pharmaceutical company.

"I haven't seen you since your trip. You still look tanned, you bitch."

I laugh. "My tan, like the memories of paradise, is fading fast."

"Was it wonderful?"

"So relaxing. I didn't realize how much I needed a break."

Someone places a glass of wine in my hand and I mingle and chat with other friends, accepting congratulations, catching up with news and talking a bit of business. My headache has dissipated somewhat and I manage to eat dinner, accept my award for outstanding contribution to the group, and make a short speech.

Whew.

It would be nice to have someone to share this experience with. My parents and Kaylee were happy for me when I told them about the award, but they're not here.

Oh well.

I'm proud of myself. I'm happy that at nearly thirty years old I can help mentor younger businesswomen and advocate for women in the business world.

After saying goodnights to all, I slip on my coat and pick up my leather tote. My Jimmy Choo heels sink into the carpet as I walk past the elegant bar, crowded with patrons.

"Lola?"

I stop, my head swinging around at the sound of my name.

It's Brandon.

I blink. What?

He's seated at the bar on a tall stool, dressed in an amazing maroon suit with a gorgeous blue tie.

That electric attraction punches through me.

"Brandon! Hi." I don't know how to greet him. Is this awkward?

"What are you doing here?" He flashes that wicked charming smile.

"I was at an awards dinner."

"Nice. Oh hey, this is my agent, Kevin Bozeman. Kevin, this is Lola McGrath."

I smile and shake hands with the man sitting next to him.

Kevin stands and pushes his wallet into his pocket. "Nice to meet you. I'm just heading up to my room."

Brandon pats the empty stool. "Have a drink with me?"

I should say no. But here I am, sliding onto the leather stool, giddy excitement fluttering in my stomach.

Brandon lifts a hand to signal the bartender. "What would you like?" he asks me.

"I'll have a Tom Collins."

He places the order and turns back to me. "I can't believe I ran into you like this." His smile and the attentiveness in his green eyes warm my insides.

I can't help but smile back. "I know."

"We had a game tonight." He picks up his glass. "My agent's in town and he's staying here so we met for a drink after." The faint tightening of his mouth tells me it might not have been a good meeting.

"I like the suit." I let my gaze wander over broad shoulders, the crisp dress shirt draping over a chest and abdomen that I know are hard and sculpted.

His face is quickly back to his usual careless smile. "Thanks. Game day."

"You have to wear a suit to games?"

"Yep. There's been talk of changing up the dress code, but it hasn't happened yet."

"What would you wear if you didn't have to wear a suit?"

"I'd still wear a suit."

I laugh. "Really?"

My drink arrives, the bartender setting it on a cocktail napkin. "Thank you," I say to him. I look back at Brandon.

"Really. I like nice clothes." He shrugs. "It makes me feel like a professional. Like I'm going to work. Which I am."

"Right." I pick up my drink and take a sip of the lemony cocktail. "I like that."

"Sweats and a T-shirt have their appeal. But not on game day."

Damn, he's gorgeous. I inwardly sigh with appreciation. "I bet you look good in sweats, too."

His eyes gleam. "Of course."

I laugh. "Cocky."

One shoulder lifts. "Maybe a little. You also look very professional." Now it's his turn to peruse me, his gaze wandering all the way down my fitted black sheathe dress to my bare calves and black stilettos, then back up. Warmth curls low inside me. "Different than Aruba in those sexy cut offs."

"Yeah, cut offs aren't appropriate attire for an awards dinner. Not to mention, it's February in Manhattan."

He lowers his voice to a velvet rasp. "Do you still have tan lines?"

My belly flip flops remembering him tracing my tan lines with his talented tongue. I smile. "Yes. But they've faded."

"Hmm. Mine, too."

"I didn't get to see your tan lines." I lift my drink to my lips. This is a dangerous, flirtatious conversation. I love it.

"I guess you'll have to take my word for it." He pauses, giving me an arch look. "Unless… you'd like to check them out now?"

Oh, I definitely would. A chance to lay eyes and hands on that magnificent body again? Yes, please! "I would," I say. "But…"

He cocks his head. "What?"

"I wouldn't want you to get the wrong idea. I don't have time for dating. Or relationships."

He smiles. "Perfect. Me either. I'm glad you put that out there. Because I wouldn't want to give you the wrong idea either."

Relief shimmers through me. I smile. "Okay, then."

He lifts a hand to signal the bartender. "Your place? I think it's closer."

He remembers that, too. "Okay."

He pays for my drink and leads me out of the bar with a light touch on the small of my back. It feels attentive, not controlling. I like it.

Holy shit, are we really doing this again?

5

BRANDON

We walk out onto Seventh Avenue into the darkness. The streets are shiny with the sleet that's been falling, reflecting all the neon and traffic lights. The damp chill wraps around us.

I can't believe I ran into Lola again. I've thought about her a lot since Aruba, which was a little bittersweet because we had so much fun that night—in fact, that was the last time I had sex—but I figured I'd never see her again. Which was the way I wanted it, but…

I smile at her. "How far is your place?"

"It's only a few blocks. We can walk."

"Are you sure?" I look at her spiky heels.

She grins and reaches into her big leather bag, pulling out a pair of sneakers. I grin too and offer my arm to hold onto as she makes a quick change under the hotel awning.

"There. All set."

"I like a woman who's prepared."

"It's my job to be prepared. If Plan A doesn't work, the alphabet has twenty-five more letters. I *always* have another plan."

"Oh, right. Superwoman." I slip my arm through hers in case the sidewalks are slick and let her direct us to her condo on 34th Street. "My back up plan is usually my original plan but with more alcohol."

She laughs. I love making her laugh.

I can't believe I'm with her again, walking to her place like we walked to her hotel room that night. Except tonight is freezing cold instead of sultry and warm. The feeling inside me is the same though—arousal, anticipation, a warm fizzing sensation flowing through my veins.

"You live really close to the arena," I say.

"I do. It's great for games and concerts."

"How long have you lived here?"

"Only about a year. I was finally able to buy my own place."

"Right, you mentioned that. I'm just renting, but I've been thinking maybe I should buy a condo. It could be an investment if I end up getting traded."

"I guess you have to think about that?"

"I do," I say wryly. "I'm not the kind of player teams build their franchise around. I've played for four different teams in my career."

"Yikes. That's a lot of moving around."

"Yep."

"That must be hard."

"I don't mind it. It can be a drag, picking up on a moment's notice sometimes, starting over in a new city, new team, but it's way easier for a single guy like me than for the married ones with kids in school. That really sucks. Some guys don't even move their families, they just live apart."

"Wow. That would be really hard."

"Yeah. I've never had anything that really tied me down, so it's not so bad."

"You've never been in a relationship?"

"Well…I guess I have. But never anything serious. For me."

"Uh oh. I bet women fall in love with you and you break their hearts."

Discomfort shifts inside me. "I don't know about that. Sometimes feelings get hurt. I never intend that. Are you warm enough?"

"I'm fine. But it's chilly out here!"

"It is. This isn't the beach. I definitely miss the sun."

"Oh, me too. I didn't even want to go on that stupid vacation, and every morning I could almost cry because I want to go back there."

"I thought you love your job."

"I do." Her smile is lopsided. "But it's stressful. I was so relaxed in Aruba."

"What's stressing you?"

"Deadlines. My boss. My staff. The client."

"Oh, is that all?"

She makes a face.

"Maybe you need to ease back a little."

"There's really no way to do that, other than quit my job. And I'm not going to do that." She lifts her chin. "I can handle it. I love a challenge."

"If you say so." I slant her a dubious glance. I noticed the faint tightness at the corners of her eyes and mouth in the bar, signs of strain that weren't there in Aruba, although her smile at seeing me was genuinely warm. Which turned me on.

"Don't worry." She smiles. "I'm good."

I lean my head closer to hers. "Oh, I *know* that."

She bites her lip. "I'm so attracted to you."

"Me too. To you."

"This wasn't supposed to happen."

"Nope."

We arrive at her building, a square concrete block.

"It doesn't look like much," she says as we cross the small lobby to the elevator. She waves to the doorman. "And I have to warn you my place is pretty tiny."

We ride to the tenth floor and she lets us into her apartment.

She turns on the light and takes off her coat, a bright red one that matches her lips, opening a closet in the small foyer to hang it. I take off my coat as well and she hangs it too, then leads me into the apartment.

I check out the space. "It's not that small." The living room is long, with windows at the far end overlooking the city.

She smiles. "It's a studio. There's no bedroom."

"Oh." I don't see a bed, either. That could be a problem…

"It was all redone before I bought it. New floors, remodeled kitchen and bathroom." She walks by me toward the windows where tons of plants sit on a narrow table. There's also a big potted spiky plant on the floor next to the sofa.

"I like it." I follow her. "Cozy."

"Hello, boys and girls."

Startled, I watch her brush her fingers over the leaves of the plants.

"How are you all doing today? Oooh, let's get rid of this yellow leaf here." She plucks it off. "Are you dry?" She pokes the soil. "No, seems good."

"You…talk to your plants?"

She turns and grins at me. "Yeah. I'm mostly sane, though, don't worry."

I shake my head.

The light shades of the apartment create an airy atmosphere—a cream sofa, a white and light wood coffee table, a white wall unit with open shelves that hold a TV, and near the windows another big white wall unit with cupboards.

Except it's not cupboards. She opens the doors and pulls down a murphy bed.

I smile. "There we go."

She faces me, pushing her creamy vanilla blond hair back. "It takes a little of the spontaneity out of things."

I move toward her and set my hands on her hips. "We both know why we're here. No need to play games."

"I like that." She meets my eyes.

"Your eyes remind my of Aruba. They're gorgeous."

"Thank you."

Our gazes hold and heat shimmers around us. Lust punches through me.

I cup her jaw and bend to kiss her. I'm not a super tall guy for a hockey player, six feet one, but she's only about five feet four and there's quite a height difference, so I bend my knees. She goes onto her toes as our mouths meet in a long press of our lips. A greeting. *Hi. Nice to see you again.*

A low groan rises in my chest and I yank her closer against me. There's just something about her, something irresistible, something potent. I've been thinking about her ever since Aruba. And now she's here in my arms.

I find the zipper at the back of her dress and slowly tug it down. It loosens around her and gapes away from her chest, revealing a black lace bra.

"Wait."

I freeze.

I draw back and meet her eyes.

She gives me a tight smile. "I just need to…use the bathroom."

"Okay." I release her, my dick throbbing.

"Oh hell. No, I don't. Just let me…" She hikes her dress up and starts shimmying her hips, taking off her underwear.

I watch in open-mouthed fascination as she steps out of a black undergarment.

"Spanx," she says, tossing them aside. "They're not exactly sexy."

Her dress is hanging half off her now. "Are you bare under there now?"

She meets my eyes and bites her lip.

With a dirty smile, I slide my hand up her thigh, then between them, finding her liquid center. "You are," I murmur. "And you're wet. And hot." I stroke gently between her legs.

She trembles and moans. "I keep thinking about your good hands."

I'm sure my smile turns even dirtier. "Good." I brush a kiss over her mouth. "I keep thinking about your sweet pussy."

She tugs at my tie, working the knot open, then unbuttoning my shirt. Her eager fingers slip inside and touch my skin. I shudder.

I withdraw my hand and lift my fingers to my mouth to suck them.

Her eyes widen and darken. "You're a bad man."

"Bad? You just said my hands are good." Her delicate taste teases my tastebuds. "I want more of this." I drag her dress off, unfasten her bra and let everything fall to the rug at our feet. "Beautiful." I trace my forefinger over her chest. "Still some tan lines."

"Let me see yours."

I shrug out of my suit jacket, whisk off my shirt, and step out of my pants in no time.

She studies me with hot eyes. Goddamn, I love the approval in her expression, the way her lips part as if she's hungry for me.

She trails her fingers over my hip, my dick bobbing enthusiastically near her hand. "You must tan easily."

"Yeah."

"Let's see the back." She turns me by my hips and sucks in a breath then lets out a long, happy sigh. "Your ass is amazing."

I grin. "Better than the front view?"

"Oh no." She gives my butt cheeks a squeeze, then turns me again. "Not better than this." And she wraps her slender fingers around my thick shaft.

"Jesus." Electricity zings through my body.

"Just as beautiful as I remember." She gives me a stroke, running her thumb over the head, spreading the drop of liquid there.

I hold her face in both hands and pull her in for another kiss, this time long and hard and hungry. Skin to skin, my tongue in her mouth, her hand working me, I'm about to explode.

"Bed," I mutter.

"Mmmm."

I grab the covers and yank them down and she slides in, all smooth skin and glorious curves. The only light is from the foyer and the city lights glimmering outside the window. The atmosphere is erotic and charged.

"There are condoms in that top drawer." She nods toward a dresser opposite the bed.

I find one quickly and bring it with me to join her in bed. She plucks it from my fingers, opens the package, and reaches for me.

"In a hurry?" I slide a hand into her hair.

"Yes."

"Good. Me too."

6

LOLA

"What's your favorite way to spend a day off?"

Brandon's hands smoothes up and down my back. I'm cuddled up against him, my cheek on his chest, legs twined together.

"Hmmm. I like to have lunch with my girlfriends. Shop. Or maybe dinner with them and a play or a concert." As soon as I say it, I realize how long it's been since we did something like that. A small ache of regret pings in my chest. "Um. I like to spend time taking care of my plants." I lift a lazy hand to gesture toward them. "And I run."

"Oh, that's good. How often?"

"Um..." I actually can't remember the last time I went for a run. "Not very often," I admit.

"It sounds like you work long hours. You need to take care of yourself."

"I know. Running is definitely good for stress relief. It's just hard to find the time. How about you? What do you do on your days off? I assume you have days off."

"Yeah, we do. Seems like things are always busy, though. And I have my dog, Martha."

"You have a dog?"

"Yeah. She's a German shepherd. I've had her for about eight years, so she's getting up there. She still likes to go to the park, though. And I volunteer with a reading group through the Bears Foundation. So some days I go to schools and read to the kids."

I lift my head and peer at his face. "Seriously?"

"Yeah."

I smile. "That's sweet."

"I'm a sweet guy."

I laugh. "Okay."

"You sound unconvinced. What do I have to do to show you how sweet I am?"

"I don't know." I think. "You *are* generous in bed."

"Yes, I am." His chin dips.

I think more. He is gentlemanly and thoughtful. So while I wouldn't have described him as sweet, I guess he sort of is. "What else do you do?"

"Not that much different than you, I guess. Hang out with my friends. I like going to Knicks games when I can. Work out."

I trace over one of his sculpted pecs. "I bet you work out a lot."

He grins. "I'll take that as a compliment."

"Do you travel a lot? I mean, outside of hockey."

"Not a lot. I've taken a few trips in the off season. Went to Europe with some of the guys one summer, and Japan another year. We try to get away during the All Star break, like we did in Aruba this year. But in summers, I mostly like hanging out at my house on the lake."

"Right. It must be nice there."

"Do you like nature? Hiking, swimming, boating?"

"I'm a city girl. I'm not really into those things. I've never even been camping."

"Really?" He sounds genuinely horrified, and I laugh.

"But I never say never. I like traveling, but there never seems to be enough time. I'm jealous of your trip to Japan."

"It was cool." He tells me about the things they did, including naked bathing in an onsen, which is apparently like a hot spring, I think? "We went to an izakaya in Piss Alley. That was amazing."

"Piss Alley?" My head jerks up to stare at him.

He grins. "Yeah. Yakitori Alley, also called Memory Lane also called "Piss Alley." There aren't a lot of restrooms, so people go off and er, relieve themselves on the train tracks."

I wrinkle my nose.

Then he tells a hilarious story about him and his friends at an all-you-can-drink karaoke bar when a drunk Japanese man stumbled into them and then dragged them to sing with him and his co-work-ers. "He kept yelling 'Sing with us, gaijin!' And we figured, what the hell, so we did. And he was all, 'We going sing with the gaijinnnnn!'"

He's so animated and expressive telling the story, I'm dying of giggles, rolling onto my back. "Stop! My face hurts."

He smiles, rolling toward me, propping his head up on an elbow. "Sorry."

"No, you're not."

"Okay, I'm not. I like making you laugh." He reaches over and pushes a strand of hair off my face. Our eyes meet.

My belly flips.

Oh God. I'm turned on again. From laughing. This man…

He leans over and kisses me. And I roll into his arms and kiss him back.

Brandon leaves later—much later—telling me to stay in bed.

"I can't. I have to lock up behind you." I roll sleepily out of bed, grab my fuzzy robe, and pull it on as I follow him to the door. He bends over and kisses my forehead. "I had fun tonight," he murmurs.

"Me too." I smile up at him.

I meet his eyes and for a few charged seconds we're fixed in place, heat melting through me.

I wouldn't mind seeing him again. I like him. I'm about to say that, and maybe ask for his number, but then I remember I was the one to stress that this is just a hook up. Nothing more. "Good night."

He leaves, I lock the door, and float back to bed on a post-orgasmic cloud only slightly dampened by disappointment.

I'm going to be a wreck in the morning, with only a few hours of sleep. Was it worth it?

Hell, yeah.

Surprisingly, I feel great when my alarm goes off. I often have insomnia and I hate how crappy I feel when I haven't had enough sleep, but today I feel amazing. I stretch in bed, and when I roll over, I breathe in Brandon's scent on the pillow next to me. Oh boy. He smells so good.

With a smile on my face, I shower, dress, and do my face, and grab my protein shake to drink on the subway ride to work.

My day is non-stop meetings, which normally is annoying, but I'm chill today, taking charge when conversations get off track and bringing us back to the issues at hand, making decisions like a boss, and getting shit done.

Wow. If this is what sex with Brandon does for me, I need to bottle that stuff and stock up on it.

Late afternoon, I'm sitting in a meeting room on the thirty-fifth floor of an office tower in Lower Manhattan, meeting with the CEO of KGP Services, our client, as well as Bob Bakker, the Managing Partner who heads their Assurance division. With me is the project manager from Synoptic, Greg Wagner.

"My next step is to do a learning needs assessment," I tell them. "With the merger, staff will be impacted by new technologies, and there'll be a significant impact to workloads. Increased use of technology can be stressful for some people. We want to identify any gaps and assess staff's ability to adapt to the new environment. Then we'll educate them on the new skills they'll require and provide change management coaching."

"We've been through a lot of changes in our organization over the years," Bob Bakker says. "We've never done this kind of thing."

I smile. "How long have you been with KGP, Bob?"

"Twenty-two years."

"Oh yes, I'm sure you've seen a lot of change in that time."

"Reorganization of job responsibilities, performance plans to increase staff competencies and skills in new areas, and recent layoffs to help balance the budget," the CEO puts in. "Also hiring younger and more diverse staff. A lot of changes."

"Layoffs are especially difficult." I smile sympathetically at the CEO, then look at Bob again. "Your experience in leading your division through these changes will be invaluable."

"I've suggested changes of my own over the last couple of years," Bob says, frowning. "I do have a lot of experience, but when I suggest ideas for improvements, my staff is really resistant."

I nod. "Can you tell me more about that? What are their reactions to your suggestions? Do they dismiss them out of hand or is there discussion?"

"They're open to discussion," he says. "But they don't think my ideas are appropriate. They say they rely too much on outdated resources and technology. Some of these younger people have different ideas about strategic thinking. They think they know so much." He shakes his head.

Okay, I'm getting the picture. The problem isn't with Bob's staff—it's with him.

"It will be important to involve them in our solutions, then." I talk about the session I want to facilitate which will include management and staff. "Including staff in the process helps with buy in." I give them details and request that they put together a list of people who will be invited to the session, with a date of when I need that by.

I sense Bob's lack of enthusiasm for my role, so I don't give him a chance to object to anything, just move ahead with what we need to do.

Greg and I leave the meeting room and exchange a look. We cross the luxurious reception area and exit to the elevator lobby where I push a down button.

"You handled that really well," he says.

"Thanks." I grimace. "My first challenge will be dealing with Bob."

"I agree."

"I'm glad the CEO was there. Support has to come right from the top. Bob needs to know that his boss is on board with the changes."

"Yep. But if anyone can handle Bob, you can."

"Thank you. I just have to figure out his WIIFM."

"His what?"

I grin. "What's In It For Me. Something he'll benefit from. Hopefully there's something good enough to persuade him this change is a good thing."

We step into the elevator.

"This is why you'd make a great VP," Greg says. "Your people skills are phenomenal."

"Oh. Thank you." I try not to sound surprised. Dealing with people is something I've actually had to work on, since I tend to be blunt and bossy. So Greg's words make me happy.

We continue to debrief about the meeting as we ride down to the ground floor.

"Are you going back to the office?" Greg asks in the lobby.

"Yes. You?"

"Nah, it's late. I'm heading home. See you tomorrow."

"Okay. Goodnight." I pull my phone out to take it off silent mode and check for emails. There's a text message from Kaylee.

Hey, we're meeting at Merry Dog for happy hour drinks, come join us. Sadie and Isla are here.

I bite my lip. I should go back to the office and make notes from our meeting and finish up a few other things. But just last night, talking to Brandon, I realized I haven't seen my friends much since our trip. I'd really like to join them. The pub they mentioned is only a few blocks away from here.

I text Kaylee back. *How long are you going to be there?*

Till they run out of beer.

I grin. *Okay. Give me an hour and I'll join you.*

Yay!

I set off toward the office. It's getting dark already and there's something about this time of day in Midtown with the tall buildings and the lights coming on that I always love. The streets are busy with cars and people ending the workday, heading to pubs for a drink, heading home to relax. I want to be one of those people pushing into a warm bar full of friends and setting work aside for a while.

I quickly type up notes from the meeting and make myself a to do list for tomorrow. I take care of a few emails that are urgent and leave the rest, then bundle up and head back outside to hustle down Madison, around the corner onto 33rd and a couple of blocks down to the Merry Dog.

Inside the light is warm, and noise assails my ear drums. I unwrap my scarf and scan the crowd, looking for my friends. Oh, there's Sadie's bright red hair. She spots me too and lifts a hand. I start toward them.

"We saved you a seat," Sadie says. "I'm so glad you made it!"

"You hardly ever join us for happy hour anymore," Isla adds with a pout.

"I know." I flash a guilty smile and hang my coat over the back of my stool. "But here I am!"

My attention is drawn to the TVs playing above the bar where a hockey game is in progress. "Is that the Bears?"

Kaylee glances at the TV, then back at me. "I have no idea."

"It is," Isla affirms. "See? Bears are winning four-one."

Brandon's playing. Right there on that TV. I stare at it.

Kaylee nudges me. "Drink?"

I blink over to the server standing at the table. "Oh. Yeah. What are you drinking?" I ask Kaylee.

"Pathological Lager."

I blink, then laugh. "Okay, I'll have one of those."

My attention returns to the TV. I now know Brandon is number twelve, but this far away the players are tiny and it's hard to make out the numbers on their jerseys.

"Ohhhh. Your hockey hook up is playing." Kaylee smacks her own forehead.

"Oh, riiiiight." Isla grins. "Have you been watching all his games since we got back from Aruba?"

"Maybe one or two," I grudgingly admit. I look around the table at them. "I ran into him last night."

"What!" Kaylee's eyes bulge.

"Where?" Isla demands.

"What happened?" Sadie asks.

I grin. "After the awards dinner. He was in the bar having a drink with his agent." I pause. "He came back to my place."

They all make high-pitched squealing noises that are luckily drowned out by the noise in the pub.

"Seriously?" Kaylee stares at me. "Wow."

"I know. Total coincidence.'"

"*Lucky* coincidence," Sadie says.

"It was." I sigh happily.

"Are you seeing him again?" Kaylee asks

"No. We still didn't exchange numbers or anything. It was just another hot night."

"You could hang around outside the arena after a game, like a groupie," Sadie jokes.

I roll my eyes. "I'm not a groupie. It was just...you know...fun. That's all."

7

BRANDON

We're sitting in the locker room after practice.

I've been thinking about the conversation I had with my agent the other night. My contract ends next year. If the Bears don't sign me again, I'll be a free agent. I haven't been worried about that; I'm adaptable. I've moved around a lot—three seasons in the AHL, three seasons in St. Louis, two seasons in Montreal. Those two years were each one-year contracts. Then when Montreal didn't sign me again, I filed for arbitration. I won, meaning they had to sign me again, but they immediately traded me here to New York. After I finished that one-year deal, the Bears signed me for three years, which was great. This'll be the longest I've stayed anywhere.

Kevin told me I need to give them a reason to want to keep me.

Do I *want* to stay here?

That's what I've been thinking about.

I like it here. I've made friends. I like New York, even though I'm not a big city guy. But I don't ever get too attached to people and places, because I always end up moving on.

"She's Vince D'Agostino's stepdaughter," Cookie says, finishing off a short speech I wasn't paying much attention to.

"Wait, what?" I stare at Cookie. (Owen Cooke; we call him Cookie.) "Are you shitting us? You're dating Mr. D'Agostino's daughter?"

"Stepdaughter," he corrects, as if he's done it a million times.

He just told us the chick he's seeing is the stepdaughter of the team owner. Jesus.

"She came to Aruba with us!"

"I know. Sorry."

"You should have told us who she is!"

"Look, it's a long story." Cookie slides a hand over his face. "And it's kind of personal, for Emerie."

I glance at the other guys. Millsy (Easton Millar) and Hellsy (Josh Heller) already knew. They nod, as if they support him.

"Wow." I shake my head. "I can't believe you're dating the owner's daughter." I pause. "Stepdaughter."

Cookie appears conflicted. He shrugs and drops his gaze.

I'm conflicted, too. I wish I'd known Emerie was Mr. D'Agostino's daughter, er stepdaughter. Did I say anything about him? No, I don't think we talked about him at all on the trip. But we could have. What else did we say that she could take back to him?

"I feel like there was a spy in our midst," I say.

Bergie snorts.

"She's not a spy, believe me," Cookie assures us.

I study him. He's dead serious. "Okay."

"Okay, I need someone to come shopping with me." Bergie changes the subject.

"Shopping for what?" I don't mind shopping for clothes, unlike some guys.

"Baby stuff."

I throw up my hands. "I'm out."

"How about you, Nate? You'd know all about baby shit."

"Ha ha. Literally."

Nate has a six-year-old daughter he shares custody of with his ex.

"But I can't," he continues. "I'm going for an MRI on my knee."

Damn. He's been having knee problems for a while.

"Red!" Bergie calls. "You have kids. Come with me."

Red's grin splits his bushy, yes, red beard. "Can't. I have to take my daughter to a doctor appointment."

Bergie all but begs everyone who's left. He turns to me one more time. "Come on. You're the only one without a legit reason not to come."

I sigh. "Fine. But after, we go to Lorenzo." I name my favorite men's wear shop. "I need new shirts."

Bergie curses. "Okay, deal."

In the baby department at Bloomingdale's, we're surrounded not only by tiny clothes, stuffed toys, and strollers, but also kids—lots of kids—babies, mom, moms looking at us, and it's freaking me out.

"This is *not* my idea of a fun day off."

Of course that makes me think about Lola, in bed, soft and satisfied and talking about what we do on our days off.

"Suck it up, buttercup," Bergie says.

"I hate this place," I mutter.

"What is wrong with you?" Bergie frowns, his attention on a stroller. "Look at these! These gloves attach to the stroller handle and you just slide your hands in."

"Wild." My skin itches. "What are we here for?"

"Stroller. Highchair. Car seat. Mandy says those are the only things she trusts me to buy. But come on, we have to have these gloves."

"It's spring."

"For next winter. The kid'll still be in a stroller." He moves on. "And hey! I like this!"

"A backpack?"

"It's a diaper bag." He picks up the black quilted bag. "It comes with a changing pad. Nice." He looks up. "Mandy already bought a diaper bag, but I'd use this one."

I nod and pull out my phone to check the time.

He's moved on to look at a crib.

"You didn't say a crib," I remind him.

"Yeah, we have a crib," he agrees.

I probably should pick up something to give them as a baby gift. I have no clue what. I look around and spy a display of blankets and stuff. I wander away from Bergie to study them. I pick up an item that has a cow head and a blanket attached. Combination toy and blankie. Huh.

"That's adorable."

My head snaps around to see Lola smiling at me. My heart jolts.

"Is it for you?" She tilts her head to one side, a teasing gleam in her eyes.

"Yeah." I hold it up. "I have a thing for cows." I give her a look.

She's so goddamn pretty, her creamy blond hair shining, her smiling lips bright red again. She's wearing black pants and a red sweater, her black trench coat open. I ran into her again! What are the odds? Probably not great, but hey, I'll take it! Maybe this shopping trip wasn't such a bad idea after all.

My mood improves considerably.

She grins and reaches out to touch the blanket. "Soft. I should get that."

"For yourself?"

She laughs. "For my co-worker. She's having a baby and I need a shower gift."

"Ah. Boy or a girl?"

"Boy."

I nod. "I'm with my buddy, Bergie." I jerk my head toward him. He's engrossed in the strollers.

"Bergie?"

"Daniel Bergen. Teammate."'

"Right."

"They're having a boy, too. In June."

"Oh, that's a nice time to have a baby."

"Could be the worst time in the world." I hand over the cow blankie. "Playoffs."

"Oh." Her eyes widen. "Yikes. They probably weren't thinking about that when they, uh…"

I laugh. "Probably not. Although some couples do. They try to plan babies for summer so it doesn't interfere with the schedule." I pause. "That doesn't always work, though."

"No, I'm sure it doesn't." She folds up the blanket and looks around. "I should probably get something else, too."

She steps over to another display and fingers some blankets. "These are nice." She picks up a set of four, which are called swaddling blankets, in various baby blue prints.

"Babies need a lot of stuff."

"I'm sure people have way too much stuff these days," she says with a light laugh. "I guess there are some necessities—diapers, bum cream, I don't know…I don't think people need…these." She moves and picks up some tiny shoes. "Why do babies need shoes? They don't even walk."

"True."

"And these towels." They have cute heads attached to them. "Are these going to dry a baby better than any other towel? I don't think so."

"Another solid point."

"Hey! Brando!"

I look over at Bergie. He realizes I'm talking to Lola and rolls his eyes.

"Brando?" She lifts an eyebrow.

"My nickname."

"Ah. Like Marlon." She tips her head. "You know, you do look like a young Marlon Brando."

I laugh. "Ah. Babe Magnet."

She laughs too. "Actually, he was." She slides me a flirty look that I very much enjoy.

"I'm supposed to be helping Bergie," I tell her. "I have no clue about this stuff. Or about kids."

A small child runs between us. We both jump back but then the little man trips and falls, spreadeagled flat on the floor.

"Uh-oh." I step over to him and lift him up. "You okay, buddy?"

His face is getting red, his bottom lip quivering.

"Yeah, you're okay," I answer myself, trying to forestall a storm of tears. I set him on his feet and crouch down to his level. He stares at me.

A harried-looking woman rushes up to us. "Alex! I told you no running." She glances at me. "Sorry."

"Hey, no problem. He's a speedy little guy." I straighten.

The woman's gaze moves over my body, her smile changing. "Yes, he is."

Oh for fuck's sake. I see the kid and the ring on her finger. I keep my smile polite and step away, moving close beside Lola. "Hope he's okay."

The woman's glance flicks to Lola, back to me, and then to her kid. "You're fine, right Alex? Thank the nice man for picking you up."

Alex gives me a suspicious look that makes me want to laugh.

They leave and I turn back to Lola. She smirks.

"What?" I frown.

"You were cute with him."

"Ugh. I don't want kids."

"Really?"

"Yeah. Marriage is a mistake. Kids are mistake. I'm perfectly happy with my life the way it is." I gauge her reaction. Lots of women get peeved when I say that. Because most women *are* looking for a relationship.

Not Lola. "Exactly! Me too. Why do people think you need to be married and have kids to have a fulfilling life?"

"I know what you mean. A bunch of my teammates have caught feelings and paired off in the last year or so. Of course, they all think I should do that too." I shake my head. "Not happening."

"Right? My parents think that. My entire huge fucking family thinks that. It's so annoying. Maybe you'll make a good uncle, because you were good with that little guy."

"I *will* be a good uncle." I grin. "I like kids. I just don't want any."

"Same!"

We exchange a look of understanding.

"Well," she says. "I better pay for these and get back the office."

And neither of us moves.

I find myself reluctant to leave her again.

"Do you have plans tonight?" I blurt out.

She bites her lip.

"Neither of us is looking for a relationship," I put in hastily. "But you can hook up with someone more than once. Right?"

Her lips twitch. "Right."

"So, would you like to…get together?"

She gives in to the smile. "That would be fun."

"Your place?"

"Sure."

"I'll come by around eight? I can bring a pizza."

"Perfect." She moves away, sliding me a smile over her shoulder.

Now I'm excited.

It's not a date. It's a…booty call. I guess. With pizza.

I amble over to Bergie, who's talking to a salesperson and arranging delivery.

"All set," he says to me. "Let's just check out the baby clothes before we leave."

"Okay, sure."

He casts me a sidelong glance as he moves to a rack. "You're in a better mood."

"Yep." I trail after him as he inspects tiny onesies, footies, and socks. I have to admit the blue tie-dye hoodie is cute.

"Who was that you were talking to?"

"Lola. Remember? From Aruba?"

"I wasn't in Aruba."

"Oh yeah. We met there."

"Ohhhh. She's the one I heard about."

"What did you hear?" I frown.

"Apparently she's a sex goddess."

My frown deepens. "Jesus."

One corner of his mouth lifts. "They had to hear that from you. Nobody else was with you that night."

Huh. Now I kind of regret sharing that. It seemed fine when I thought I'd never see her again, but now it feels tacky. Although it *is* true. "Well, yeah, she's good at it. That's why we're getting together tonight."

"Of course you are."

I spot a giant giraffe, like, my height. That's it. That's what I'm buying Bergie's kid. I'll have to come back. Wait, maybe I can order it online and I don't have to ever set foot in this place again. Excellent.

"Are you buying those?" I point at the socks Bergie's holding.

"Nah. We have tons of socks." He sets them down.

"Good. On to Lorenzo's."

"Oh yeah." He sounds as enthusiastic as I did about coming here.

"It'll be fun!" I slap a hand on his shoulder. "And you owe me. Let's go."

8

LOLA

Brandon arrives a few minutes after eight, and he is indeed carrying a big flat box that smells like spicy tomato sauce.

"Oh my God, I'm starving." I take the pizza so he can hang up his coat. I admire the shape of his shoulders in a soft black puffer jacket, the way his sable brown hair's tousled on top from the wind, the stubble shading his lean jaw.

"Me too," he says, his tone suggestive enough for me to give him a look. He smirks.

It's a cocky, brash, slightly swaggering smirk, and yet it's so goddamn cute I want to lick him all over.

There's no denying the sexual attraction between us.

I shake my head. He's also carrying a bottle of wine. "Oh, this is nice. Thank you." I carry it all into my tiny kitchen. He follows and sits on a stool at the counter. I hand him a corkscrew and the bottle of wine to open, then pull plates and wineglasses from cupboards.

"Did your friend get the baby things he needed?" I ask.

"Yeah. The things his wife allowed him to buy. She's decorating the nursery."

"Another thing babies don't need."

He grins. "Probably true. I'm sure they don't care about wallpaper or carpet or what color the bedding is."

"Right?" I open the pizza box. "Still hot! Nice job."

"Thanks. I stopped a little place near here."

"Nico's. It's my favorite."

"I knew that."

I laugh. "You're just lucky."

"I definitely am." His wink is flirty. "And going to get luckier."

"Yes. You are." I wink back at him.

This is fun.

We move to the living room couch to eat. "Should I put the TV on?" I ask.

"Sure."

I flick through channels, pausing at a hockey game. I give him a questioning look.

He shakes his head. "I'm off duty."

That makes me smile. "I get that." I find a crime show that he approves of, and we start watching it, but our conversation soon distracts us.

"You're not playing tonight," I observe.

"Nope. We had an optional practice this morning, but that's it."

"But I don't think that was how you like to spend your days off."

"Exactly." He points at me. "I was thinking that as I was suffering through the kids' department at Bloomingdales. But then I ran into you, and the shopping trip got a whole lot better."

Mine too. "When do you play again?"

"We leave tomorrow on a road trip. First Dallas. Then Winnipeg, St. Louis, Minneapolis."

"Whoa. You'll be gone a while."

"Yep. A week." He's always so carefree and cheerful, but I swear a shadow passes over his face.

"What's wrong?"

"Hmm? Nothing's wrong." He takes a bite of pizza.

Do I push it? He apparently doesn't want to talk about whatever's bothering him.

"Is it hard traveling that much?"

"Not for me." He gives me a cheeky smile. "Road trips are good. We get to all hang out together. Bond."

I nod. "I guess so."

"Maybe it'll help us play better," he says, looking briefly glum again.

"Problems?"

"Nah." He scrunches his face up. "It's getting close to the playoffs. We need to be playing our best if we want to make it, and if we want to make a deep run. Which we do."

I study his face. This guy doesn't like to talk about heavy stuff. I can see this is important to him, but he's keeping it light. "When do the playoffs start?"

"Early April. Our last game is the seventh. Then they start shortly after that."

I nod. "You want to win the Stanley Cup."

"Sure. Every player does."

His cell phone rings. He frowns. "Shit. That's my mom."

"Do you need to get it?"

"Nah."

I blink. "Go ahead."

"She's probably calling to bitch about my dad."

"Oh."

"They're divorced. But they can't stay away from each other."

"Oh."

"They hate each other."

The phone stops ringing.

"It sort of sounds like they love each other."

"I have no idea. They just drive me crazy."

The phone rings again, with the same ring tone.

Heaving a sigh, he pulls out his phone. "Hey, Mom."

He stands and walks over to the window. I watch him lift a hand to rub the back of his neck while he listens, his biceps bunching, his back muscles rippling. I sigh with pleasure, but then frown when he finally speaks, his tone weary.

"I know he wants to retire. That's his decision, Mom."

I can hear her higher-pitched voice faintly.

"I can help you out financially. You know that." He shakes his head, listening. "Look, this isn't a great time to talk. Can I call you tomorrow?" He turns and gives me a crooked smile. "Yeah, sorry, Mom. Tomorrow. Okay? Okay. Good night."

He ends the call and drops his hands. "Sorry about that. I never know what it's going to be about."

"Is everything okay?"

"Yeah." He walks back and sits beside me again. "She's all worked up about something that isn't going to happen for months, and maybe not even then. My dad keeps talking about retiring, but she's worried he won't pay her spousal support if he does."

"Oh."

"But I think he just says that to get her all riled up. He loves his job. He's a firefighter."

I smile. "Do you have siblings?"

"No. Only child."

"Like me."

"I wish I had a sibling so they could call him. Or her." He rolls his eyes. He smiles, but there's a faint tightness to his mouth that tells me he's feeling more than he lets on. Again.

Much later, both of us naked and sweaty in my bed, he says, "I should go, I guess."

"Okay." I slide out of bed and grab my fluffy robe as he dresses. I wish he'd stay. Not only for more sex, but to talk. I feel like he needs someone to talk to about the things that are bothering him. It sounds like the issues with his parents are more than the odd phone call. Not that I can help, but I could empathize and be a sounding board, since I too am an only child, and my parents bug me, too, sometimes. But he probably has friends he talks to and I'm being too nosy. That's not what this is about. This is about hooking up. Physical intimacy, not emotional intimacy.

I walk with him to the door and he stops there to set his hands on my waist. He smiles down at me.

"Give me your number," I blurt out unexpectedly.

"Um…"

"Like you said…we can hook up more than once."

"Or twice, even." His lips quirk.

"Yeah."

I enter his number into my phone. "Thanks."

"Thanks for having me over."

"Thanks for coming. And thanks for the pizza and wine."

He brushes a kiss over my mouth, then another, and another, this one clinging longer. I curl my hands over his shoulders and hang on as I melt against him.

"Let me know you got home safely," I say jokingly. "You know how I worry."

"You need to text me so I have your number."

"Right. I will."

"Goodnight, superwoman."

I let him out and lock the door, then walk into the bathroom.

Superwoman.

He called me that in Aruba. I'm not superwoman. My parents brought me up to believe I could do anything. That I was the best at everything. When I got to college, out in the real world, away from their coddling, I discovered that wasn't true.

I hated it.

I felt like an imposter. I felt like a loser. My failure to get into med school, like my parents hoped for me, still gives me loser vibes even years later and I've struggled with that ever since, with proving myself, to others but also to myself, trying to be perfect, trying to *really* be the best. This promotion will definitely prove that.

So when Brandon called me superwoman, it made my heart feel full and my knees feel weak.

Because I want to be superwoman.

Well, I don't want leap tall buildings or fly. I just want to be *good* at something. Something I've accomplished on my own. Like this promotion.

I pick up my phone and send him a text. *This is me, Lola.*

I catch sight of the goofy smile on my face in the mirror. I feel like my blood is carbonated, fizzing in my veins, my stomach doing happy little flips. I touch my lips where he just kissed me, my eyes bright as I regard my image. Then I spot my computer and the work I brought home that didn't get done. Shit.

What was I thinking earlier, wanting Brandon's number? I don't have time for that. But honestly, before this I never met anyone I *wanted* to have time for. Regret twinges inside me.

I need to stay focused on my goal. I need to *kill* on this project. I need to show them my leadership skills and my commitment to the company so I can get that promotion. Vice president.

Half an hour later, I get a text message.

Made it home, safe and sound. I know how you worry.

I smile at my phone. I send a smile emoji. I hesitate, then send another message. *Good luck on your trip tomorrow Marlon.*

He texts back an eyeroll emoji, then, *Thanks, we need it.*

9

BRANDON

Our road trip sucks.

We're fighting Pittsburgh for a playoff spot. They're a good team with a hot goalie. We need every point we can get to stay ahead of them.

We won our first road game in Dallas in OT, then lost tonight in Winnipeg. I'm frustrated because I felt like I was playing well but just couldn't get the puck in the net. Alone in my hotel room at the Fairmont, I pick up my phone and stretch out on the bed. I look at Lola's name. Ah, what the hell. I tap in a message.

Hey. How's it going?

She replies right away. *I'm okay. How are you? Sorry about the loss.*

Did you watch the game?

Yeah.

I smile. I like that. *Cool. I just wish we'd won.*

You can't win them all. Wait, that's a cliché, right?

Yeah, but it's true. A coach used to tell us sometimes you win, sometimes you learn.

That's a good attitude.

I'm trying to figure out what we learned tonight.

And...?

I pause, because I still haven't figured it out. *I guess we need more of a sense of urgency. I tried.*

I don't think it can be just one guy who does it.

I nod, although she can't see me. True. It has to be the whole team. Including me.

What more can you do? I mean that sincerely...is there more?

Good question.

I mean, even off the ice.

This gives me pause. Bergie's a great leader and he's playing hard, too. JBo, our other alternate captain, definitely had an off night. And our other alternate captain, Nate, has problems with his knee.

Leaders lead by example, she messages me.

Yeah. My mind goes back to my conversation with Kevin and him telling me I need to put in extra effort if I want to stay in New York. I find I kind of do want to stay. I've seen how hard Lola works toward her goals. So yeah, I've been working harder during practices, playing harder in our games. It's not helping. What can I do off the ice to set an example?

You're always so upbeat, Lola messages. *That's a good strength, I'd say.*

I read her message a few times. I do like to keep things light. But that doesn't mean I don't feel the urgency. I think about the atmosphere in the dressing room after the game. It was dismal. We were down on ourselves. It's hard not to be. I slowly tap in a message. *Maybe I can do more to keep things positive.* I pause. *But still urgent.*

She sends me a smile emoji.

My frustration has eased and I relax into the pillows on the bed. *Thanks.*

For what?

Just for letting me talk it out.

Any time, Marlon.

We lose again in St. Louis.

I tried to be positive in the dressing room. I feel like I'm playing my best hockey of the year. But some of our guys aren't.

One of them is Cookie.

What is up with him? We aren't best buds, but even I can see he's distracted. He's slow, playing sloppy, screwing up. He turned over the puck at our blue line and cost us a goal in the St. Louis game. I know he was pissed about it; he's harder on himself than anyone else.

Does this have anything to do with his new girlfriend? Who happens to be the team owner's stepdaughter? That whole thing is a recipe for disaster.

Our general manager pulled him out of the dressing room to talk to him in St. Louis. It couldn't be about his play; that would be Coach's job. There haven't been trade rumors floating, that I know of. I'm curious what it was about, but it doesn't seem to have helped Cookie's focus because tonight in Minneapolis he's even more off his game

Again, things aren't going our way. Little things keep costing us and our frustration is growing.

The game is nearly over and we're down three-two. We've pulled our goalie, Gunner, for the extra attacker. I'm on the bench watching the play. Fletcher from the Caribou shoots the puck down the ice and another Caribou snags it and heads to the empty net.

Every nerve ending is on alert as I watch what happens, hoping he somehow doesn't score. Then Cookie flies down the ice toward Schneider. He's a fast skater but I don't know if he can get there in time to stop Schneider from putting the puck in the net.

It happens fast. Cookie and Schneider collide right at the net, and the puck is in. The goal horn blares, but Schneider's down, sliding into the boards. He doesn't move.

Jesus fuck.

The Caribou immediately swarm Cookie, pissed at him, and of course our guys are stepping in. On the bench, we're all standing, trying to see what's going on. The refs blow whistles and try to get things under control, but everyone's still pushing and shoving. Finally, they separate the players. A linesman guides Cookie off the ice.

I watch the replay on the screen above us and wince. That looks bad. I know Cookie was just trying to stop the goal, but that was a brutal hit.

Fletcher is screaming at the ref, irate, while a trainer from the Caribou hurries over to Schneider, still motionless. A couple of players stand near him. The arena goes quiet. There is *nothing* as quiet as an arena full of fifteen thousand hockey fans when a player gets hurt.

My heart hammers, watching this. Nobody likes seeing another player injured. Eventually, a stretcher is brought out and Schneider is taken off the ice on it. That has to be bad. Every player in the league would try to skate off even if both legs were broken.

Now I have to focus on the last couple of minutes of the game. Shit like this happens. You don't like it, but you have to separate it. But scoring two goals in two minutes is a tough task at the best of times.

We lose. Again. And we've probably lost Cookie, after that. I can't imagine he's only going to get a slap on the wrist. *Fuck!*

The dressing room feels like a funeral. This isn't the time to be making jokes, so I keep my mouth shut. I'm not on the list to talk to the media, so I shower and change and head to the bus. Everyone's quiet, especially Cookie. He's shook. I guess we'll deal with everything tomorrow.

It's three in the morning when I'm driving home from the private airport in Long Island we fly in and out of. I feel weird. Unsettled. Antsy. I should be tired, but instead I'm wired. I cruise along 9A, make the U-turn at West 56th, then drive the couple of blocks to my apartment. Before I pull into the underground parking garage, I stop on the road, dark and deserted right now. I pull out my phone.

I scroll to Lola's name.

I shouldn't do this. It's the middle of the night.

No. Even I'm not that much of an asshole.

I drop my phone, park, and go up to my apartment.

I'm greeted by my ecstatic German Shepherd. "Martha!"

She's older and slower now, but she still gets excited when I come home, whether it's after a half hour trip to the bodega or a seven-day road trip. I crouch down and rub behind her ears and boop her nose with mine. "Have you been a good girl? Huh? Were you good for Lilley and Zaria?"

Lilley is Millsy's girlfriend, who owns a dog walking and day care business. Zaria is a college student who works for her.

"They take good care of you, don't they, Queen Martha?"

After sufficient attention to my pupper, I head to the bedroom. Martha follows me and curls up in her own bed in the corner. I take off my suit and fall into bed naked, but I can't sleep. After a couple of hours of flopping around like a flounder I drift off, but my dreams are so weird. I'm lying on my back on the ice, paralyzed, but everyone's ignoring me. The play goes on. Nobody cares.

I wake up sweating. Christ. What time is it?

It's only eight in the morning. I've had about an hour of terrible sleep. I feel like shit. Not only from the lack of sleep, but I took a couple of hard hits into the boards and my ribs and shoulder are tender.

I pull on a pair of gray sweatpants and an old T-shirt and make myself a cup of coffee. I pick up my phone, but I know last night's events are going to be all over social media. I don't want to see it. I set it down on the counter and stare into space as I drink my java.

I rub my face. God, I'm tired. So tired.

After my coffee, I shower even though I showered a few hours ago after the game, hoping that will make me feel more normal, but nope. Back in my sweatpants, I take Martha for a walk. I wander around my apartment. I stare out the window. Try to distract myself with a Netflix series that everyone's talking about. Finally, I turn off the TV and heave a sigh.

I keep thinking about Lola.

I pick up my phone again. It's nearly noon.

I was happy to give her my number that night. Running into her randomly probably isn't going to keep happening. It's not like I want a girlfriend. It's just that we're so sexually compatible. I love fucking her. She's amazing.

I run my thumb over the screen and then press on the last message we exchanged. I purse my lips in indecision. Ah, fuck it, I want to see her. I bring up a new message box and type in *Hey, what are you up to today?*

It takes a few minutes for her to reply. *Not much. How are you? I saw the game last night.*

Ohhh. Really? I nod slowly as if she can see me. Ha. *I feel like shit.* No. Delete, delete, delete. *I'm okay.*

Want some company?

Oh hell yeah. I blow out a long breath of relief. *Yeah. I do. Come over?*

Sure.

I text her my address and she says she'll see me in a while.

Great. I drop my phone and clasp my hands together. I check out the place. It's decent. My cleaning lady was here a couple of days ago so it's not bad, but I left some dishes in the sink. I'm not trying to impress Lola, but I need to occupy myself waiting for her, so I clean up and wipe down the counters. I pop a couple of Advil so I'm not too much of a downer when Lola arrives.

About an hour later, the doorman calls up that she's here. My gut clenches and I head to the door to let her in.

"Hi." I sweep my gaze over her. Damn, she's gorgeous. She's wearing a light jacket, a big, loose scarf in shades of pink and red, and jeans. Her lips shine pink as she smiles at me.

"Hi."

"Come in."

She stops short as Martha comes padding up to inspect her. "Oh."

"This is Martha."

"She's…big."

"Do you like dogs?"

"Um. Yeah."

"She's really friendly. And old." I rub Martha's head.

Lola hands me one of the Starbucks' cups she's carrying. "I don't even know if you like coffee, but I wanted one, so I stopped at the Starbucks."

"Thanks. I love coffee."

"It's just black but I have cream and sugar." She pulls a paper bag out of her purse.

She cautiously holds out a hand to Martha, letting her sniff. Martha approves with a couple of gentle licks, but that's not a surprise because she loves everyone.

"I just need some milk." I take the bag and my coffee to the kitchen counter that separates my kitchen from the living room to doctor my coffee.

"Nice place." Lola sets her cup on the coffee table and unwinds her scarf, looking around. "Love the windows."

"Oh, let me take your jacket."

She hands it over and I hang it in the closet.

"Think of the plants you could grow in here!" She wanders to the windows. I have a corner unit, so there are floor to ceiling windows on both sides, today giving a view of clear blue sky and the river.

I smile. "Yeah, that's true. I don't think I could keep plants alive, though."

"Sure, you could. They just need a little attention." She turns and smiles, her eyes warm. "You have a lot more room than I do."

"Yeah. Your place is cozy, though."

"Yours is very...white."

I laugh and take a seat on the couch. "Yes, it is. I like things clean and bright."

She sits next to me and picks up her coffee. "It is definitely that. I like clean and bright, too." She sips her drink, regarding me over the lid of her cup. "When did you get home?"

"About three in the morning." I rub my jaw. "And I haven't been able to sleep."

"Oh, no." Her forehead creases. She reaches out and rubs my arm. "Tell me about what happened last night."

"You said you watched the game."

"Yeah, I did. But I don't really know that much about hockey. What happened?"

I tell her what I saw from the bench and how shook everyone was, especially Cookie.

"Cookie." The corners of her mouth lift. "Cute."

"Not last night, he wasn't," I mutter.

She pauses. "Are you mad at him?"

"No." I shake my head and slump back into the couch cushions. "Maybe? I don't know."

"The people talking about it on TV made it sound really bad. Like he did it on purpose."

"Well, yeah, he hit the guy on purpose. But he didn't mean to hurt him. He's not like that. I can one hundred percent say that."

"That's good."

"Obviously you don't want someone to get hurt. No one does. But it happens. And now Cookie's probably going to get suspended. We only have five games left. He's one of our top scorers. We're fucked."

She looks like she wants to smile. "I'm sure missing one player doesn't mean you're completely fucked. Where's that positive attitude?"

I grimace. "Right, right. Positive."

Her smile breaks free.

Reluctantly, I smile back at her. I reach for her hand and squeeze it. "Thanks for coming over."

"I figured you needed some distraction." She leans over and kisses me, a slow, lingering kiss.

Yep, my dick is now distracted. "That could work," I agree in a low voice.

LOLA

I stretch in Brandon's bed. It's a big bed and feels luxurious, with soft sheets and a cloud-like duvet. I rub my calf along his and turn to look at him.

He's asleep.

He looked exhausted when I got here—tired eyes with shadows under them, scruffy jaw, and messy hair. Last night must have been hard for him.

I study his face now. The scruff is the same, his hair is even more tousled from me running my fingers through it. I'm tempted to do that again. But his features are more relaxed, his mouth soft. He's a beautiful man—I admire the curve of his upper lip, the neat edges of his sideburns, the slope of his nose, and thick eyebrows.

Physically, he's gorgeous and I'm attracted to him. I'm attracted to his easy smile and fun banter. He has something about him that appeals to me and I'm sure it appeals to a lot of people—a sort of brightness that draws you in. But seeing him so troubled bothered me. A tenderness swells inside my ribcage.

There's more to him than surface charm. There are depths and shadows and complications. I'm hooked by that. Curious. Concerned.

We're sex buddies, nothing more. I know that. But I care about him.

I don't want to disturb his sleep. Maybe I should leave? That wasn't the best sex we've had, but it was still better than pretty much every other guy I've been with. Sinking my teeth into my bottom lip, I slowly slide the covers aside and ease toward the edge of the bed.

His eyes pop open.

"Where're you goin'?" he asks drowsily.

"I was going to go home…"

"Stay." He reaches for me and as always, I'm helpless. I didn't really want to go home that much anyway. I snuggle into him, he wraps his arms around me, and his breathing slows again.

I don't need a nap, but being enveloped in this warm, soft cocoon, the slow thud of his heart against my chest, make me a little sleepy too, so I close my eyes and let myself fall.

I wake up with Brandon watching me. He smiles.

I touch his cheek. "You look better."

"Uh oh. How did I look before?"

"Tired."

"Yeah." One corner of his mouth lifts higher. "I was. I feel a lot better now."

"Good."

"Sorry I fell asleep."

"That's okay. You needed sleep."

"Yeah. And now I'm starving."

I grin. "Oh."

"But I don't want to get out of bed."

I narrow my eyes at him. "Are you asking me to cook for you?"

"No!" He stares back at me. "That's not what I meant."

"I *could* cook," I say.

He shakes his head. "No. I'll order something in." He reaches for his phone on the bedside table and unlocks it. "Aw, fuck."

"What?"

"My phone's been blowing up. I didn't want to look at anything this morning." He wrinkles his nose. "Maybe I can handle it now. But first…food." He scrolls through his screen. "There's a place near here…do you like Greek food?"

"Sure." I guess I'm staying.

I lay and watch him swiping at his phone to place the order. Then he settles back into his pillows, stuffing a couple of big fat ones behind him. "Okay. I'm going in."

I laugh. "You sound like you're heading into battle."

"Social media is pretty much the same thing."

I pout and frown. "I guess I've never experienced what you guys do, being famous."

"It's fucking scary, sometimes. Stay close, I might need you."

Amused, I shift closer. "I'm here for you, big guy."

"Okay. Well, the good news is that Schneider's okay. He has a concussion. They released him last night after checking him out."

"That is good." I watch his face as he reads and talks, enthralled, if I'm being completely honest.

"The guys are all texting Cookie to see how he is and standing up for him." His eyebrows pull together over his nose. "He's not replying to anything." He keeps reading, sometimes aloud to share comments with me. "Jesus. Some of these people…" He closes his eyes. "Some of the fans are so pissed off at Cookie they want their team to hurt him the next time they play us."

My stomach rolls. "That's terrible."

"I guess it's not surprising. Fighting's part of hockey, and sometimes we do fight to avenge a teammate. But they're saying some really ugly things. Shit. Maybe I shouldn't have looked." He drops his phone. Then he picks it up. "No, I need to know what's going on. Cookie's suspended. And he's having a hearing tomorrow."

"A hearing? Jeez. This sounds serious."

"It is. The Department of Player Safety will meet with him to hear his side of the story and decide what his punishment will be."

"Oh boy."

"Yeah. Like I said, we're fucked."

"Brandon."

He looks over at me, then smiles. "Okay, fine. We all need to step up and do our best as a team."

"That's better." I give a firm nod.

He leans over and kisses my nose. "You're adorable."

Warmth flows from my chest and through my veins. "Um, thank you."

He laughs.

A whine next to the bed has us both lifting and peering over at Martha. She smiles and her tail wags.

"You need to go out, girl?" Brandon sets his phone down. "I'll take you."

He pulls on his gray sweatpants and yum! I've never seen a man look so good in them. His ass is firm, his thighs are beefy, and the view from the front with no underwear on is also impressive. Nice dick print. "We'll be right back." He tosses me a T-shirt from a drawer.

"Okay."

I watch Martha follow him eagerly out of the bedroom.

I pull on the T-shirt. It's huge. Wonderfully scented. I run a hand over the soft cotton and inspect the graphic on the front that says TALK EARTHY TO ME. Brandon is a tree hugger? Interesting.

I slide out of bed, the hem of the shirt falling around my thighs, and use the bathroom. I smooth my hair down and run a finger over a smudge of mascara beneath one eye. I didn't wear much makeup to come here, but I never go anywhere without mascara.

This bathroom is gorgeous—more white, with gleaming white tiles on the walls and floor, and a white vanity with white marble top. There's some color in the thick taupe towels and the mat on the floor.

I return to his bed. His bedroom has color—deep taupe walls, dark brown furniture, and lighter taupe bedding—which makes it feel more intimate, the late afternoon light shining pale and weak through the window. I amuse myself on my phone until he and Martha return. I hear sounds in the kitchen—I think he's feeding her—then he appears and rejoins me on the bed.

He talks more as he looks through various sites, more about last night, about how he almost called me at three in the morning. He plays me a video of his coach talking about the hit and defending his player. I like listening to him open up. What would I have done if he'd called me at three in the morning? I like my sleep. But as I've already noted, I'm defenseless when it comes to Brandon's charm.

Our food arrives and Brandon goes to the door to get it. I'm about to get out of bed when he steps back into the room, carrying a sack of food. "Let's eat in bed." He sets the big sack of food on the dresser.

I blink. "What?"

"Eat. In Bed." He lifts a provocative eyebrow.

"That sounds…decadent."

"Yeah. I like it."

I kind of like it, too.

Brandon grins. "Be right back."

I sniff the delicious scent of beef. Martha is interested too, pacing in front of the dresser, her tail swishing. She could probably reach the bag and steal it, but she's a good girl.

Brandon returns with a big wooden tray, a bottle of wine and two glasses.

"Wow." I fold my hands on the duvet, watching him set up. Soon we have gyro sliders with tzatziki on warm pita, and fries with feta and truffles in front of us, along with big glasses of Malbec. I pick up a fry and munch on it. "This is amazing."

"I like their food. And they're close."

"You don't cook?"

He grimaces. "Not as much as I should. I know how to make a few things, but I'm lazy. How about you?"

"I love cooking. But it's not much fun for one person. I admit I order takeout too often, as well."

He picks up a pita. "That shirt looks good on you."

I glance down at it. "Does this shirt mean you're an environmentalist?"

He grins. "Big time."

"Really?" I tilt my head.

"Why do you sound surprised?"

"I don't know." I lift my shoulders. "I just wouldn't have thought that."

"We have to protect this world. It's the only one we have."

"True." I take a bite of a slider. "Oh my God, this is good."

"Back home in Michigan, I got involved with a local activism group that advocates for protecting waterways—the Great Lakes, plus Michigan has about thirty-five thousand inland lakes."

This is unexpected but strangely sweet. I let him talk about stormwater runoff and planting native flowers and shrubs that don't need fertilizer, rising emissions, and lots of other stuff.

"Sorry," he eventually says. "That was probably boring as hell."

"Not at all. I'm fascinated. I need to step up more."

"We can all do small things." He pauses. "Wow, I actually forgot about the shit show happening in the hockey world for a while."

I smile. "Probably good to get away from it for a bit." I pick up my wine and take a sip. "This is also delicious."

"I just happened to have that. I think someone left it when I had a party."

"Lucky us."

"At least I *can* get away from it. I bet Cookie is beating himself up over this. He can't handle it when he's not perfect."

"Ugh. I relate to that."

He gives me a look. "Nobody's perfect."

I grimace.

He sighs. "This has to be killing him."

His concern for his teammate is also sweet.

"You can be there for him tomorrow." I reach out and squeeze his forearm. His sexy, strong forearm. I let my fingers linger there.

He gives me a look as if he knows what I'm thinking, and I meet his eyes. Might as well be open about the fact that I want to ride the flagpole.

He points a fry at me. "Finish eating."

"Yes, sir."

He laughs.

I pick up another fry and ask the question that's been on my mind since he texted. "Why did you text me and invite me over?"

He gives me a filthy look. "You have to ask that?"

I meet his gaze steadily. "Is that really all you wanted?"

He doesn't reply.

"We've seen each other a few times now," I add softly. "We're still in agreement about what we want, right?"

"Right." He studies me. "Okay, it wasn't all I wanted. I like you, Lola." He rubs his fingertips over my cheek. "I felt like I needed a friend. And a hug. One of those hugs that turns into sex."

I smile. "I like those hugs, too. With you."

He hesitates, then says, "Have you been with anyone else?"

I know what he's asking. "No. You?"

"No." His forehead puckers. "Look, I get that neither of us wants to get serious. Although, the sex is seriously hot."

"No argument there." I fan myself with my hand.

"But we can be friends, right?"

"Friends with benefits." I roll my eyes.

"Basically, yeah. Why not? We like each other and we have great chemistry."

"You're pretty sure of yourself, there, big boy." I give his shoulder a little shove, not wanting to give in to him that easily. "You think I like you?"

"I think you do." He leans over and smooches my lips. "Admit it. You like me."

I can't help but smile against his mouth. My belly is fluttering, my chest warm. "Okay, fine, I like you."

"And you like fucking me."

"I do." I sigh.

"So why not be fuck buddies?"

I blink at him, studying him. I've never had that kind of relationship. I have no problem with it. I'd like to think women can have that kind of relationship as easily as men can, although I know people say women can't be friends with benefits because their emotions will always get involved. But mine won't. I'm focused on my career. Marriage or long term is definitely not what I want right now.

I could be working right now. But I made the choice to come here. To see Brandon. I've done that a few times, even blowing off work to watch hockey games. I can't keep doing that.

"No commitment," he says, watching my face. "No strings."

I pull in a long slow breath through my nose. I feel like this *is* a commitment. A commitment to have sex and not get emotionally entangled—that still takes time. And what if one of us does get emotionally entangled? That could get complicated.

But deep down inside, I want this. He's right—I like him. I like fucking him. I want more. "Okay. Why not?"

He kisses me again, this time slower. Deeper. "Just one thing, though."

"What?" My voice is breathy.

"We're exclusive. I'm not asking for a long-term commitment," he adds hastily. "I just don't want to be one of many."

I tilt my head and purse my lips. "I suppose that's fair. You as well, right?"

"Of course." He looks mildly offended. "Deal?"

My insides tremble. "Deal."

BRANDON

The fallout from the hit on Schneider has the team's mood lower than snail shit. Cookie's been suspended for eight games, meaning the rest of the regular season and into the playoffs if we make it. There's a general sense that this punishment is unfair, considering things other players have done, and considering Cookie is one the cleanest players in the league. Stuff like that is frustrating because it's out of our control, and it can make you crazy if you let it. It's done and we have to deal with it. We have to win our next game and Pittsburgh has to lose, and then we've clinched a spot.

I hate this for Cookie. I hate it for all of us. I want to put my fist through a wall or throw something. But that won't help things. I remember Lola chiding me about my doomsday forecast. It's almost like a superstition; like, if you expect the worst it won't happen. But this is a good time for me to show some leadership, so I refrain from joining the whining.

"Okay, guys." I speak up just before we go on the ice for practice. "We can't change what happened. We've vented about the suspension, but we need to let it go and move forward. Bitching about it won't help."

I get somewhat surprised looks from some of the guys, nods from others.

"I know this is a shitty situation, but enough of the gloom and doom, okay? Gunner, you played fantastic the other night. Really solid in net. You kept us going. We need you to stay like that. Jammer, you were on their offense like pastrami on rye."

That gets a surprised laugh from the guys.

"Seriously. Just keep that up. What did we learn from that last game?"

"Uh…"

"Before things went to shit," I add.

"We're good when we play our game," Bergie says, helping me out. "Up-tempo, fast-paced, lots of physicality."

"Right. We need to stick to that. This is it, guys. We can't just *hope* we make the playoffs. We have to *work* for it."

"Yeah!" Bergie punches the air. "Let's work for it! Let's do it!"

We head out onto the ice and I try to set an example there, too, busting my ass.

After practice, the media frenzy outside the dressing room is wild. Cookie is talking to the media shortly and the room where the press conference is being held is packed. I give Cookie a clap on the shoulder as he walks by me. "You got this."

He barely nods. I can see the strain on his face.

The rest of us eat the lunch the team provides in the player lounge. The atmosphere feels marginally lighter than earlier, but I can tell we're all thinking about Cookie facing a firing squad across the hall.

"I'd be peeing my pants," Beav says. "Thank fuck that time I got arrested I didn't have to face the media like this."

"You got arrested?" Hellsy asks. "What the hell for?"

Beav's eyes shift. "Uh, it was nothing."

"Assaulting a woman," Morrie says easily.

Hellsy's mouth falls open. "Seriously?"

"No!" Beav scowls. "I mean, that's what the charge was, but it wasn't like it sounds. We were flirting—"

"*You* were flirting," Bergie corrects.

"Okay, yeah," Beav admits. "I was drunk, okay? I thought she was interested. I grabbed her ass."

A collective "ohhhhh" fills the room.

"I know, stupid." Beav rubs his forehead. "After that we left, but I went back to apologize to her and she called the cops."

Now it's an "oooooh."

"I had to do a public apology," he continues. "But that wasn't as bad as this."

"Wow," Hellsy says. "I did not know that."

"You were new here at the time," Beav says.

"Public apologies are scary shit," Bergie adds.

"Not as scary as being chased by Freddy Krueger," Nate says.

We all look at him. He grins. "Right? Who's scarier? Freddy Krueger, Jason Vorhees, Michael Myers, or Ghostface?"

We all ponder that.

"Oh Christ, Freddy Krueger is the scariest," I say with a shudder. "I had nightmares about him."

"On Elm Street?" Bergie asks.

"You know it." I smirk.

The others groan.

We get into a heated discussion about who's the scariest until we hear the sounds of the presser breaking up.

"Do you think Cookie will come back?" I ask.

"Doubtful." Millsy shrugs. He's probably the closest to Cookie. "He and Emerie broke up."

I gape at him. "Jesus. Really?" Cookie and Emerie haven't been together that long, but Cookie seems really into her. And, despite being the team owner's stepdaughter, she seems like a sweetheart. "That sucks. Especially now." I guess it's none of my business what happened.

"He's being an idiot," Millsy says. "But he's kind of fucked up right now. We'll give him some time. Keep an eye on him."

He, Hellsy, and Cookie all live in the same apartment building. "Good. Let us know if there's anything we can do."

"Thanks, man."

We go to the meeting room for Coach to talk to us.

"I know some of you are thinking we have a big challenge to deal with," he says. "But it's actually an opportunity. A chance for us to rise. To show what we're really made of. No excuses. This team doesn't depend on any one person to win. We do it together." He looks around the room. "All of us. Remember—tough times don't last. Tough teams do."

We're all listening. Coach does have a way of motivating us. We can do this. We all have to step up.

Bergie reinforces Coach's message like the leader he is, along with Nate and JBo. Like Bergie, Nate's been around while with a lot of experience, so they're great at helping the younger guys deal with stuff like this. I've been around a while too. Nobody's ever seen me as a leader in the room, despite the fact that I'm older than a lot of the guys. I'm just the unattached single guy who likes to have a good time. Maybe it's time for me to step up even more.

We have our last road trip of the season to Pittsburgh and Detroit. I get one goal in Pittsburgh, helping us win three-one. Dad drives into Detroit to come to the game with my Uncle Brian and my cousins Ryan and Caleb, who are a little younger than me. We all get together in the afternoon. They're excited to watch me play live.

"It's really cool ending the season here," I say.

As a Michigan boy who grew up a Detroit fan, it's always fun to come "home" to play. It always gives me a little extra zip in my game. I'll never forget the first time I played here. Half of Grand Rapids came to watch. Such a rush.

We talk about what happened to Cookie, which has been a huge nightmare for him and his family because of rabid fans on social media.

"And not even online," Dad adds. "People were actually threatening his parents." He shakes his head.

"What is wrong with people?" Uncle Brian shakes his head. "I mean, this city has some enthusiastic fans, too. But that's just never acceptable."

I get two goals and an assist for the win.

We make the playoffs.

The adrenaline is flowing. Things are clicking for us. This is a good time to be peaking.

We've shown ourselves we can do this without Cookie. He seems to be doing better. He's coming to practices, watching the home games from the press box. We'll be glad to have him back in the lineup, though.

We feel like celebrating after the game, but we have a flight. We get home around eleven since it was an early game, and this time I give in to my impulse and text Lola.

Hey Marlon! Sure come over, she texts back.

The Marlon bit makes me smile. *How about we go out for a drink somewhere? I feel like celebrating.*

I was in bed...but okay.

Sure?

Yes! You need to celebrate!

Instead of exiting 9A near my place, I stay on it until 34th, and there I am, at Lola's.

Wait. I can't show up emptyhanded. I think there's a bodega around the corner...I take a quick walk and yeah, I find the place still open, the lone clerk inside behind the counter staring at his phone. I glance around and spy a rack with a few bouquets of flowers. Not a lot of choice. It's cheesy, but I think she likes red, so I grab the bright bunch of red, purple, and yellow blooms.

"Hi," she greets me, smiling. "Congratulations."

"Thanks." I grin back at her. She apparently got dressed, now wearing a pair of jeans and a sweater. She looks soft and casual and so, so beautiful. "These are for you."

"Aw. Thank you. They're so pretty. Let me put them in some water quickly." She moves into her kitchen. "Two goals! You played great."

"And an assist. Don't forget the assist."

"Right, right."

"And thanks to Vancouver for beating Pittsburgh."

She laughs softly. "That too."

"I hate it when our success depends on someone else losing."

"How much do you hate it?" she teases.

I smirk. "Not that much."

She sets the flowers into a vase. "I'll arrange these later. Let's go. There's a little pub around the corner."

"Perfect."

LOLA

It's a mild spring day. I just finished a client meeting, and I stride along Stone Street, taking in the old buildings and narrow streets. I love this area, with all its history. It's not far to the steakhouse on Broadway where I'm meeting Kaylee for lunch. I enter, tugging my light scarf loose and looking around for her. There she is.

My heels tap on the black and white tiled floor as I cross to the small table for two covered with a white cloth. This place just reeks of money and power, with the amber lighting, dark wood, leather, and all the suits. Kaylee waves at me as I approach.

"Hi!" I hang my coat on a hook nearby and take the seat opposite her. "How are you?"

"I'm great. How did your meeting go?"

"I think it went well." I pick up a menu just as a server approaches. We both order coffee and he leaves us to look at the menu. "This client is a challenge. But I like a challenge."

I decide on the lobster bisque and a salad of field greens.

"So what's new with your hockey player?" Kaylee asks, once we've ordered.

"*My* hockey player?" I grin. "He came over last night."

"Oooh. This is getting serious."

"No." I hold up a hand. "This is not getting serious. We're both on the same page about that. We are booty buddies. That's it."

She lifts an eyebrow. "Really?"

"Really." I give a firm nod. "We spelled it out. Exclusive. But still just booty buddies."

"Hmmm."

"Why the skepticism?"

She purses her lips. "I don't know. I guess I just worry about you getting hurt."

"Hurt? Me?" I laugh. "This is perfect for me! I get some mattress action and no strings attached."

"Honestly? I *am* skeptical about whether it's possible to have a sexual relationship with someone without catching feelings."

I sit back in my chair, a bit surprised and hurt by Kaylee's doubts about this. "We're not going to catch feelings. We're both clear on that."

"I thought that kind of relationship is non-committal and non-monogamous. But you say you're exclusive."

"Yes." I nibble my bottom lip. "Neither of us wants to be one of many. Part of it is safe sex, you know what I mean?"

"Yes. And I do hope you're being safe."

"Two kinds of birth control—my IUD and condoms."

"Okay, that's good. Did you two talk about boundaries?"

"Um." My teeth worry my lip again. "Other than being exclusive?"

She gives me a look. "Yes."

"Not really. But we understand each other."

"I think it's important to make sure you do. Things can get complicated if you're misreading signals or expecting something he's not prepared to give."

"Hmmm. I get that."

"So you're saying you're not dating?"

"Nope."

"You two have never gone on a date?"

"Uh..."

She narrows her eyes at me.

"Well, last night we went out for a drink. To celebrate them making the playoffs! That was the only time, though."

"Did you both spell that out?"

I hesitate. "No."

She gives me that chiding look again. "You need to have rules. Do you do sleepovers?"

"No…" I did have a nap at his place. But that doesn't count.

"Sleepovers probably aren't a good idea."

Damn. That's disappointing.

"No dating. No sleepovers. No acting like a couple—holding hands, PDAs."

"You're a tough cookie."

She laughs. "It's about protecting yourself."

"I don't think I need to do that. I'm totally focused on work right now." Other than the night I ignored my work to have sex with Brandon. And the nights I didn't stay late because I wanted to watch his hockey game. "But you're right…we should discuss those things." I pause. "It's not a relationship. It's a shagship." I grin at my own inventiveness.

"Haha. That's good. I have to remember that." Her eyes sparkle. "I gather the shagging is good?"

"Oh my God." My belly flip flops just remembering how good. "Amazing. He really does have good hands." And other good parts. "I have to nail this project," I tell her. "Keith confirmed his retirement date. He'll be leaving in September. They'll be posting his position soon."

"Oooh! That's so good!"

"I'm excited." I give a little shimmy. "Anyway, that's what I'm focused on right now."

"With a little bedroom rodeo."

"It's good for stress relief."

"Can't argue with that." Kaylee pauses. "Have you told your parents?"

My mouth gapes open like a Japanese koi. *"About Brandon?"*

Kaylee collapses into laughter. "Oh my God, your face. No! About Keith retiring."

"Oh." Now I laugh too. "No."

"They'd be impressed, though, right? Vice president?"

"I think so. But I'm not telling them anything until it's a done deal. Otherwise it'll just be another failure."

She tilts her head sympathetically. "They're your biggest supporters."

"I know. Too big, sometimes." I sigh. "I don't want to disappoint them." I change the subject. "How's Leo?"

"Oh, he's okay."

Her lack of enthusiasm has me narrowing my eyes at her. "What's wrong?" Their relationship is pretty new, but I thought things were going great. She seemed to really like Leo.

"I don't know." She gives a lopsided smile. "I thought he was so nice at first."

"Are you still not over Carter?" I keep my tone gentle. She and Carter were together for years, and she took the breakup hard.

"Leo is the first guy I've really been with since Carter," she says. "Maybe he's my rebound."

"Hmmm. That could be."

"There's nothing at all wrong with him," she continues. "He's a nice guy. I'm just not feeling the...excitement."

"Oh. Damn. Are you going to break up with him?"

"I guess I should. It's not fair to lead him on if I'm never going to fall in love with him. But maybe I *am* going to fall in love with him." She meets my eyes, hers full of uncertainty.

"I've never been in that position. I've never let myself consider falling in love with someone." There've been men I casually dated, and there've been men who wanted more and got pissed when I made it clear that wasn't going to happen, which made ending things easy. "So I don't know what you're feeling, and I don't have any advice." I smile sympathetically. "Except trust your gut, I guess. If you know, you know."

She nods. "Right."

We catch up with other news over lunch and then go our separate ways, Kaylee back to her office, me to mine up on Madison Avenue.

Now I'm thinking about Brandon. And rules. Kaylee does make a good point. Brandon and I may think we're on the same page, but we haven't exactly talked about details.

But…talking about details makes it seem like a bigger deal than it is. It's casual. Fun. Hot.

Smoking hot.

I'll just casually bring it up next time I see him. *If* I see him. Wait. That's a depressing thought.

Which clearly means that's something we should talk about. If one of us wants to end this shagship, we need to be up front and tell the other person. Okay, maybe we do need to have some boundaries.

13

———

BRANDON

There's a meme I've seen that says LIFE WILL BE POSTPONED DUE TO PLAYOFF HOCKEY UNTIL FURTHER NOTICE. It's for fans, but it applies even more to the players. We now have no life outside of hockey.

We have home ice advantage and we're playing against the New Jersey Storm. Those are two factors in our favor. We don't need to leave home basically for the first round of the playoffs. On the other hand, that can be a negative. There are distractions here: wives, girl-friends, kids, a baby due to arrive any day.

Lola.

Lola's not a distraction in a bad way, though. She makes no demands on me, expects nothing from me other than sex. She's a *good* distraction because we all know that myth about athletes not having sex before a game is indeed a myth. That said, she has a life and she's busy. In fairness, I can't make demands on her or expect that she'll be around and DTF any time I want. I'm not an asshole.

And now I have an unexpected complication.

"We're coming to watch you play!" Mom says on the phone Monday afternoon. "We get in tomorrow around noon."

My eyes shoot open wide. "Who's coming?"

"Dad and I!"

I blink a few times, processing this. "You and Dad."

"Right. We're still your parents. And we're so proud of you. We want to watch you play in the playoffs and cheer you on."

Sure, *now* she's proud of me. "Okay. Well. Good. That's great. I can get tickets for you. How long are you staying?"

"You play tomorrow night and Thursday in New York, then Sunday and Tuesday in New Jersey, right?" It sounds like she's looking at the schedule.

"Right."

"We'll probably stay a week then, and see those four games. Maybe you'll win all four!"

Ha ha. Possible, but not likely. "Maybe."

"We're going to stay with you."

I squeeze my eyes closed. "Okay."

This is going to fuck with my hockey mojo. Jesus. I rub my forehead.

"We're so excited for you!"

She gives me her flight details and says they'll make their own way here to my place, and we end the call.

They're excited for me. Wow. When I was growing up, they were always too busy being pissed off at each other to pay any attention to me. And if they did come to my games, embarrassing shit happened. One time they had an argument in the stands while they were watching my game. Even I could hear them on the ice. I wanted to skate off and never come back. I got a lot of sympathetic looks from other parents after the game, which burned so fucking bad. Mom didn't come to many games after that. I was relieved; but I was also crushed.

And now it's playoffs. And they're coming to stay with me? I am fucked.

There's one person I need to be with right now. One person I can relax with and forget the rest of the world with. So I text her.

I have a business dinner tonight, she responds with a sad emoji. *But it should be done by about nine. Is that too late?*

Is it? Nope. *That'll work.*

For the first time, I feel a twinge of guilt. Am I using her? I guess I sort of am—but she's doing the same. We agreed what this is. I don't need to feel guilty.

I take Martha for a walk to pass some time, heading down to the river. I love being around water, although the Hudson River isn't Lake Michigan. We follow the path along the Greenway, breathing in spring air. Things are getting green, spring wildflowers sprouting here and there. We wander down to Clinton Cove and find a place to sit and gaze out over the water, New Jersey on the opposite side. I love finding little nature spots in this big urban space. It helps me chill out. Martha likes it, too

I ponder the problem of Mom and Dad and what that's going to be like. I manage to get myself worked up again, even though I'm supposed to be relaxing. Dammit! Why'd they have to come? Why did they have to come together? And why couldn't they have stayed in a hotel? Frustration makes my skin feel too tight.

Don't think about them. I try to recall the strategies I've learned over the years to control the adrenaline. Motivational self-talk. Being here by the water is something that's helped me in the past, like some guys use music. Relaxation techniques.

I've got this.

And I get to see Lola in about...I check my phone...five hours. Jesus. That's way too long.

I jump up and start hiking home at a brisk pace, but I soon have to slow my speed for Martha. The signs of her aging give me a little stab in my heart region. What the hell am I going to do when she's gone?

As I pass a flower shop, I pause. We step inside. Wow, it smells amazing in here, so green and fresh. I look around. I spy an arrangement of small plants and move toward them.

"Are you interested in succulents?"

I look up at the salesclerk, smiling at me. Why does that sound dirty? Jesus, I'm a pig. "I don't even know what they are." I smile back. "My..." I pause, then for the sake of simplicity say, "My girlfriend likes plants. But she doesn't have one like these." I point to one with thick leaves edged with red. "That's nice."

"That's an aeonium urbicum. Also called a salad bowl."

"Okay, I'll take that one."

She wraps it up and I take it home. I pass more time by cleaning my apartment, making up the bed in one spare bedroom with clean sheets, and eating a healthy dinner of salmon, brown rice, and broccoli. I spend some time reading a book I just got, written by Victoria Wynn. She's a sports psychologist and the mother of two hockey players, and her ex-husband is the coach of the Long Beach Golden Eagles.

I'm interrupted by a text from Lola.

Meeting done early! I'm on my way home now.

Great. See you soon.

And I'm out the door faster than a bee-stung stallion.

I nearly lose my mind trying to find parking and end up in a parking garage a couple of blocks away from Lola's place. Stupid drivers are pissing me off and the parking lot attendant is an asshole. In the back of my mind it occurs to me that staying home and meditating might have been a better choice for this evening.

Too late now.

Finally Lola lets me into her apartment. It hasn't even been a week since I was last here. We tried to get together on the weekend, but I was busy with the team and she had something going on with her friends.

"Hey," she greets me with that sunny smile.

"Hi, beautiful." Instantly tensions eases out of my body. I just want to look at her and smile at her. And yeah, fuck her. But not yet. Not right away. First I just want to be with her. I kiss her forehead. "How are you?"

"I'm good. Come on in."

"Here."

She tips her head. "You brought me something again!"

"Yeah. It's small."

She opens the paper wrapping to see the small plant. "Oh! It's so pretty."

"There's information in there about the kind of plant it is and how much water it needs."

"I love it. Thank you." She goes on her toes and kisses me. My chest goes spongy and warm.

She's wearing a soft lounge outfit, gray, with leggings and a long, loose top. The waves of her hair are messy and she looks so pretty.

A laptop sits open on the coffee table in front of the couch.

"Working?"

"Yeah." She rolls her eyes with a guilty little smile. "Guess what?"

"What?" I sit on the couch.

"They posted Keith's position. The VP job."

"Oh wow! The one you've been waiting for."

"Yes." She gives an excited little grin and dance. It's so fucking cute. "So I'm working on my resume."

"Don't they already know everything about you?"

"Yes, but we still have to formally apply. So I'm trying to tune up my resume with all my accomplishments and awards over the years."

"I bet you have lots, superwoman." I smile.

She laughs. "I have a few."

"When is he leaving?"

She tells me all about it, along with things that have been happening with the project she's working on. I'm interested. I ask her questions to understand more of what she's talking about. She's so damn smart.

"Would you like a drink? Beer? Wine?"

"No, thanks. No alcohol today. Tomorrow's a big day."

"Right, right. Are you ready?"

"Fuck no." I sigh and tell her about the call from my mom.

"Oh my God! They're coming together?"

"Yes. I can't believe it."

"Hmmm. Didn't I say it sounds like they still love each other?"

"Fuck me, you did." I lean my head back and laugh dryly. "If that's love, I want nothing to do with it."

"Oh, Brandon." Her voice is like velvet. "Is it that bad?"

I don't look at her, my head still back. "You don't want to hear about my messed-up family."

"Tell me. I can see this is bothering you."

When people poke at me, about things I don't want to talk about, I close up. I feel that happening now. Even though it's Lola and I know she's not being nosy, that it's because she cares, it bugs me. "I'm fine." I lift my head and grin. "Our family motto is 'well, that escalated quickly.'"

She laughs, though her eyes are still shadowed with concern. "I'm sorry. And now they're coming to stay with you."

"Yeah."

"You should have told them no."

I tilt my head. "I don't think they actually asked."

She laughs lightly. "Even so, it's your place. You could say it doesn't work for you to have them staying with you when it's the playoffs."

I let her words sink in. "You're right. I guess I could have said that."

"It's about boundaries." She pauses, nibbling her bottom lip. "Speaking of boundaries, you and I need to have a conversation about that."

"What?" I frown. Is she pissed that I pick random times to come over? "Shit. I knew I was being an asshole."

"No, no! You're not. Why would you say that? It's just...well, I was talking to Kaylee about it and she made some good points, and I thought to prevent misunderstandings, maybe we should clarify a few things. Like, we did agree we'd be exclusive while we're doing this FWB thing."

"FWB?"

"Friends with benefits."

My lips twitch. "Right, right. So...what else?"

"Well, safe sex. We've been using condoms, but I didn't tell you that I have an IUD. You should know that."

"Okay. Fair enough." I pause. "Does that mean we can forego condoms?"

She purses her lips. "Maybe? If we both have test results and we're definite about being exclusive."

"I can do that."

"Okay. Me too. And, um, dating. We're not dating. Right?"

"Right. But…" I consider that. "It would be okay if we went out to eat occasionally, right?"

She purses her lips. "That sounds like a date."

"It's a meal."

Her small chin sets. "I suppose once in a while a meal would be okay. I mean, it's not that much different than eating a pizza here."

"Right."

"Also, Kaylee says no sleepovers."

"What? Hell no!"

Her eyes fly open. "No?"

"No!"

"We haven't done that."

"But we might. Sometimes it's a pain in the ass getting up in the middle of the night to go home."

"True."

I fold my arms and set my jaw. "I'm not agreeing to that one."

Her long eyelashes flutter. "Um. Okay."

She's a super businesswoman but I think I've rattled her. I try not to smile. "Anything else?"

"Well, if one of us wants to end this, we should be up front with the other and say so. Rather than just ghosting. Agreed?"

"Definitely." I wait. "Are we good?"

She nods, her mouth curving into a reluctant smile. "Yeah, we're good."

"Good." I lean over and smooch her mouth. "Now get your cute little butt in that bed."

"Hey! I at least need some foreplay." Her eyes sparkle.

"Oh, I'll give you foreplay."

14

———

LOLA

I stare at Keith in dismay. "I can't take on another project right now."

As soon as I say the words, I want to take them back. That's not the kind of manager I want to be. I want to be able to do anything. I *can* do anything. But in all honesty, this current project is taking all my time and more. Maybe I could take on another project—but could I do a good job of it? And I don't want to do just a good job. I want to do the *best* job.

"I know your plate is pretty full with the KGP project," Keith says. "But you're efficient and organized. You're our go to when we need to get something done and done right."

His words are flattering and I respond to them even though I recognize he's buttering me up.

Am I efficient, though? Or do I spend too much of my own time getting things done? This question makes me uneasy and I push it to the back of my mind.

I also have this feeling that if I don't do it, they'll find someone else who will. I'm still a term employee, and even though I've been here a long time, my contract can end tomorrow. Which is one of the reasons I'd like to have the VP position. And trying to get out of work isn't going to convince them I'm VP material.

Maybe if I work smarter I can handle it.

I've tried to follow the rule of never going to my boss with a problem unless I have a potential solution to it. And right now, I don't have a solution to this, other than suggesting someone else take it on. The truth is, no one else can handle it either. We all have a lot on our plates right now. Like most organizations, Synoptic has been trying to do more with less.

"Okay." I give him a confident smile. "I've got this."

"Thanks, Lola. I know I can count on you."

"Of course."

I leave his office and return to mine to sink into my chair. I feel tired. Very, very tired.

It'll all be worth it. I can use this as an opportunity to show them what I'm capable of. That they really can count on me. I already work hard. I'll just work smarter. My new mantra. But how?

I'll figure it out.

I sort of wanted to go to the hockey game tonight because it's the playoffs. Kaylee said she'd go with me. But now, I'll spend my evening here in my office reviewing all the project materials and start working on my change management strategy.

Around six, Zayn pokes his head into my office. "Oh hey, you're still here."

"Yeah. I will be for a while." I smile. "You're heading out?"

"Yeah. A few of us are going to Fitzgerald's to watch the hockey game. Bears versus Storm. Want to join us?"

"I didn't know you're a hockey fan."

"Oh yeah. I love hockey."

It's tempting. I don't hang out with people from work often and it would be fun. Plus…Brandon's playing and I want to watch the game.

I swallow a sigh and shake my head. "Thanks, but I have so much to do with this new project."

"Yeah. Look, tomorrow I can take some stuff off your hands. I can work on the survey results for your stakeholder report."

Hmm. Maybe. I smile. "Okay, we'll talk tomorrow."

A while later, I pop out to pick up a Baja shrimp salad from a nearby taqueria. I eat it at my desk, thinking about Brandon. Is he nervous? Does he get nervous before a game? Before a playoff game? How are things going with his parents? I'm glad they're here for him and hopefully they're aware of what he needs and more concerned about that right now than their own issues.

I hope he plays well tonight.

Now that we had our discussion about "boundaries" and we're both on the same page, I feel like we're good. We can do this shagship. It'll all be fine.

I can't ignore the lump of disappointment sitting in my belly that I can't watch the game. I keep checking the NHL app for updates on the score as I work, which isn't helping my focus.

Did I mention that I'm tired?

Around nine, with the Bears leading two-one, I call it a night and leave the office. I find a radio station that's playing the game and listen on my earbuds as I ride the train home, embarrassing myself by cheering out loud when the Bears score. It sounded like Brandon scored! Turns out he assisted, but that's still good. I want them to win!

The game ends as I walk into my apartment, a three-one victory. Yay! I'm exhausted but that lifts my mood. I toss my coat onto a chair, kick off my shoes and leave them on the carpet, and head to my plants.

"Hello, boys and girls," I croon. "I'm home late, I know. How are you doing today?" I touch my philodendron. "Phoebe, you're looking a little scraggly. You need a trim. We'll do that this weekend."

I'll have a glass of wine and read in bed for a while, then get an early night so I can be ready for tomorrow. After washing and moisturizing, changing into pajamas, and settling into bed, I open my e-reader. I have two books in progress—one on high performance leadership, and a fun rom com. I should read the leadership book. But I'm tired. The rom com wins.

I sip my wine and sink into my deliciously soft bed as I read.

I'm startled by my phone buzzing. I reach over for it.

I'm downstairs. Can I come up?

Brandon. Huh. I didn't expect to see him at all during the playoffs. I text back, *Sure.*

A tingle of excitement shoots through me. I throw my legs over the side of the bed, push my feet into fluffy pink slippers, and cross to the door to await him. It only takes a minute for him to arrive.

He walks in, freshly showered and smelling spicy clean, his hair a bit damp at his temples. He's dressed in another fabulous suit, this one a deep, deep green. His crisp white shirt is background to a rust brown tie that matches his leather shoes.

He lifts his arms in a cheer.

I laugh. "I heard. Congratulations. Come in."

He grins and walks in, unbuttoning his suit jacket.

I close the door behind him. "I didn't expect to see you."

"I didn't either." He makes a face and sits on my couch, apparently quite at home.

I like that.

"I can't go home," he says. "My parents are fighting."

"Oh my God." I sit cross-legged on the couch, facing him, a knot tightening in my stomach. "You're kidding."

"I wish." He rubs his face. "They fought all day."

"What are they fighting about?"

"How to get to the arena. What to eat before. Which goalie the Storm will start. Who should sleep on the couch. You name it. They were even arguing about whether I should have a game day nap."

My eyes widen. "You always have a game day nap."

"Right? I'm not messing with my routine now."

"Those are…"

"I know. Ridiculous." His head falls back. "I just wanted some peace and quiet before I go home. I told them not to wait up for me."

"Oh. I'm so sorry. This sucks that you can't even go home after a game." And here I was so hopeful that they were here for him.

"I guess I did it to myself." He closes his eyes. "I'll know better next time."

"Well, at least they're here. Obviously they care about you." I don't know what their problem is, but I'm annoyed on Brandon's behalf. I slide in closer and snuggle up to him.

"Eh."

"What does that mean?"

"Nothing."

There he goes being evasive again. I want to know what's going on with him!

He slides his arms around me and we sit in silence. Finally, he says, "I won't stay long. Just needed a little respite."

"I get it."

As always around him, I'm turned on. A faint heaviness aches low in my belly. I'm ready for him to carry me over to the bed. But he's not making any move to do that. That's okay. He just expended a lot of energy.

"How was your day?" he murmurs, eyes still closed.

"Shitty."

He opens one eye to peer at me.

I smile. "But fine."

"What happened?"

"My boss gave me another project to work on."

"Oh. That's bad?"

"I'm on overload as it is. I'm not sure how I'm going to handle more." A small sigh escapes me. "But I'll figure it out."

"You work so hard, superwoman." His fingers slide through my hair.

"I know. I'm going to try to work smarter." I give a dry laugh.

Now both his eyes open. "Are you really worried about it?"

I thought I was hiding that. "I'm a little worried, yeah."

He gazes at me. "Don't let your job make you sick, or something."

"Of course not! It's fine."

"Hmmm."

That sounds like he doesn't believe me.

"I have to show them I can do it," I say quietly. "You know why."

"The VP job."

"Yes."

"I get it. That's your goal." He pauses. "Why is that so important to you?"

Because once upon a time I thought I really was supergirl. Because when I got to college I discovered I wasn't the best at everything I did. Because I want to be the best. Because...I want my achievements to be real.

I say none of those things. "It's a permanent job. And I'd be in charge."

He nods slowly, stroking my hair again. Tension eases out of me, tension I didn't even realize I was storing in my muscles. I relax into him, my cheek on his chest. "This is nice."

"Yeah."

His hand slips under my pajama shirt and strokes my bare back. Tingles flow through my veins, but he doesn't take it any further than that, and when his hand stops, I realize he's dozed off. My heavy eyelids drop down and I doze off, too.

I wake with a small start. I think I drooled on Brandon's beautiful shirt. I rub my fingers over it. "Hey," I whisper. "Do you want to go to bed?"

His eyelids flicker, then open. "Shit. I fell asleep. I'm sorry."

"That's okay."

"I better get home." He kisses my forehead.

"Okay." I drag myself away from him, feeling a tug like a magnet.

He stands and stretches, then winces.

"What's wrong?"

"Just a twinge in my shoulder. Took a hard hit into the boards from that asshole Garnier."

"Are you okay?"

"Oh yeah. I'll get it checked out tomorrow. They'll do some magic shit to it." He smiles.

I stand and follow him to the door. "Be safe out there."

"Yeah. I'm good. Thanks for putting up with me."

"No problem." I smile up at him and touch my fingertips to his beard stubble. "Good luck in your next game."

"Thanks. Good luck to you too, with your new project."

"Thank you."

I lean against the door when he's gone. It's just after midnight. He wasn't here that long. We didn't bang. That's...weird. But inside I feel strangely warm and content.

Superwoman. That's right, dammit.

15

BRANDON

I survive my parents' visit.

They talk about coming back if we make it to the next round of the playoffs. Which we will, if we win tomorrow, since we won the first three games. I'm thinking maybe I'd rather lose.

Just kidding.

But we lose.

That makes us more determined to wrap things up, and we win game six in New Jersey. Pittsburgh and Washington are still playing, so we have a break for a few days before the second round.

But when I say break, I mean, we're busting our asses in practices. And now that my folks are gone, I'm really trying to focus on hockey and staying healthy—light workouts, lots of stretching, physical therapy sessions for the minor bumps and strains we all have, massages, and eating healthy.

What I'm not doing? Fucking.

I feel stupid for going over to Lola's place that night. I showed up unannounced, fell asleep on her couch, and left without giving her a single orgasm. What the fuck?

I have texted her. Just casually. We talked on the phone a couple of times because I don't have the patience to type long messages. She congratulated me on our series win. Sounds like she's working long hours. I don't like that for her, but she says she loves her job, and I get that. I'm focused and dedicated, too, right now. I hope this pays off for both of us.

It turns out my dad can't get time off from work to come to New York again so soon, so I don't have to deal with that distraction. And yet, I kind of liked it that they cared enough to come, and that they were both in the stands watching me play. That didn't happen very often when I was a kid.

Pathetic. I don't need my parents cheering me on.

I see Lola once before the next round of playoffs start. I convince her to let me take her out for dinner—it's not a date!

We end up playing Pittsburgh in the second round. They've been a pain in our asses all season. There's some bad blood between us, after some intense physical games, and I start the first game off with a hard hit against one of their top scorers. That sets the tone and there's a lot of slamming and smashing through the whole series. Playoff hockey is intense, physically and mentally, and by the time we've won round two in six games again, I'm exhausted.

And yet I'm wired. We're getting closer to the ultimate prize—the Stanley Cup.

With a few days before the third round starts, I invite Lola over to my place. I order in food.

She comes straight from the office. She walks in and hands me...a plant.

"What's this?"

"A pothos. I grew it myself, from cuttings. It's super easy to take care of. Even you can't kill it."

I take the small concrete pot, eyeing it. "Don't tempt fate."

She laughs lightly. "Put it in the window. It'll be fine." She crouches to rub Martha's ears. Martha sits happily, soaking up the attention. "You're such a good girl, aren't you. And so pretty. Look at your pretty eyes."

Fuck. I love it that she likes my dog.

I set the plant on a table and turn. I eye her up and down. "That suit is hot."

She straightens and smiles. "Why, thank you. I like you in a suit, too."

"Not tonight, thank fuck." I heave a tired sigh. "Come on in, I ordered Mexican food."

"Is that on your approved diet?"

I grin. "No. But we have a day off tomorrow, so I'm living it up."

I watch her ass sway in the tight pencil skirt as she walks over to the couch. She stops and points. "What is that?"

She's gesturing at the six-foot giraffe sitting in the corner.

"That's my gift for Bergie and Mandy's baby. The baby's due in a few weeks."

She turns, smiling. "That's your gift?"

"Yeah. I think it's cool."

"It's...amazing."

"I know it's not practical, but I think the little guy will love it."

"I think he will, too." She takes off her suit jacket, which pulls the silky fabric of her blouse taut across her breasts.

"Jesus," I mutter, my dick thickening.

"What's wrong?"

"You make me have thoughts that are so fucking filthy." I pause. "Thank you."

She laughs, a light delighted sound. "It's been a while. Are we eating or fucking first?"

"Hmm." I prowl toward her and set my hands on her hips. "How about a foregasm? Then we can eat?"

She gives a strangled laugh. "A what?"

"Foregasm." I bend and kiss her lightly, then deeper. "Figure it out, superwoman." I swing her up into my arms and carry her into my bedroom.

When I've got her out of her sexy little suit and lacy lingerie, I push her down onto the bed and move between her legs. "I've missed this pretty pussy." I stroke my fingers up her cleft. "Jesus. So soft. Open your legs wider."

She obeys, parting her thighs, watching me with dark eyes, her bottom lip separating from the top one. Christ, she's so fucking sexy.

I play with her, bending over to lavish attention on her sweet tits, my fingers delving and stroking her pussy, until she's moaning and writhing and wet. So wet. Then I kiss her between her legs, breathing in her now familiar scent, licking her sweet juices, finding her swollen clit and sucking.

She comes hard, hips lifting, her body shuddering, soft cries falling from her lips.

"Goddamn, I like making you come." I sit up and wipe my mouth.

"Uuuungh."

I smile. "I'll get the food."

She makes a noise of protest and lifts her head. "What about you?"

"I can wait."

"Ohhhh." Her head falls back as if her neck is Jell-o.

Yeah, my dick is throbbing and impatient, but I wanted to give that to her.

"Are we eating in bed again?"

"Do you want to?"

"I don't think I can move, so yes."

Perfect. I gather up the steak tacos, rice and beans, and some eating utensils and take everything into the bedroom. Lola's now beneath the covers, her pale hair spread against the dark pillowcase.

She lifts her head and peers at me. "Yay. Food. It smells amazing."

"I even have margaritas."

"You're really going wild."

"Our next game's not till Wednesday. I figured one drink would be okay. Man, I can't wait to taste that tequila."

She pulls the sheet up and tucks it under her arms, and I'm totally distracted by her bare shoulders as we eat.

"You're still dressed," she says, giving me a look.

"So I am. Do you want me naked?"

"Of course I want you naked."

"You don't have to ask twice." I strip and join her in bed, fully aware of her perusal of my semi-hard cock.

She sips her drink and gives a happy sigh. "This is the best margarita I've ever had."

"Top shelf tequila. Fresh lime. Really good."

We demolish everything I ordered. It's so good I could cry.

"What do you want when your season's done?" she asks me. "What forbidden treat?"

"Ice cream. I fucking love ice cream."

"What's your favorite kind?"

"Haagen-Dazs pralines and cream," I answer immediately. "But I wouldn't say no to any kind of ice cream."

"Yum."

"How about you? Do you have a favorite ice cream?"

"I like my ice cream dipped in chocolate. Haagen-Dazs has those bars…they're all good. I love the crunch of the hard chocolate mixed with the ice cream."

"Huh. What would you think about margarita ice cream?"

Her eyes twinkle and she cocks her head. "I would try it."

"When I was in Japan, we had wasabi ice cream. It was terrible. I can't handle hot spices."

She grins. "Hot and spicy ice cream. You'd think the creaminess would help with the heat."

"It did not. We also tried soy sauce ice cream, and sesame ice cream. That was surprisingly good."

"Hmmm. I once had corn on the cob ice cream. It was kind of like creamed corn."

"Ugh."

"I thought you said you wouldn't turn down any kind of ice cream."

"I guess I lied."

She points to my plate. "You're not eating your jalapeños."

"I ate one. That was enough."

She reaches over and snags some of the pepper slices and pops them into her mouth.

My jaw drops in horror. "What are you doing?"

"I like jalapeños."

"You're going to burn your mouth."

"Nope. I like it hot."

"Haha. I like it hot too. But not like that."

She smirks. "I'm superwoman, remember?"

"I never forget that, believe me." I kiss her and get a slight tingle of heat on my lips. "That mouth is not coming anywhere near my junk."

She pouts. "Damn. I was ready to repay you for the foregasm."

I wince. "I'm probably more disappointed than you are."

With a light laugh she rubs her tits against my arm. "How long do you think it takes for the heat to wear off?"

"No idea. We could google it." I give her a hopeful look.

"Hand me my phone."

I reach and then hand it over. She taps her bottom lip. "I'm not sure exactly what to enter in the search."

"Blow jobs and hot spices."

She taps on her phone, then frowns. "Oh, that was a bad idea." She taps again and shows me a graphic clip from a porn movie.

I choke. "Oh."

She turns the phone back to her.

"Wait," I say, leaning over.

She gives me a look.

"Kidding. Although I don't mind the odd triple X movie."

She's repressing a smile as she searches again. "Okay, it says it takes twenty minutes."

"Oh hey. That's not long."

"What should we do until then?" She slides down under the covers and gives me an innocent look.

"Good thing I love that pussy."

"I meant a hand job."

"Oh. Okay then! But…could you go wash your hands?"

Giggling uncontrollably, she rolls out of bed and disappears into my bathroom.

"Use lots of soap!"

16

LOLA

How can I not watch the games? They're in the third round of the playoffs. If they win this round, they go to the Stanley Cup finals. This is big!

But I'm losing my mind at work. So...much...work.

I take work home with me and try to do it in front of the TV. I don't get much done. I keep watching the game, cheering for the Bears, groaning when Tampa Bay scores. The Bears lose the first game, which isn't a good omen, but they win the second, so that's good.

Brandon texts me. *Hey guess what. Bergie had his kid!*

I smile. *Congratulations to them! Everyone doing okay?*

The baby was a little early. I think he's okay, but Bergie's going to miss our game tonight.

Oh, right. Well, he should be with his wife and baby.

I guess.

I smile at his lack of enthusiasm. Hockey is clearly more important to him than a baby.

Daniel, or Bergie as Brandon calls him, ends up missing a bunch of games, because their baby has to stay in the hospital with some problems because of his prematurity. Brandon's not very forthcoming about the details and I feel terrible for everyone. I'm sure Daniel's first concern is for his child, but it has to be killing him to miss these important games. And he's their captain and one of their best players. I hope the team can win without him.

They pulled together when Owen Cooke was suspended, so they can do it again.

Now there's no way I can not watch the games on TV. They win game three. Brandon scores two goals and gets two assists. I'm nearly bursting with pride for him.

They win game four. Again, Brandon's playing great. I listen to the TV commentators talking about how he's stepping up, one of their more experienced players, showing leadership to the younger guys, leading by example.

They win game five. Then they play game six which is a nail biter, because this could be the championship for them. They're in Florida and they show the actual Stanley Cup on TV. It's there!

But they lose.

Dammit. The disappointment flooding me is shocking in how intense it is. You'd think I had something riding on this game. Of course, I do—I want this for Brandon.

They come back to New York for game seven. Brandon texts me to tell me his parents are coming to see this game again. *And guess what?*

What?

I told them they need to stay in a hotel.

I grin. *Good for you!*

We end up talking on the phone. I know he doesn't have much patience for long text messages.

"You made me realize I could do that," he tells me. "And you know what? When I explained to Mom that I need to keep to my routine, she understood. I figured she'd be pissed that I wouldn't let them stay with me, but they're fine with it."

"There you go. Respecting your boundaries."

"Right."

"They must be excited. This is the last game of the series."

"Mom says she's nervous."

"I get that." I laugh. "So am I."

"Aw."

"Never mind us. How about you? Do you get nervous?"

"Sure. If I wasn't nervous there'd be something wrong with me. I just have to control the energy. Too much adrenaline can lead to mistakes. But you need *some* adrenaline to perform your best."

We chat for a while. When we end the call, I say, "Good luck. I'll be watching."

"Thanks, superwoman. I like knowing that."

I'm so nervous about this, I invite Kaylee, Sadie, and Isla over to watch the game with me. I'm not even going to pretend I'm going to work tonight. I pick up snacks and wine, and they bring more wine.

We arrange our food and beverages on the coffee table and settle in on the couch. I turn on the TV in time for the national anthem.

"So how are things with Leo?" Isla asks Kaylee.

"I'm going to break up with him."

"Oh no!" We all gaze at her in dismay.

"It's okay. It's for the best. I like him, but I feel like we're more friends than lovers. I want what you have with Brandon—headboard banging, sheet-twisting sex."

"We all want what she's having with Brandon," Sadie says dryly.

I laugh. "But you want love, too."

"That could come." Kaylee pauses, opens her mouth again.

I lift my hand. "No. Don't say it. Brandon and I are just bang buddies."

She purses her lips. "Okay."

"I'm sorry about Leo."

"Yeah, me too. He's such a nice guy. But he'll give some other woman toe-curling orgasms. Maybe."

Yikes.

They drop the puck to start the game and we all focus on the TV. I'm on the edge of the couch the whole game, except when I'm jumping up to cheer. Everything rides on this game.

It's fast. It's hard. They're hitting each other and it feels like they're skating up and down the ice, end to end, the entire game. These two teams are evenly matched and in the third period, the score is tied one all.

Aaaaah!

"I can't handle this!"

The others aren't quite as invested as I am, but they're enthusiastically cheering, too. Kaylee grabs my arm and squeezes when the Bears almost score. They curse along with me when the ref doesn't call a play against Tampa Bay that was clearly tripping.

Then Brandon gets the puck and flies toward the Tampa Bay net alone—a breakaway!

"Oh my God."

We all stare at the TV, wide-eyed. My hands curl into fists as Brandon skates in on the goalie alone, does some fancy fake move, then shoots the puck into the net.

"Yesssss!" I pump my hands in the air.

We all leap up and hug and jump up and down, cheering. God, I love my friends.

"Okay, okay. We got this. Eight more minutes."

But eight minutes is a lot in a hockey game, and with only two left in the third period, Tampa Bay ties it up.

I slump onto the couch. "Noooooo."

"Breathe," Sadie says. "Two minutes. Lots of time."

"Haha. Sure."

They try. They try so hard. Brandon gets a shot on net that's beautiful, but the goalie makes an amazing save.

The third period ends in a tie.

Overtime. "Jesus," I mutter. "This is terrible."

"It's okay, it's okay," Isla chants. "More wine?" She holds up the bottle.

We all agree and she fills glasses generously.

"One goal," I say. "That ends this whole thing. One lucky break."

"Or one mistake," Kaylee says.

I wince. "Yeah."

My stomach is a mass of knots as the overtime period starts.

The Bears have a chance on net. The goalie stops the shot. Another chance. Another save. They're putting pressure on, again and again. Then Tampa Bay desperately clears the puck and Nate Karmeinski on the blue line tries to stop it, actually diving to the ice with his stick outstretched. Ouch. He misses it. The puck slides over the line, and a Tampa Bay player scoops it up and sails down the ice. Jamal Jordan, the other defenseman, is on him but can't quite catch him. It's a break-away, Jamal desperately trying to stop him and using his stick. He either takes the guy down and gets a penalty, or doesn't and…

He scores.

The crowd in the Apex Center goes quiet as the Tampa Bay players start jumping up and down and tossing their gloves on the ice. Their excitement is our misery. The camera pans across the Bears' bench. There's Brandon, head down, shoulders slumped.

My heart squeezes and I think I might actually cry. I brush a tear from one eye. Damn, damn, damn.

My apartment is also quiet.

"Well, that's it then." I sigh.

"I'm sorry," Kaylee says glumly. "That's so heartbreaking."

"Yeah. Their season is over. Not the way they wanted to end it, but hey… they did great to get this far."

Heaviness fills me as we watch the players form lines to shake hands. I catch of glimpse of Brandon, his face sweaty and stoic. I press a hand to the ache in my chest.

My friends all give me sympathetic smiles and shoulder squeezes, and refill my wine glass. They stay a while longer, but I'm exhausted. I feel like I played that whole game with Brandon.

When they're gone, I get ready for bed. Before I turn the lights out, I reach for my phone and send Brandon a message. *I'm so sorry. You worked so hard.*

I don't know what else to say. I don't get a response, but I didn't expect that. I'm sure he's busy with the media and his team.

In the dark, I can't stop thinking about him. I have trouble sleeping at the best of times but it's usually because I'm figuring out a work problem. Tonight, I'm imagining how disappointed he must be. I feel his chagrin like it's my own. I might even shed a few tears into my pillow, which is *very* unusual for me.

I hear from Brandon the next day at work when he texts me.

Hey.

I text back. *How are you?*

Bummed.

I give a pouty smile. *I'm sure you are.*

Can I see you tonight?

I'm supposed to go to a PWNA meeting, but I've already canceled because I need to get work done. I've been falling behind with all these hockey games. But I want to see Brandon. If there's anything I can do to make him feel better, I want to do that. And I'm not even thinking of a blow job or anal. Well, those things *might* make him feel better. I just want to see him and tell him how amazing I think he is.

Of course. My place?

Sounds good. 7?

See you then.

I set my phone on my desk and smile. Now I better bust my butt getting shit done.

My heart goes soft in my chest when Brandon walks into my place. "Hi."

"Hi." He's carrying food, bless him, a big bag from Feldstein's.

I take it from him and set it on the counter, along with the beer he brought. I smile at that. Then I turn and move toward him to wrap him up in a hug. His arms slide around me and he pulls me close, letting out a long sigh.

"You played great," I offer. "That probably doesn't make you feel better."

"At least I know I did everything I could. I left it all out there on the ice."

"It looked like it."

We stand, hugging, for a moment, then draw apart. I meet his eyes. "I'm still super proud and impressed."

"Thanks." He brushes my hair back, a slight smile curving his lips. "I like hearing that."

"What did you bring us to eat?"

"Ruben sandwiches."

"Yum."

We sit on the stools at my counter to eat. I accept a beer and offer a toast. "To the Bears."

He clinks my bottle with his. "Thanks."

"Talking about next season probably doesn't help."

"Nope."

He's usually so fun and upbeat, never taking things seriously, that seeing him down like this is killing me. I pick a loose piece of sauerkraut off my sandwich and pop it in my mouth. "How is Daniel's baby doing?"

"He's doing better. Apparently he had some breathing problems."

"Oh wow. That's scary."

"Yeah. I talked to Bergie before the game and he sounded pretty choked up. It must be hard to be a parent and see your brand new baby sick."

"I can't even imagine."

"When the baby comes home, I'll take the giraffe over."

That brings a smile to my face. "That giraffe is ridiculous."

"I know." He smiles too. "I'll be the fun uncle."

He *would* be the fun uncle.

With our sandwiches finished, I move into the kitchen. "I have a surprise for you."

"New sexy lingerie?"

The hopeful expression on his face cracks me up. "If I knew that would cheer you up, I would have made a trip to Victoria's Secret."

"Damn."

"No, it's this." I open my freezer and produce a container of Haagen-Dazs pralines and cream ice cream.

His eyes light up and oh my God, so does my heart.

"You *are* superwoman," he breathes. "Hand it over."

"Maybe a bowl?" I ask. "Or just a spoon?"

"Just a spoon. Oh wait—you want some?"

I laugh. "Maybe a taste." I grab two spoons from the drawer and return to the stool next to him, where we proceed to eat ice cream from the container.

"This is so fucking good," he says.

Our eyes meet. And hold. "I'm glad," I whisper. "I hate it that you're sad."

One corner of his mouth lifts. "I'm okay." He pauses. "Let's see if I can guess which part of your body you like being kissed the most."

17

BRANDON

"Should you be with your parents?"

I rub my cheek against Lola's silky hair. "They flew home this morning. It was all the time off Dad could get."

"Oh. Okay." She pauses. "You don't seem really close with your parents."

Her words feel like a poke in the chest. "Remember what I said about our family motto?"

"Oh right. 'Well, that escalated quickly.'"

"Exactly. The less time spent with them the better," I say lightly. "And I'll see them soon anyway. I'll be heading to Michigan for the summer."

"Oh. Right." She pauses. "When are you leaving?"

"I think next week. I have a few things to get done. We have to clean out our lockers, meet with Coach. Barbie and Nadia are having a party tomorrow night to wrap up the season."

She gives a little nod. "How long will you stay there?"

"Probably until August. Although I do have a wedding to come to in July. Hellsy and Sara are getting married."

"Oh, that's nice. Where's the wedding?"

"They're having it here."

"Nice."

"I'm not a big fan of weddings," I confess. "But Hellsy's a good guy and I pretty much have to go."

"Oh God, I hate weddings, too." She groans. "My cousin got married a few months ago. It was a huge family wedding and all anyone wanted to talk to me about was why *I'm* not married."

"What did you tell them?"

"I told them I'm just lucky."

I laugh. "Good one."

"Do people ask men that question all the time, too?"

"Hmm. Not so much."

"Bah. I hate that."

"I hate it for you."

"Thank you."

"Thanks again for the ice cream."

"You're welcome."

"I guess I should go." I swallow a sigh. Getting up and leaving her bed is getting old. If it was a weekend, I'd push for a sleepover, but she has to get up and go to work in the morning.

"Okay."

She follows me to the door and I indulge in a long, hot kiss before leaving.

As I walk to the parking garage, I'm a lot calmer than I was when I got here. It's kind of amazing how much better I feel. Our season was going to end at some point. And there's more to life than hockey. I look forward to summers at the lake, working on my house and the yard, fishing and golfing.

But if it's hard leaving Lola's bed, how hard is it going to be to leave and not see her for months?

On Friday night, I have dinner with Kevin. He's in town touching base with his clients now that the season's over here. We discuss the possibility of signing again early, if the team is interested. We go over some terms and he says he'll feel them out and let me know how it goes. It would be great to get things locked up before fall so next season I can play without the worry of that at the back of my mind. But Kevin's honest that the team's not so eager.

"When I met with Coach the other day he said they were impressed with how I stepped up when Cookie was suspended," I tell him. "He said they like how I kept things upbeat in the room, and focused on staying positive when shit happened."

"That's great to hear." He pauses. "Have you heard any rumors about financial problems?"

I frown. "Financial problems for who?"

"For the team. I'm hearing rumblings that there are some unhappy creditors. Vince D'Agostino apparently held them off because he thought he had a line on a cash investor, but it didn't come through."

"I haven't," I say slowly. "But I've been pretty focused on the playoffs."

"Oh yeah, I get it."

"What would that mean for the team?"

"I don't know. Possibly selling it. Or bankruptcy protection while trying to refinance."

"Huh."

As he's paying the check, I excuse myself to use the restroom, and when I round a corner of the dining room the hotel, my gaze lands on Lola. Seeing her is like a jolt to my senses, and a happy feeling slides through my veins. I check out who she's with—an older couple who must be her parents. She looks like her dad, although his hair is light brown.

She glances up and sees me, too, her head giving a tic, then a smile breaking across her face.

I cross toward them, smiling back at her.

"Hi," I say, standing next to the table. "How are you?"

"I'm good! You?"

"Yeah, great. Just had dinner with Kevin." I glance at her parents, who watch our exchange with puzzled smiles. "Hi. I'm Brandon Smith."

"Oh, these are my parents, Carrie and Rick McGrath."

"Nice to meet you." I shake each of their hands.

"Aren't you…don't you play for the Bears?" Mr. McGrath asks.

"Yeah." I smile. "That's me."

"Sorry you're out of the playoffs," he says. "But it was a good run this year."

"Thanks. Appreciate that."

"How do you know Brandon, Lola?" Mrs. McGrath asks.

"We met in Aruba," she says honestly, looking at me, not her mother.

"Oh. Right. I forgot about that trip."

"It was during our break," I put in. "Nice to get away and get some sun."

"Lola never mentioned you."

"Really? I'm hurt." I press a hand to my chest.

Lola rolls her eyes, and luckily her parents know I'm joking.

"Lola never tells us anything," Mrs. McGrath says dryly, with a look at her daughter. "Would you like to join us for dessert?"

Lola's eyes widen and meet mine. I study her, trying to get a clue from her about how to answer. She gives a tiny lift of one shoulder and a crooked smile.

"Sure, I'd love that. Just let me say goodnight to Kevin." I return to the table where he's waiting.

He tosses back the last of his drink as I approach.

"I just ran into a friend," I say. "I'm going to join them for dessert."

"You didn't want dessert." He grins. "I guess the friend is a woman."

Yes. Yes, she is. But it's not like that. Whatever. "Thanks for dinner, and the talk. Keep me posted. I'm heading to the lake next week, but I'm back in town in July for Hellsy's wedding."

"A Heller family wedding. That will be quite the event."

I return to Lola's table and take the empty chair next to her. They're all looking at the dessert menu and Lola hands me hers.

"Well hello, we have another guest," the server says, stopping at the table. He smiles at me. "Would you like a coffee or a drink?"

I eye the coffee cups. "Sure, coffee would be great, thanks."

"I'll have a refill," Lola says. "Thank you."

We order two desserts to share.

What am I doing here? That was a crazy impulse to say yes to Lola's mom's invitation. I'm so damn curious to meet them, though.

"Have you heard anything more about the VP position?" I ask her, knowing she's submitted her resume. "Any interview scheduled yet?"

"What's this?" Mr. McGrath says. "VP position?"

Lola's lips tighten and she glances at me. "Our VP is retiring," she tells her parents slowly. "In September."

"And you applied for his job?" Mr. McGrath asks.

Uh oh. She hadn't told them. Why not? She's excited about this!

I feel the waves of unhappiness Lola's giving off. Shit. I slide her an apologetic glance.

I guess her mom wasn't lying when she said Lola doesn't tell them much. But why?

"Do you think you have a chance of getting the job, Lola?" Mrs. McGrath asks carefully.

Lola tenses even more next to me.

"Of course she does!" I say heartily. "She's a top candidate."

Mrs. McGrath tilts her head, eyeing me curiously.

"What do you do, Mr. McGrath?" I ask, trying to change the subject.

"Call me Rick," he says. "I'm a dermatologist."

Oops. Dr. McGrath. Turns out Mrs. McGrath is also Dr. McGrath. She's a rheumatologist.

We make small talk about her parents' work and hockey as we eat the desserts. I'm not really hungry, but I fork up some delicious cherry cheesecake and chocolate lava cake. Lola only takes one bite, I think.

Fuck. She's upset.

We've finished dessert and our coffees and I learn it's Rick's birthday and that's why they're having dinner. "Oh hey, happy birthday," I wish him.

Lola picks up her purse, getting ready to leave. "It's been so nice to see you," she says to her parents. "Happy birthday again, Dad."

We all stand and leave the hotel. On the street, they do a bunch of hugs and kisses, and a valet brings their car around.

"Nice to meet you!" I call, waving.

When they've driven away, Lola turns to me, glaring, her mask of composure dropping. "Why did you say that?"

I wince. "About the promotion? Sorry. I didn't know you hadn't told them."

She makes a small growling sound that's a little terrifying and turns away, starting to march down the sidewalk.

I hasten after her. "Hey. Why is that so bad? Why didn't you tell them?"

"It's a long story."

"That's not an answer."

"I know."

"Slow down. I'll walk you home."

"You don't need to do that."

My gut tightens into a big knot. "Okay, you're mad at me, I get it. I just want to understand why."

"I don't want to talk about it." She stalks along the sidewalk in her pretty flowered dress and flat shoes, not looking at me.

My jaw clenches and my chest tightens. I stick with her, though.

"Hey. You said we need to be open and honest with each other. What's happening here?"

"Arrrgh. I'm mad! Okay?"

"I get that."

We walk silently the few blocks to her place. I want to say more but pushing her doesn't seem to be the right thing to do. And I know myself how I shut down when people press for personal details I don't want to share.

I'm just hoping this isn't the end of us, over a stupid, thoughtless comment.

We arrive at her apartment building. We both stop at the door. She stares at the sidewalk, then lifts her head. "I'm sorry."

I wait.

"Come in. I'll tell you why I'm so mad."

She doesn't seem as angry now. I follow her inside, into the elevator, and then into her apartment. She crosses the living room and turns on the lamp next to the couch. She sits down.

I sit near her, patiently relaxing and stretching an arm along the back of the couch. Inside, my guts are still twisted.

"Okay." She shifts on the couch, pulling one leg up under her. "I'm an only child."

I nod. I knew that.

"My parents always told me how amazing I was. They doted on me. Coddled me. They told me I was smart and talented and I could do anything."

I nod again. That seems like a good thing…?

"But it wasn't true."

What? She's superwoman! I blink, keeping my face neutral.

She huffs a little laugh and picks up a cushion, hugging it to her. "They wanted me to be a doctor, like they are."

Of course they did.

"I couldn't get into med school," she says. "In fact, when I got to college, I discovered I really wasn't the best. At anything."

"What the fuck," I mutter. "Lola—"

She lifts a hand and shoots me a rueful smile. "It's true. I didn't really want to be a doctor, anyway, but it was still humiliating that I couldn't. Then they wanted me to go to law school. I flunked my LSAT. They told me I could try again. I didn't want to try again." She sighs. "It was a very rude awakening, discovering that I really *couldn't* do anything I wanted. I was taking business classes and I had to work my ass off to pass them, never mind have a perfect GPA. My parents had always advocated for me. They'd been involved in my schools, with my teachers, helping me with homework and hiring tutors. Then they weren't there, and I was on my own, and I felt like a big loser."

My chest aches. The droop of her lips makes my throat tighten. I want to pull her into my arms and comfort her and assure her she is *so* not a loser.

She swallows and keeps talking. "They were disappointed that I ended up with a business degree, even though they tried to act like they were proud of me."

"I'm sure they were proud of you," I can't resist saying.

She smiles. "Well, yeah. I know they love me. Anyway, I started working right away at Synoptic. I wanted to prove I could have a successful career despite not being a doctor or a lawyer or graduating at the top of my class. I've worked so hard there to get ahead."

"And you have."

"I want that VP job...*that* will be successful. But I didn't tell them because if I don't get the job, it'll be another disappointment. They were so sorry for me when I didn't get into med school, or law school. If I tell them how much I want this job, and then I don't get it, I can't handle their pity."

"Not pity," I correct her, frowning.

She dips her head again. "I hate it."

I'm silent for a moment. "Fuck. I'm sorry, Lola. I shouldn't have mentioned it."

She reaches out and squeezes my hand. "You didn't know. I'm sorry I was so angry about it."

"I didn't intend to cause problems for you."

"I know."

"I shouldn't have joined you," I add. "Then this wouldn't have happened. I don't know what I was thinking."

Well, I do know. I was thinking I wanted to see Lola and meet her parents. But that's not part of our booty buddies deal. I fucked up.

"It's okay. I sort of wanted you to join us." She peeks at me from behind her hair. "I wanted to see you."

My insides relax somewhat. "I wanted to see you, too."

I pull her closer and wrap my arms around her. Everything settles down with her in my arms and things okay between us. "Can I ask you another question?"

"Okay."

"Your goal of getting this VP job—is it for your parents? Or for you?"

18

LOLA

I stare at Brandon. "It's for me."

"Okay." He touches my cheek with his fingertips.

"It is," I say. "I love what I do. I have ideas for how to lead and grow our division and I want to do that. I want to prove to *myself* I can do this."

He smiles. "You know I think you're a superwoman."

I smile back at him, my chest filling with a warm fizz. His confidence in me doesn't feel patronizing. It feels empowering. "I think you're pretty super, too."

"There's nothing wrong with wanting your parents to be proud of you, though."

"I know." I eye him.

"I bitched about my parents coming to watch me play, but honestly, deep down inside I was happy they wanted to. Growing up, it often felt like they were too busy fighting to have time to be proud of me."

I lay my hand on his thick thigh and squeeze, my heart aching. "I'm sorry."

"One time they had an argument in the stands during my game. They were actually yelling at each other and making a big scene. Mom stormed out. I was so fucking mortified. I wanted to skate off the ice and never come back."

My heart squeezes painfully.

"She didn't come to many games after that, and it was better. Except when I scored the game winning goal and we won the championship, she wasn't even there." He pauses. "Don't get me wrong, I love my parents. It's just…complicated."

I see that. He's talking more about his parents than he has in the past.

"So much bickering and yelling and tension. All the time. There were times it made me feel like I was going to puke."

I make a soft sound in my throat. "Oh no." I lean into him and wrap my arms around his waist.

"There were times I actually wished they'd get a divorce. Which made me feel guilty." He sighs. "And scared. Then they did split up. I was relieved, but still miserable. Then I hoped that things would finally be calm and quiet between them, thinking this was for the best. Instead, they just kept at each other, both of them complaining to me about the other. All the fucking time."

"Oh, boy." I smooth a hand over the front of his button-down shirt.

"I try hard not to take sides. In fact, I want nothing to do with their squabbles. Which makes my relationship with them pretty strained."

He's usually so vague about personal things, but now he's telling me this, and my heart hurts for him, both as a kid, so disturbed by their arguments that he felt sick, and as an adult.

I hesitate. "Is that what motivated you to work so hard at hockey?"

He's quiet for a long moment, then says, "I think hockey was actually an escape from it. It was somewhere for *me*, where my accomplishments were real—like goals and assists. Like praise from my coach or cheering from the crowd."

"Yeah." Something inside me clicks. "I get that. I want real accomplishments."

"It *is* why I don't ever want to get married. Or have kids."

I nibble my bottom lip. "I get that, too," I say softly. "I'm too busy for kids right now, and maybe I always will be." Although having children would be an accomplishment, maybe the biggest there is—it scares the hell out of me. Because failure at being a mother is probably the biggest failure there is.

Our eyes meet. And hold.

I like this man. So much. He's become so important to me. A voice in the back of my mind tells me this isn't part of our deal. But we're friends. I wouldn't have sex with him if I didn't *like* him. It's fine. The air thickens around us, the room shrinking in on us. My hands tingle with the need to touch him.

"Is it getting horny in here or is it just me?"

I burst out laughing, surprised. Trust him to make light of the charged moment. "It's not just you."

"Ah." His eyes gleam as his gaze drops to my mouth. He runs his thumb over my bottom lip. Desire pools between my legs and a fever sweeps over my skin. I want him to kiss me so badly right now. "Glad to hear that."

"Brandon..."

"Yeah?"

My heart knocks under my ribs and I'm filled with a deep, hot yearning. There's so much I want to say to him. This feels...different. I feel so close to him right now. I feel like more than friends. But I'm afraid to say that because we had a deal. "Take me to bed."

His slow smile melts the panties right off me. He stands and takes both my hands, pulling me to my feet, then walking backward, leading me to the bed. It's still up in the wall, so he reaches for the handle and pulls it down. Kicking off my shoes, I watch him. God, he's beautiful.

He starts unbuttoning his shirt. I move closer and give him my back so he can pull down my zipper. I could do it, but...I want him to.

He slowly lowers the zipper, bending to press kisses against my spine inch by inch. I brush the lightweight fabric off my shoulders and the dress floats to the floor. I step out of it and turn to face him, setting my palms on his chest. His skin is hot satin.

"Mmm. This is pretty." He touches the edge of my pink lace demi bra.

I rub my hands over him and he groans.

I was so angry that my goal was divulged to my parents, but after a while stewing, I couldn't blame Brandon. He didn't know I hadn't told them. And even though I was angry, he stuck with me because he wanted to know why. And I told him. I told him some of my deepest, most painful secrets—that I felt like a failure. And he's still here. I want to bring him as close as I can, hug him and kiss him all over his beautiful face.

He thinks I'm superwoman.

Emotion swells up inside me.

I want to be with him, like this, tonight, more than any other night we've been together. I want his strength and understanding. His admiration and approval. His acceptance of who I am.

I want to thank him. To show him *my* appreciation. To show him *my* admiration for how he's dealt with parents that were too wrapped up in each other to give him everything he needed.

I want to give him everything he needs.

That's a lofty goal and too bold for what we have. I know it. But still…that's what I want. All I can do right now is give him this.

I run my hands over his strong shoulders, pushing his shirt back and off. It joins my dress on the floor and I work open the belt and zipper of his gray pants. They too fall to the rug. Heat radiates off his body and I breathe in the scent of his skin, which I know so well now. I cup his butt and pull him closer.

He smiles down at me and God, that smile! Brushing my hair back, he bends his head to kiss me, hot, lazy, thorough. A tight, achy knot of need forms deep inside me.

He bites my lower lip, licks it, then takes my mouth with his again, deep and seeking. I kiss him back, giving myself up to him, pressing myself against him, skin to skin. Except for a little pink lace, which he's already working on. He flicks open the clasp at my back and tugs my bra from between us.

It's luscious, the brush of air over my sensitive nipples, the heat of his skin against mine, the pressure of his chest flattening my breasts. I shiver and tremble, my pussy quivering.

With a gentle push he takes me down to the bed, following me, stretching out next to me, sliding an arm under my shoulders. He finds my mouth with his in a long, consuming kiss, sets his other hand on my waist, then slips it down to my butt, bare except for my thong, pulling me toward him. I lift my leg over his hip and he sneaks his fingers under my panties to find my center where I'm wet and aching.

He makes a low rumble of appreciation. He plays there, making me clench and shake, and then I push my hand on his chest, nudging him onto his back, and climb over him. I straddle his hips and lean down to kiss him. He holds my hair back from my face and slides his tongue over mine, another growling sound vibrating in his chest.

I plant my hands into the mattress and shift so my breasts are right at his face and he captures one swollen nipple in his lips and tugs. Sensation unfurls inside me, right to my aching pussy. A moan leaks from my lips. He grips my butt cheeks and my hips press needily into him. I want to feel his arousal too, and I shift onto one arm to reach between us and find his thick shaft beneath the soft cotton of his boxer briefs. I rub over it, down to the soft fullness of his balls, up to the head poking out the elastic edge of his briefs.

He makes rough noises as I caress him there, then I sit up straight and rub my palms over his abs and chest. He watches me with hot eyes, his mouth full and soft. I bend to kiss him again, wet, sloppy, with growing impatience. I'm still aching, so I rub my pussy over his hard cock, trying to graze my clit where I need to be touched so badly.

"Fuck," he groans, hands on my ass again, squeezing, fondling, fingers slipping beneath my thong.

"Oh yeah." My mouth still rests against his, our breath mingling. I kiss him again. And again.

I rise up again and shift backward, kneeling beside him to peel his briefs down. I reveal his cock, and my lungs seize. "So beautiful," I whisper, gazing at him as I finish stripping off his underwear. His shaft lays long and thick against his belly. I want to hold him and taste him and feel him in my mouth.

So I do. I stroke up and down, bending to kiss the tip, then lick. I glance at his face and meet his eyes and the air around us shimmers with heat as I hold his gaze and slowly run my tongue over the head.

"Christ, Lo. Your mouth…"

I lick more, wetting him, then open wider and take him in. Again he holds my hair back, watching intently, his body tight and straining.

God, there's no feeling like this, him in my mouth, big and virile, pulsing and leaking. I explore the shape of him with my tongue, glide my lips down as low as I can and slide them back up.

His fingers tighten in my hair and his guttural sounds inflame my arousal even more. I love doing this, I love how it feels, and I love how it makes him feel. Tensions rises in his body and with a harsh groan he pulls me off him. "I want to fuck you."

I smile, my lips wet, and slowly straddle him again.

He eases aside my lace panties, but then impatiently curls his fingers into them and snaps the tiny strap at my hip.

My belly flips. "Hot," I breathe.

He doesn't smile, his face focused and austere. I lift myself over him and he helps with his hands on my hips.

"No condom," I whisper. We've taken care of sharing test results.

"Fuck, yeah."

His crown notches at my opening. I love how the fit is perfect and right and easy…but then I lower myself and he pushes up inside me and it's not quite so easy. Even so, the tight stretching feeling, the feeling of being filled, is perfect.

He lets out a long breath, his gaze focused where we're joined. "Christ. That feels amazing."

I press my hands onto his chest again, rising, lowering. Deeper. Fuller. I curl down to kiss him again, and our mouths meet and hold as we move together until he's all the way inside me. I press a hand to my belly where I feel so gorged. So exquisitely, extravagantly sated. "So deep," I whisper. "I feel you here."

His eyes flicker and then he's tired of me being on top I guess, as he sits up, bands an arm around my waist and flips me onto my back without separating us. I gasp out a little laugh. "Show off."

The corners of his mouth twitch. Now he's kneeling between my legs. He pushes my thighs up and back. I hook one hand under a knee to hold it there, and his hips rock, sliding in and out of me.

"Oh. God. Oh…" I probably sound like a porn movie, but I can't stop the noises that escape me, the sensation of him inside me so lovely, so dirty, so transcendent.

We're not just having sex.

He lowers his mouth to mine, kissing me with tongue, slippery and sloppy and raunchy, and yet divine. Every nerve ending is electric, every sense is on overload. I can't think.

He rubs his pubic bone over my mound, catching my clit, and holy hell, it's good, so good, firing up every cell in my body, that coil of heat low inside me curling tighter.

He moves faster, my breath coming in vociferous pants that he takes into his mouth between kisses, our mouths so close. Sweetness swells and rushes toward me, building into a peak of almost painful pleasure that wracks me. I shudder and clench around him, my orgasm going on and on.

His own follows closely as he shouts, his body tightening and pulsing against me and inside me. He buries his face in the side of my neck, panting, gasping. I love it.

I could fall in love with this man.

19

BRANDON

I roll Lola flat onto her stomach on the bed. She's limp and boneless from her first orgasm. I'm going to do this all night long. No sleep-overs? Fuck that. I'm not leaving her bed until there's daylight outside and maybe not even then.

I slide a hand over her ass, admiring the smooth curves. Then I straddle her legs and rub the head of my cock through her slit, still pressed closed. The friction is delicious, especially without a condom.

I watch my cock enter her. Bareback. I've never had bareback sex and I'm glad it's with her. It's incredible.

She's tight around me, so goddamn hot, and I groan with pleasure as I push inside. I look up at her, taking in the sweep of her naked back, the pale gold hair draped over her face. She's making those sweet sex sounds again, sounds that make me lose my mind and want to pound inside her. And I will. Later. Because I know she likes that too. But right now, I want to take care. I want to savor every moment, every touch, every slide and push, every lick and nip.

"This is even deeper," she moans, her fingers at her mouth. "Oh, God, Brandon...so deep."

"I like that. I want to be so deep inside you, you can feel me in your throat." I give a sharper push, making her gasp and moan. "Yeah. I fucking love that."

"I love it, too."

And I love that about her. I almost say it out loud, but...whoa. That's going too far. I take a breath that the bump of my heart stole.

Excitement pounds through me, my insides twisting themselves into knots. I brace myself on one hand and smooth my hand down her back and up, then down to squeeze her hip as I move inside her and sensation grows.

She pushes her hands into the mattress to lift herself and twists, and I lean down to kiss her. That mouth...Christ. Soft and hot, sweet and spicy. She's temptation and solace and sin and sustenance. She's everything, right now. Everything I need. Everything I want.

She drops flat again, now slipping a hand beneath her, pushing her ass in the air against me.

"Yeah," I groan.

I feel her touching herself, her fingertips brushing my cock as I move in and out. She squeezes me as she comes, the sounds falling from her lips lighting me on fire.

I stretch out over her, pressing her into the bed with my weight, rocking against her ass, and then I'm hurtling over the edge, my vision black, a thundering in my ears. "Christ! Lola...*fuck.*"

I fight for breath, time measured in pounding heartbeats.

"I'm sorry," I manage to say. "Can you breathe?"

"Breathing is overrated," she mumbles.

I chuckle and lift myself off her. Our skin is sticky with sweat and I slowly pull out and flop down next to her on my back. I lay my forearm over my eyes, my heart still thudding. "Jesus."

"I know." She turns her head so she's facing me, letting one limp arm drape over my chest. "Holy shit."

I swallow. That was intense. Even for us. Our chemistry has been amazing from the start, but it seems like it's just getting hotter and hotter. "Just so you know," I rasp out, trying for casual. "I'm not leaving tonight."

Her eyes are closed, but her mouth curves into a smile. "Me either."

"You live here, babe."

Her lips lift more. "Oh, right. I forgot where I am."

"I'm that good." I lean over to kiss her.

"Yes. You are."

I pull her closer and she melts into me, shaping herself to me like soft wax. I feel like something else is melting inside me.

I can't get enough of her. We just fucked each other senseless, twice, and yet I'm kissing her again, pulling her close. She coasts her hand up over my shoulder, fingers sifting through my hair, sending tingles sliding down my spine. This time our kisses are hot and deep but not desperate. I need her taste on my tongue. I need to breathe in her scent. I need her hands on me.

She snuggles into me, skin to skin, and we're wrapped around each other like a tensor bandage.

I can't believe I told her about my parents. But after meeting hers, and hearing about her struggles, my heart was squashed like a bug. Her vulnerability and honesty were like a hook inside me, tugging at me, snaring me. She may be superwoman, but seeing that soft side of her wrecked me. And for some reason after that I trusted her, trusted that if I told her about my own parents she wouldn't think I'm a sappy chump, or an ungrateful asshole. Somehow I knew she would understand why my perception of marriage and kids is so cynical.

She does understand.

And that really fucking freaks me out.

And yet, I'm not running out the door.

I feel like something changed tonight, but…did it? Did it for her? We had an agreement. No strings. Just sex. I can't screw things up now.

I'm leaving to go to the lake on Sunday. The day after tomorrow.

That's probably a good thing.

Yeah. That'll give us some distance. Some breathing space. Even though breathing is overrated.

Lola makes me breakfast in the morning. This is a first.

"You're a fantastic cook." I just ate the best eggs Benedict I've ever had. "Isn't Hollandaise sauce hard to make?"

"Nah. Using the blender is pretty easy."

I watched her whizz up a bunch of ingredients and then drizzle hot melted butter in and it turned out perfect and creamy. I finish my glass of orange juice. "That was delicious."

She smiles. "Thanks. I like cooking. Sometime I'll make you dinner."

"That would be great." I pause. I guess I better get it out there. "I'm leaving for Michigan the day after tomorrow."

"Ohhhh, right." Her eyes flicker and she drops her gaze. "I forgot about that."

"We should talk about that."

She tilts her head and meets my eyes with a neutral expression.

I fucking hate that neutral expression. Last night she was open and vulnerable and passionate. I swallow a sigh.

"Talk about what?" she asks.

"About this." I gesture between us. Why does this feel awkward? It didn't feel this way when we first talked about our arrangement. "We agreed to be exclusive, but…I, uh, don't expect you to, uh, be that…" I scrunch my forehead. "While I'm gone."

She lifts her chin in acknowledgement. "That's fair."

Fair. Okay. That's good.

"And of course, same for you. You don't have to be exclusive either, while you're gone."

I feel like I just took a butt end in the gut. I can't…I can't even think about sleeping with someone other than Lola. I give a terse nod, my fingers gripping the edge of her counter tightly enough to crack the granite.

"Are you driving there?" She picks up her mug of coffee and lifts it to her lips.

"Yeah."

"That's a long drive."

"I've done it in one day before. But this time I'm going to stop and visit a buddy in Cleveland, which is about halfway."

"That's good."

"And I'll stay a night in Grand Rapids with Dad. My place is about an hour north of there."

"Have you got good snacks for the trip?"

Snacks? I blink. "No."

She smiles. "You have to have good snacks for a road trip."

"Absolutely. I'll have to pick some up."

Her lighthearted conversation eases my mood. A little. I gaze at her, wanting to say more, something, except I don't know what.

"You have my number," I say. "I'm going to text you my address. Just in case."

"In case what?" Her eyebrows pull together.

"I don't know." I shrug. "Just in case. Whatever."

I don't even know myself why I'm doing that, but I pick up my phone and send her the address of my place in Pelican Beach.

"I'm going to miss you," she says with a soft smile.

Aw fuck. "Me too," I rasp out. "We can stay in touch."

"Sure."

Goddammit, this is gruesome. "I'll help you clean up."

"No, no. Don't worry about that. It's Saturday. I've got all day."

"What do you have planned today?" I hold up a hand. "Please don't tell me work."

She makes a cringy face. "Maybe a little? But I'm going out with Kaylee and Isla and Sadie tonight."

"That's good." I slide off my stool and stand next to hers, setting my hands on her waist. "Promise me you won't work too hard."

"Ha. I can't promise that. I'm swamped and they're apparently going to be scheduling preliminary interviews in the next couple of weeks. It's been a while since I interviewed for a job. I need to prep."

"Right. Okay. But take care of yourself. And if you want to practice interview questions, you can call me. Any time. I have Wi-fi at the lake."

"Oooh all the modern conveniences."

"You know it. I even have running water."

"No outhouse?"

"Hell, no."

She laughs. "Good to know."

Our eyes meet and the air changes around us, going thick and warm. Unspoken messages pass between us but neither of us say them aloud. I bend and kiss her. Softly. Once. Twice. Fuck, it's hard to drag myself away this time. "Take care, superwoman."

She slowly unwinds her arms from around my neck. "You too, Marlon."

BRANDON

Before I leave for Michigan I have one last duty—attending Bergie's baby shower. They're calling it a Jack and Jill shower because it's co-ed.

I study the giraffe in my apartment. There's no way I can wrap it, so I'm just going to carry it in like that. I have a card, and I find some ribbon to tie around the giraffe's neck and attach the card to it. That'll have to do.

Yes, I feel like a goofball in the elevator when some of my neighbors get in and see the big spotted toy standing next to me. I shrug and grin at them.

The shower's being held at Nadia and Barbie's place. When Nadia opens the door to me, she bursts out laughing.

"Vat is this?" She cackles more. "Oh, I love it."

I carry the thing into the living room. Some people are seated, others are gathered around the big dining table which has been covered with food. My eyes widen seeing the decorations—masses of balloons in shades of blue, white, and silver and all different sizes, formed into a big arch over a chair where Mandy sits with a tiny bundle in her arms. Next to the chair are giant blue and white building block decorations. I take in the three-tiered blue cake on the table, a big teddy bear holding more blue balloons, and a massive arrangement of blue and white flowers. Another table holds a pile of wrapped packages and gift bags.

I head toward Mandy. Babies scare the hell out of me, but I have to meet Benjamin.

She looks up and sees me lugging the giraffe. She too cracks up. "Oh my God. Brandon!"

"This is for Ben." I smile and peer down at him. "How's he doing?"

"He's great. Thankfully."

"Scary start for the little guy. I'm glad everything's okay."

"Us, too."

Bergie joins us, laying a hand on my shoulder. "What the hell, Brando?"

"Don't you love it?" I grin at the giraffe. "I saw it that day when we were shopping at Bloomingdale's and had to have it."

"I do love it," Mandy says. "Thank you so much. Do you want to hold Benjamin?"

I lift my hands. "No! That's okay."

She laughs.

"I'm afraid I'll make him cry," I add. "Or break him."

"Let's get a drink." Bergie pushes me toward the kitchen.

"Let me just put this dude in the corner out of the way." I stash the giraffe.

A few of the guys are gathered around the kitchen island. Bergie opens the fridge and pulls out two beers, handing me one. You'd think he lives here, he's so comfortable helping himself, but we're all like that here, since Nadia and Barbie entertain us a lot.

Two toddlers barrel through the kitchen and Red comes chasing after them. "Hey, Brando," he says as he passes by. "Stop running, Anna! Chris! Stop!"

Yikes.

There are more kids here—Nate has his daughter Quinn so they're here, Murph and his wife Mia have two boys, Coach has two girls, Grace and Hazel. Grace is the oldest and she, Hazel, and Quinn are playing with Murph's boys, Jason and Joel, with Mia keeping an eye on them from the couch.

The Bears family is growing. Every year someone has a baby. There are still single guys on the team, but Hellsy's getting married so they'll probably start a family, and I wouldn't be surprised if Millsy does soon, too. Also Morrie—he and Kate seem pretty solid.

I'm single.

That's okay. I like it.

I gulp down my beer.

"So? Off to the lake tomorrow?" Nate asks.

"Yep. I can't wait."

"We're coming in August," Bergie reminds me. "After the wedding."

"Yep. The other guys are coming in July. It'll be fun." I help myself to some potato chips from a bowl.

"Okay guys, you have to buy a square." Lilly approaches us with a big card.

"Huh?"

"You buy a square for fifty dollars."

"Fifty bucks!" I stare at her.

She laughs. "We're guessing how many onesies and how many bottles Mandy and Daniel get today. The winner wins the pot."

"Oh. Okay. Can I take two squares?"

"You can take as many as you want." I pull out some cash and hand it over, and mark my name and guesses on the card. The other guys do the same.

"I can't wait to win that." I rub my hands together.

"We're playing baby Pictionary!" Nadia calls out. "Over here!"

On the far side of the room she has an easel and a white board set up.

"Do we have to?" Hellsy mutters.

"Oh hell yeah." I start toward Nadia. "I didn't know there'd be games!"

We get into teams. One player from the team takes a card and then has to draw the item on the card, all of which are baby-related items, for the other person to guess.

Millsy reads his card. He frowns, then shoots Lilly a helpless look.

She laughs. "Go for it!"

He takes the marker and draws some weird lines.

"Highchair!" she yells. "Stroller!"

He shakes his head, his brow creased with frustration as he adds more lines.

"Um…" Lilly squints. "A diaper?"

"Time!" Nadia calls.

"It's a pacifier," Millsy says. "Jeez, can't you see that?"

Lilly collapses in laughter. "Um, no, honey."

The game continues hilariously. Then it's my turn. I beer at my card. "Jesus," I mutter.

I have no clue. I take the marker and start drawing.

I'm paired with Nate. "Baby food. Diaper bag. A crib!"

I shake my head. Then I draw, clearly and unmistakably, two breasts with nipples.

"Breast pump!" Nate shouts.

"Yeah!" We high five.

"Oh my God," Nadia mutters.

After the game, which we win, I fill my stomach with sliders, buffalo chicken wings, more chips, then cake.

"Did you have an episiotomy?" Red's wife Elena asks Mandy.

I lift an eyebrow at Bergie.

"It's an incision in the perinium," he explains in a low voice. "When the baby's coming out."

"Christ." I wince. "That doesn't sound fun."

"None of it was fun," he agrees.

"I did," Mandy says. "But I still had a lot of tearing."

"Oh no."

"I can't listen to this," I mutter, moving away. "I need another beer."

Standing by the fridge, I take a moment for myself, surveying the others all eating, drinking, talking. Damn. Despite all the kids and babies, I like these people. I really want to stay here. In this city. With this team.

I wish Lola was here.

What?

At least she'd be the same as me—she feels the same about kids. But she'd still have fun. She'd get along with everyone here.

"Excuse me. Could I have another drink?"

I look down at the small girl in a pink poufy dress standing in front of me. Blond curls are held back from her face by a headband with a pink bow on it. Nate's little girl, Quinn. Goddamn she's cute. She gets her looks from her mom, that's for sure.

"What do you want? Beer?"

She blinks. "Yes, please."

I chuckle. "How about some punch." I move to the island and pour some fruit punch from a pitcher. I hand it to her.

"Thank you."

She takes it with two hands and lifts it to her little heart-shaped lips.

A little punch slops over the edge of the cup and onto her dress. She stares down in dismay. "Ohhh noooo."

"It's okay. We got this." I grab a cloth and dampen it, then try to sponge the juice off her dress. It mostly comes out and I use a dry towel to rub it dry. "Look. Almost gone."

"Thank you!" She gulps down more juice. "Could I also have another piece of cake?"

"Uh…" I don't know how much cake she's had. I glance around. "Where's your dad? Oh, there." I head over to Nate. Quinn slips her hand into mine and skips beside me.

"Quinn wants more cake," I tell Nate. "Is that okay?"

Nate gives Quinn a direct look. "You've had three pieces. And you didn't finish the last one."

"I like the icing," she says and bites her lip, giving her dad big brown eyes.

"I think you've had enough," Nate says firmly.

I look down at Quinn. How can he say no to that face? "Sorry, kid. Dads are like that."

She pouts, then shrugs and skips off.

"It was worth a try." Nate grins. "Thanks for checking."

The party winds down and people start leaving. It's a nice evening so I walked here, and I stroll home with a weird brew of emotions inside me. My teammates and buddies are good guys. I like their wives and girlfriends. I even like their kids.

So why do I feel so alone?

LOLA

This is terrible.

I keep thinking about Brandon. I miss him so much. We didn't even see each other that often, but I miss him. It's been nearly three weeks since he left.

I'm losing my mind at work with everything I have to do, plus stress about the job interview. And this distraction and melancholy feeling isn't helping.

He's texted me a few times and I'm shockingly thrilled about each one of them. I eagerly read them and text him back. He made it to his lake house and texted me a picture of Martha on the beach, beautiful blue water behind her. I also eagerly re-read each exchange, which is not productive. But enjoyable.

I forgot about a dentist appointment last week. I'm super organized, so that's not like me. Also, I desperately need to see my hair stylist. My natural color is blond, but not *this* blond, so when roots start showing it looks terrible. I just haven't had time.

Yesterday, I missed the due date for my change management plan on the new project. I should have easily been able to have the plan done for now—the planning is the easy part! This has never happened before. I groveled to Keith and promised to have it finished by end of business today.

"What can I help with?" Zayn asks, poking his head into my office. "I know you're slammed."

"Just finish working on the staff survey." I tell him with a tight smile. "But thanks."

"Are you sure? I could handle formatting it."

"That's okay."

He hesitates, then nods and disappears.

It's another late night, but I get it done. Jeff will have it in the morning. And tomorrow I'll get caught up on all the other tasks I put off doing today.

I walk into my dark apartment, tired and downcast. I wish Brandon was coming over. But that's not going to happen for a while. Maybe never again. Maybe he'll meet someone else this summer and he won't be interested in a booty buddy when he comes back.

That makes me want to cry.

What? I never cry.

I heat up some leftover chicken lo mein and sit on my couch to eat it. I turn on the TV, and the channel with the hockey game comes on. The Stanley Cup finals. Is Brandon watching?

I sigh. I have to stop thinking about him.

That night before he left, when he stayed all night and we talked and talked, I felt my feelings change for him. I felt I could fall in love with him. Maybe I already was falling in love with him. Would that be so bad?

I don't want marriage or commitment. But I want Brandon. I know he has feelings for me too, even if it's just friendship with a little lust mixed in. Okay, a lot of lust. We are definitely combustible together in bed.

But I was too afraid to talk to him about that. I'd already confessed how my parents had babied me and how I felt like a loser when I got out into the real world. That if I don't get this promotion, I'll feel like a failure all over again. I'd already opened myself up and I was afraid to go even further and tell him I might be falling for him.

And now he's gone.

I poke my chopsticks at the noodles, my appetite miniscule, a heaviness in my stomach.

I toss the rest of the lo mein, guzzle down a glass of water, and head into the bathroom to wash off my makeup. My bottle of cleanser is empty and I dig around in the vanity for another bottle I know is there. I knock over a box of tampons, scattering them across the bathroom floor.

Shit.

With a sigh, I crouch to pick them up. My hands go still and I stare at one of the tampons. Isn't my period due?

Now I vaguely remember the notification I got on my tracking app. Last week. My period was due last week. And it hasn't started yet.

Christ. I'm so fucking stressed I'm missing periods. What am I doing with my life?

After I get into bed, I grab my phone and check the app. Yep. My period is a week late.

I have an IUD, plus we used condoms up until that last time, so I know I'm not pregnant. I'm not worried about it. Missing a period due to stress is no big deal. I have bigger things to worry about. Like nailing this promotion.

And not missing Brandon.

***

My interview goes well, I think.

It's intimidating, being interviewed by the CEO, Keith, and the VP of Human Capital. But I know them all and have worked with them as project sponsors over the years. I wear one of my favorite suits, a summery pale blue one with a fitted jacket and a blue and white silky shell under it.

I have a lot of examples of ways I've demonstrated problem solving, leadership, creativity, and innovation. I know my strengths—interpersonal communication and motivating others. Convincing people to go along with change is a definite test of how to motivate others. The one question I stumble a bit on is when they ask about delegation. I delegate all the time, of course. But coming up with a really strong example of that has me floundering. I recover, though, so I think it worked out.

I'm ready for a big glass of wine after that.

I stop at a wine store on my way home, but as I study the various bottles on the shelves, I pause. My period is still late. It's now almost a whole month overdue. I haven't been worried about it because I know I can't be pregnant. But the idea of drinking a few glasses of wine makes me stop and think.

Maybe I should take a pregnancy test. Just in case.

Two lines.

I squint at the pregnancy test. Two lines means pregnant. One line means not pregnant.

There are two lines.

I shake my head slowly. That can't be right.

Luckily, I bought two tests. Just in case.

I use the other one and wait a few minutes for the results.

It's the same.

My legs go weak. I sit on the toilet. This can't be.

Really. It can't be.

How can it be?

It's wrong. Somehow.

Shit! Now what? I'm going to have to go to the doctor. No period and a positive pregnancy test are fairly conclusive, but I know it's wrong. Maybe there's something else wrong with me?

A knot of worry tightens in my stomach. Cancer? Definitely stress can cause missed periods. Thyroid issues? I don't have any other symptoms. Pregnancy...? That's as worrying as cancer.

No. Don't be ridiculous. Cancer is a terrible disease. Pregnancy can be terminated.

Jesus. Would I do that?

It doesn't matter. Because I'm definitely not pregnant.

"You're pregnant."

I stare at Dr. Geller, my OB/Gyn, a few days later.

She's not smiling, as if she knows this isn't news I'm ecstatic about.

"But I have an IUD."

"Yes. Less than one percent of women with an IUD get pregnant."

I feel dazed. Like the room is swirling around me. "One percent. I'm the one percent."

"Sometimes IUDs can slip out of place," she says, her tone calm and pragmatic. "Have you had any symptoms such as vaginal bleeding, cramping, pain or soreness in your lower abdomen?"

I rub my stomach. "No."

"Have you been checking monthly to see if you can feel the strings?"

"I was," I say slowly. "I might have forgotten..." I can't remember the last time I checked. "Can sex cause it to slip?"

"No, it shouldn't. It can slip if you have a tilted uterus, or a small uteral cavity. Yours is somewhat small. Or if you have very heavy cramps with your period."

"I have cramps, but not that bad."

"Sometimes we don't know why. In any case, we need to remove it, since you're pregnant. There can be risks associated with it."

"I..." I stop. "I don't know if I want..." I meet her eyes.

She nods. "You don't have to make that decision right now. But we should remove it. If it stays in, you're more likely to have a miscarriage, or lose the pregnancy. There's also a higher chance of premature birth and infection. Also, you're more likely to have an ectopic pregnancy than a regular pregnancy if you have an IUD, so we'll need to do an ultrasound."

I nod. I knew someone who had an ectopic pregnancy and it was scary. My heart lurches into a quick pace and my hands grow clammy. I swipe at my forehead. "Okay."

"The ultrasound will tell us where the pregnancy is, and also help see the IUD if it's moved. We'll remove it then."

I nod.

"According to my handy app here, based on the date of your last period your due date is March first. So you're…about nine weeks along right now."

"Um. I think I know when it happened. It wasn't nine weeks ago."

"We calculate the pregnancy starting on the first day of your last menstrual period."

"Oh. Okay."

"Any other questions?"

"Um. Probably a million, as soon as I leave here."

She smiles. "Write them down and we'll talk more next time."

I leave the clinic in a haze of shock. It's three o'clock and I planned to go back to the office, but right now I can barely remember my own name. I stumble into a tiny restaurant on Second Avenue.

I guess I shouldn't have coffee? I rub my aching forehead again. "I'll have a…glass of milk."

The girl doesn't bat an eyelash and I take my milk outside and sit at a small table on the sidewalk. It's a gorgeous June day, warm and sunny. I watch traffic pass in a blur, my mind churning.

This is…bizarre. This can't be happening. I'm sweating. And shivering. My hands shake as I pick up my milk. I can barely swallow it.

What am I going to do?

22

LOLA

"*What?*"

Kaylee nearly falls out of her chair.

We're at Roots, a cool vegetarian restaurant in Chelsea.

She gapes at me.

I give her a weak smile.

"When you said you needed to talk to me about something, that was *not* what I expected." She picks up her glass of wine and downs it. "That's why you didn't order wine?"

"Yep." I eye her empty glass longingly.

"How the hell did that happen?"

I lift an eyebrow.

"You know what I mean." She levels a glare at me.

"My IUD slipped."

"Holy shit." She closes her eyes. "You have got to be kidding me."

"I wish I was." I take a gulp of water.

"What about condoms?"

I wince. "We agreed since we were exclusive and I have an IUD we didn't need to use them anymore."

"Ohhhh."

"Yeah. It's been confirmed by ultrasound. There was a possibility it could be ectopic, but it's a normal pregnancy. I'm about nine weeks."

"Oh. My. God."

"I know. I've been saying that a lot."

She leans forward. "It is Brandon's, right?"

"Of course!" I frown. "I haven't been with anyone else."

"Oh boy." She sucks in a long breath. "Whoa." Her eyes widen. "Does he know?"

I bite my lip. "No. He's gone home to Michigan for the summer."

"Oh, shit."

"I can get hold of him," I add. "I just don't know what to tell him."

She tilts her head, her eyes softening. "Oh, hon."

My bottom lip trembles. "Gah, I keep getting all emotional about this. It's annoying me! I should be able to analyze this problem, figure out the pros and cons, and come up with the best solution."

"It's hormones," she says. "Also, a baby isn't the same as a business problem."

My throat thickens and I nod, looking down at my water. "And my boobs hurt and I have to pee all the time and I'm tired."

"Have you been throwing up?"

"No, thank God."

"Well. Let's get right to it. Are you going through with the pregnancy?"

I have to smile at her forthrightness. "I don't know."

"Well, let's talk it out."

"I knew I could count on you."

Kaylee doesn't try to convince me either way, and I love her for that. She listens to me when I talk about my job and my promotion and how I'm barely hanging on and that's *without* a baby.

"And what about having the baby?" she asks softly. "Would you keep it?"

"If I have this baby, I'm not giving it up," I say flatly.

She nods.

"What are the pros of having a baby?" I ask. "I can't think of any. They're a lot of work. And time."

She nibbles her bottom lip. "Um…well, I guess the biggest pro is…love?"

My eyes sting and grow wet. "Oh, for fuck's sake, I'm crying again." I grab a tissue from my purse.

"Love's the most important thing in the world," she adds.

I'm not all mushy about this. They did an ultrasound a week ago, but at eight weeks there wasn't much to see. Apparently, the embryo is the size of a peanut right now. I'm not picturing a baby growing inside me. Yet.

Even so… *shit*. More tears leak out.

"It's okay, Lo," Kaylee says. "It's okay to love your baby already."

"I don't know if I love him. Or her. Them."

Her smile says she doesn't believe me. "What about Brandon? Should he have some say in this?"

"My body." Then I sigh. "Yes, I do think he has a right to know. It's my decision, though."

"Absolutely. And I am here for you whatever you decide."

"Thank you." I blink back more tears. "I love you."

"I know."

I laugh.

We talk more about what could happen if I do have the baby— what my life would look like, what options I would have, how I could manage.

"I'm overwhelmed." I cover my face with my hands. "How do people do this?"

"I'm not saying it's easy. But a lot of people do it."

"True." I finish my Tex-Mex chopped salad, loaded with corn, black beans, and tomatoes. Nice and healthy. "That was so good."

"I love this place."

"When does Brandon come back?"

"Not until August."

"Ohhh."

"Yeah. I have to tell him before then." I sigh. "Fun."

BRANDON

"This is the life."

I lean back in my chair, sitting on the beach in front of my house. My buddy James Baumgartner, who plays for the Chicago Aces, sits near me. We both have a beer in our hands, legs stretched out in front of us, feet in the sand, a big bowl of potato chips on the table.

The lake and the sky stretch endlessly blue in front of us. Up here where we're sitting, the beach is a little scrubby, with shrubs and grasses growing through the sand, but down the little bank lined with big rocks the sand is a soft white border along the water. Martha lies off to the side on the grass, in the shade of a tree.

I love this lake. Day and night. In the day it reflects everything around it. In the night it's a void, a huge pool of mystery. It's serene and calm and stormy and wild.

"This is a great place." Bomber adjusts his sunglasses. "And that's a really nice golf course."

We did eighteen holes this morning and stopped for lunch at the clubhouse. "Yeah, I like it."

"You had to cheat to beat me."

I snort. "As if. You had more slices than a loaf of bread."

"Har. Good one."

"You think I'll let you forget that score on the ninth hole? The par three?"

"What will it take for you to never mention it again?"

"Hmm. I'll think of something."

"The house is looking good," he says, gesturing behind us. "You've done a lot."

"Still needs a lot of work. It's old."

"It's huge. Seven bedrooms. That's ridiculous for a single guy. You planning on having a bunch of kids or something?"

"Hell, no." I shudder. "I just thought it was a great house, and I got it for a good price because it needed work. It fills my time here, fixing shit. Plus there's lots of room for guests. Some of the guys are coming over the summer."

"That'll be fun."

"This place used to be one big party all summer, not now everyone's getting married and having kids so things aren't so wild."

We shoot the shit for a while, then go back up to the house to barbecue steaks on the gas grill I got last summer. I point out where I cleared trees so the low deck has a view of the lake and we have a couple more beers while we eat.

I love it here. I've never been a big city guy, although I have gotten used to living in New York, and I admit there are cool things about it, but this is home. It's the scent of water and sun and grass, the wind in the trees, the soft rhythm of the waves on the shore when the weather is good, and the powerful crashing swells when Lake Michigan is ornery. I even like it in the winter, although I don't get here often in the winter.

It was true what I said about this being party central in the past. For some reason, this summer feels lonely. I've still had visitors—Bomber for one, my parents, and others are coming—Bergie, Mandy, and the baby, Nate and his little girl that he has for the summer, some of the guys. And I don't mind being alone. But the huge house feels empty and sitting on the deck or the beach with Martha isn't as relaxing as it usually is. I keep thinking about New York. And Lola.

It's been a few weeks now. I know she's okay, because I've texted her a few times. I've sent her funny memes I think she'd like. I wished her luck with her interview. I'm already thinking abut when I'm back in New York for Hellsy's wedding later this month, and if I'll see her.

I even thought about asking her to come to the wedding with me.

But that would be a date. We don't do dates.

I've also thought about inviting her to come here for a few days. That wouldn't exactly be a date, would it?

I'll admit that I also fantasized about her. How could I not? She's so fucking hot, and the things we've done in bed together will fuel my spank bank for a long, long time. I get wood just thinking about them, so of course I need to play squirt hockey. A lot.

After we eat steaks along with potatoes and carrots I picked up at a nearby farmers' market, we take another beer down to the beach. There's a fire pit here and it's nice to watch the sun set over the lake with a fire going.

"What the hell are you wearing?" Bomber eyes my joggers, a black pair with pizzas on them. They're a narrower style so they're stretched over my butt and thighs, but they're super soft and comfortable.

"These are great pants." I glance down. "Moisture wicking."

He lifts an eyebrow. "Okay."

"I need to chop some wood." I set down the cooler with a few beers in it. "Or maybe you want to? Get in a workout so you don't get all soft and doughy over the summer?"

He snorts. "Guess you better think again. I'm not chopping off a hand or a foot during the off season."

"So you're going to let me do it."

"Whose hands do you think are worth more?" he muses, lounging back in his beach chair.

I shake my head and fetch the axe to chop some wood. I actually enjoy it. It's a great physical activity for burning off some energy. There's no gym close to here, although I've created one in one of the bedrooms with some equipment, so it's good to get a workout with the axe.

I raise my arms and bring the axe down on the piece of wood sitting on the stump I use as a base. Then I let out a hair-raising scream, drop the axe and fall to the ground. I roll around. "My foot! My foot!"

Bomber jumps up and dashes over to me, and at the look on his face I collapse into laughter, lying on the sand.

"Fuck you." He shakes his head, trudging back to his chair. "Asshole."

Still chuckling, I get up and brush the sand off my pants and pick up the axe again. This time when I bring the axe down on the log, it splits with a satisfying crack. I repeat this a few times, building up a pile of split wood. I'm about to bring the axe down one last time when a voice behind me says,

"Whoa, I didn't know you're also a hot lumberjack, Marlon."

23

BRANDON

I nearly take off my foot for real as the axe comes down and misses the log.

I jerk upright and turn to see Lola in the shadows gathering as dusk approaches. The breeze off the lake teases her hair off her face, the low sun gliding her in gold. She's wearing jeans and a pale pink T-shirt that says SMASH THE PATRIARCHY.

Martha jumps up and trots over to Lola, moving fast for her, her tail swishing in excitement. Lola bends to greet her and rub her head.

"Jesus Christ," Bomber says. "Did you actually chop your foot?"

I'm still staring at Lola. "No. What are you doing here?"

She smiles. "Surprise!"

I shake my head. "I've had a few beers but I'm not that drunk. Are you real?" I close the distance between us. As I get closer, I see the faint tightness at the corners of her eyes and mouth. She's nervous.

I hold out my arms wide and she takes a couple of steps and then she's in my arms and I'm hugging her. "What the hell, superwoman? Did you fly here?"

"Yes." She chuckles. "On an airplane. Then I rented a car and drove."

I smile down at her. "You missed me, didn't you? I knew it."

She rolls her eyes. "Maybe a little."

I laugh softly.

Bomber clears his throat.

"Oh, hey. Bomber, this is Lola. Lola, Bomber. He plays for the Aces in Chicago."

"I'm guessing your name isn't really Bomber," she says dryly.

"James," he says. "Call me either. Nice to meet you."

"You as well."

"I didn't know you were expecting another visitor," Bomber says.

"I wasn't. This is a total surprise. But a nice one." I'm downplaying it. Excitement fizzes in my belly, happiness flowing through my veins. I can't believe she's here, but I'm so fucking glad she is.

I want to ask again why she's here, but I postpone that since Bomber's here and giving her an interested look and I need to shut that down. "Would you like a beer?"

"Oh. No thanks. Maybe some water?"

"Bomber, go get her a bottle of water while I build the fire."

He shoots me an irked look, but jogs back to the house.

I grab her hands and pull her close again. "What is this?"

"A vacation?"

"Ha. Somehow I don't think you take many vacations." I narrow my eyes. "Did you get good news?"

She blinks. "Oh, about the promotion? No."

"Damn. I thought maybe you came to celebrate."

She smiles. "They haven't made a decision yet."

I see Bomber coming back. "We can talk later."

"Okay."

"Come have a seat." I pull another chair up closer to the firepit. "I was about to build a fire."

"Nice." She gazes around. "This is gorgeous."

"Isn't it? I love it."

"So quiet and peaceful."

"Yeah." I arrange wood and kindling and set a match to it. It smolders, flares up brightly, then lowers again as the wood starts to burn.

"Here you go, Lola." Bomber hands her a bottle. "I brought a few more beers for the cooler while I was up there." He deposits them into the cooler sitting on the sand.

"Good man." I use the poker to jab the logs, sending a shower of sparks swirling into the air, then take my seat again. "There. Boy Scout worthy."

"Were you a Boy Scout?" Lola asks. Martha sits next to her, and Lola absently strokes her.

"No. I had no time. Did you have any trouble finding this place?"

"No. Google maps helped me out."

"Awesome. How long are you here for?"

She gives me an uncertain look. "Can I stay tonight?"

"Jesus. Of course! You can stay as long as you want."

"You might not think that—" She stops. "I can stay the weekend. I took today off."

"Holy shit. A three-day weekend. Are you feeling okay?"

"Hey."

"I'm teasing. But you do work hard, babe."

"What do you do, Lola?" Bomber asks.

She tells him about her job. I half-listen. Two days, she's here. Like, one day really, depending when she leaves on Sunday. That's not enough.

The sky shimmers pink and orange at the horizon. With no clouds, the sun is a fireball slowly sinking into the water.

"Look at that sunset," Lola says. "Wow. What a view. Do you sit here every night and watch this?"

"Pretty much. If it's raining, I watch up on the deck."

She lets out a sigh of contentment. "This is glorious."

A feeling of lightness flows through me. Damn, it makes me happy that she likes it here.

She asks Bomber questions about where he's from and how long he's been in Chicago, which is a long time. Conversation flows easily as it grows darker.

Then Lola slaps at her arm. "Ouch! I think I just got a mosquito bite."

"Probably." I set my beer down and reach for the can of insect repellant sitting in the sand. "Here. Want me to spray you down?"

"Ugh. I hate the smell of that stuff."

"Do you want to go inside?"

"No. It's so nice here." She wiggles her fingers. "I'll do it." She takes the can and moves away from the fire to mist herself with the bug spray. She hands it back to me and I use some as well, then hand it to Bomber.

"They never bite me," he says, but he gives himself a couple of spritzes. "I don't know why."

"You're not tasty enough," I say. "Maybe if you showered more."

He laughs.

"What's new in the big Apple?" I ask Lola. "How's the project going?"

She catches me up and tells me a funny work story and gives a review of the Broadway play she went to last weekend. When Bomber and I have finished off the beer and it's coal dark, I suggest heading back to the house.

I douse what's left of the fire with lake water and take Lola's hand to lead her to the house.

"Are there bears here?" she asks.

"Oh yeah."

"Eeeek."

I grin. "It's fine, they won't bother us."

The house is mostly dark, with only the kitchen light on. A motion sensor light outside pops on as we near, illuminating the deck and yard.

"Your house is huge," Lola says. "Not what I expected."

"What did you expect?"

"I thought it would be a little log cabin."

I choke. "Ooookay."

"I also thought maybe it was a brand-new modern mansion." She shoots me a look as we cross the deck to sliding doors. "I had no idea."

I open the screen door and let her in. Bomber follows us, carrying the cooler of empties.

"Long day," he says with an enormous yawn and exaggerated stretch. "Think I'll call it a night."

"Okay." I repress my smile. I'll thank him tomorrow. "Good night."

"Night." He disappears up the stairs.

Lola turns to survey the interior of the house as I turn on some lights. "Wow. This is amazing."

"There's still a lot of reno to do, but it keeps me busy."

"I love it."

"Did you bring a bag?"

"Oh, right. I left it in the car."

"I'll get it for you."

She pulls the car key out of her jeans pocket and hands it to me. I jog out to the rental car parked in the driveway behind my SUV and retrieve a small suitcase from the trunk. Inside, I set it at the bottom of the stairs.

"Are we talking now?" I ask her.

Her lips pucker into a tiny smile. "Sure."

"Do you want a drink now?"

"No, thanks."

"Have a seat." I gesture at the huge sectional that takes up half the living room. It faces the fireplace, with doors to the sunroom on either side of it.

"Um, can I use your bathroom first?"

"Of course." I shake my head. "Sorry. Upstairs, turn left, and it's the second door."

She disappears and I sit. I don't know what's going on, and while I'm happy to see her, I'm starting to get a little uneasy.

Lola returns moments later and takes a seat near me. Is she pale? She looks pale. She twists her fingers together, meets my eyes, then looks away.

My uneasiness intensifies.

"There's no way to ease into this," she finally says. "So I'll just say it. I'm pregnant."

Everything freezes. Stops. Even my breathing. I stare at her.

She gives an unsteady smile. "Yeah, you heard right. Sorry to be so blunt, but I didn't have any kind of lead in, like 'remember that time the condom broke' or...anything." She clears her throat. "My IUD slipped. I didn't know."

I can't find any words, even though I have a million questions. My mouth dries up and my breath evaporates. A baby? She's going to have a baby? My baby?

For a moment, I'm almost delirious with excitement. Happiness. I can't help but look at her stomach, where there is no sign of pregnancy whatsoever.

Then reality smacks me in the back of my head. I can't have a baby. The last thing I want in the world is to be a father. A *terrible* father. I can't do that.

Now a block of ice forms in my gut and the coldness spreads through my veins and over my skin.

"I just found out," she says. "My period was late, but I thought it was stress so I didn't worry about it." She swallows. "I'm about nine weeks."

I blink.

She licks her lips and swallows again. After a thick silence, she goes on. "I haven't decided what I'm going to do yet. But I thought you should know."

I lift a hand that feels weirdly heavy and rub the back of my neck, looking away from her. She's having my baby.

It *is* my baby. I have no doubt of that. We agreed to be exclusive while we were together and I trust Lola that she was.

Holy fuck.

She's pregnant.

I can't quite get past that stupendous fact. "You're sure?" I manage to say. "I mean..."

She nods, one corner of her mouth lifting. "Yes. I've been to the doctor. We had to do an ultrasound because getting pregnant with an IUD means there's a risk of an ectopic pregnancy."

I nod, although I have no fucking clue what that is.

"But it's a normal pregnancy, everything's fine. So. Yeah."

Everything's fine.

I didn't know how much hearing those words mattered. Okay. Okay. Everything's fine. I think. "Do you feel okay?"

"Yes. Just normal stuff. No morning sickness."

I suck in air. "Okay. Good." I rub my mouth. "Wow. This is…wow."

"I know." She exhales sharply. "Believe me, I know. I'm still stunned."

I search her face. "Stunned. Yeah. Are you…you said you don't know what you're going to do."

She nods slowly. "This wasn't part of my plan."

I nod slowly. "Or mine."

She flinches.

"Sorry," I mutter.

"No. I know it's true. This wasn't part of the plan for either of us."

Is this really happening?

I've had buddies who knocked up chicks. Some got married. Some didn't. It was almost always a mess. Nate married his ex when she got pregnant and look how that worked out. I press my fingers to my temples. "I don't understand how this could happen. We were always careful."

"I know." She stares at me, looking like she's sitting on sharp nails. "I know. We didn't plan this, but it happened. It's not what either of us wanted. But we have to deal with it."

I nod slowly, our eyes meeting in a shared affinity. Yes. Neither of us wanted this. And yet…here we are. We made a baby. "Christ on a bike."

"I know." She pauses. "We have options."

I suck air back into my lungs. "Right."

Then her eyes get glossy. Ah, hell. Is she going to cry?

She blinks rapidly. "Sorry," she mutters, dashing a hand across her eyes. "I get really emotional lately. Apparently, it's hormones."

"It's a big thing."

"It is." Her voice catches. "Really big. Like, I don't think I can handle it, big."

My shock fades in the face of her vulnerability. "You can handle it." I instill confidence into my voice. "You're superwoman. You can do anything."

Me, on the other hand? I'm not so sure about me.

LOLA

Oh, geez, now I'm really going to cry. How was I supposed to know that hearing Brandon tell me I can do anything was exactly what I needed to hear? How did *he* know?

I did it. I told him. It's done.

He's…rattled.

"Maybe we should sleep on this," I say carefully. "We can talk more in the morning. It took me a while to come to terms with it all."

"Uh. Yeah. Okay, sure." He stares at me for another long moment, shakes his head, and stands. "I'll…get a room ready for you."

Oh. A room. Not his room.

Why did I assume I'd sleep with him? That was obviously an error. I feel a pinch in my chest at this. I stand, too, and follow him to the stairs. He grabs my carry-on bag and brings it up. At the top he pushes open the door on the right. "One of the guest rooms," he says. "Oh, the bed is made. I'll just get some towels for you to use." He stops, shakes his head again, then leaves.

The room is basic, a good-sized bedroom with white walls and hardwood floors. I turn on the lamp beside the bed then pull down the old-fashioned roller blinds on the two windows. The bed has an old-looking bronze metal headboard and footboard. I run a hand over the smooth, plain white comforter.

Brandon returns with some thick towels and sets them on the old oak dresser. His usual easy grin and twinkling eyes are absent. He still looks like someone just shone a spotlight in his eyes.

My chest aches. More tears threaten. Dammit. "Anything else you need?" he asks, his voice rocky.

"I don't think so. Thank you."

"Okay. Good night."

He leaves like a snarling dog is snapping at his ankles, closing the door behind him.

I sink down onto the bed, my head drooping. Well. I knew this wasn't going to have him jumping up and down with excitement. I sort of thought we'd be more of a team in this, though. I thought... well, I don't know what I thought. I don't know anything, anymore. I just know I'm tired.

So tired.

I wake to sunlight glowing around the edges of the blinds. For a moment I'm confused abut where I am, then I roll to my back and stare at the ceiling when I remember. A knot immediately tightens in my belly.

I don't want to leave this bed. I don't want to face Brandon again. Maybe I can sneak out.

Can I actually do that? If I make it downstairs with my suitcase and don't run into him, I will bolt out the front door and head straight back to Grand Rapids. I get dressed, pad carefully to the bathroom down the hall, wash up and brush my teeth, then shove things back into the bag. I raise the blinds. One window is on the back of the house and looks over the lake.

Oh wow. It's so beautiful. I stare out for a moment and endless blue, the sky clear, the trees an incredible bright green. I let out a sigh, then pick up my bag and descend the stairs. I pause in the hall.

So far, no Brandon. Or James. I hear muted voices coming from the far end of the hall, which is a door leading onto a porch, I think. This place is so big.

Can I really do it? Just run?

It'd be easier, but I guess that's not fair. With a sigh, I leave my suitcase by the door and follow the voices.

The porch is screened in, surrounded by shrubs and trees. A fresh morning breeze drifts in. Brandon and James are sitting on comfortable-looking wicker chairs, drinking coffee. Martha slowly rises from her place on the floor in a square of sunlight and plods over to me, her tail wagging.

Brandon's head jerks up as he catches sight of me. "Morning."

"Good morning." I smile at him and James, keeping my chin up and my shoulders squared. I reach down and scratch under Martha's snout.

"Did you sleep okay?" Brandon asks, standing.

"I slept great, thanks. Could I have some of that coffee?"

"Absolutely." He disappears through another door. As I walk closer I see the kitchen. Whoa. What a kitchen.

He's already renovated this space, it appears, as the cabinets are all new and white with marble countertops and black pendant lights over a massive island. As I take it all in, my gaze lands on the plant on the windowsill above the sink.

Polly the pothos.

My heart jolts. I stare at the plant, looking full and green and healthy.

Brandon pulls a bright yellow mug from a shelf and fills it with coffee, sets it on the island then moves to the big stainless-steel fridge to pull out a carton of milk.

"Thank you. I love this kitchen."

"Thanks. It had to be done first. The original kitchen was unusable. The first summer I was here, it was like camping."

I take a sip of the steamy brew. Our eyes meet. The air in the room shifts and heats. I drop my gaze. "I'm going to head home today. I just wanted to tell you in person." I raise my eyes. "I'm sorry to drop this on you."

"Wait, wait, wait. You can't just go." He frowns. "This impacts me, too."

"I know that."

Keeping his tone low, he says, "Bomber's leaving this morning. We can talk more after that."

I swallow. "Okay. I'm sorry about that, too. I didn't expect to interrupt your visit."

He shakes his head. "Stop apologizing."

I bite my lip.

He tips his head back, eyes closed. "Do you want some breakfast?"

I'm not hungry, but I should eat. "Okay. Did you already eat? I can make myself something."

"No, we haven't eaten yet."

"I would love to cook in this kitchen. If you have food." That was a joke, but it doesn't land right.

"Of course I have food."

I swallow a sigh. "Sorry. I was kidding."

"I have eggs, ham, bread. Scrambled eggs?"

"How about I make omelets?" I move to the fridge.

"You don't have to cook for us."

"I like cooking. Remember?" I slide a chiding glance over my shoulder. We're acting like strangers, like the last few months didn't happen.

"Right. Fuck." He drops his head. "I'm sorry."

"Stop apologizing."

His head jerks up. Our eyes meet. My lips quirk and then his face finally relaxes into something closer to his usual charming, upbeat expression. And my heart bumps.

He grins. "Okay."

I pull out a carton of eggs and quickly find some vegetables, cheese, and the ham he mentioned. As he makes toast, I whip up some eggs and chop onions and peppers.

"I've been abandoned." James steps into the kitchen. "What's up?"

"We're making you breakfast," Brandon replies.

"What can I do?"

"Can you get the juice of the fridge?" Brandon says.

"What kind of omelet would you like?" I list off all the ingredients and get some butter sizzling in a pan. The kitchen is well stocked with high end cooking utensils, although they don't seem well used.

Martha hangs out at my feet and I "accidentally" drop a piece or two of ham on the floor, which she inhales. Soon we're sitting on stools at the island and it turns out I *am* hungry. I devour my three-egg veggie and cheese omelet, two pieces of toast, and a big glass of orange juice.

"This is fantastic," James says. "You're a great cook, Lola."

"Thanks." I beam a smile at him.

What has Brandon told him about me? About our relationship? And why I'm here?

James helps clean up then goes to get his stuff.

Brandon picks up the coffee pot. "More?"

"No, thanks. I'm limiting myself to one cup of coffee a day."

"Oh." He blinks. "Right. I guess that's why you didn't have a beer last night."

"Yep."

Once James has departed, Brandon leads us back out to the porch. I sink down into a cushioned chair and breathe in the scent of pine and lake water.

"Okay." Brandon sits, too. "First, I'm sorry about my reaction last night. Needless to say, I'm kind of knocked for a loop."

"I know."

"Tell me what you're thinking. Tell me what you want."

I open my mouth to tell him that I don't know. That I've been thinking about nothing else and I haven't figured it out yet. But I do know. Somehow I came to this decision in my subconscious without even realizing it, but at this moment…I'm certain. "I want to have the baby."

He blows out a breath. "Are you sure? Because I would totally understand if you made a different decision. But having said that, I also want you to know that if you have this baby, I will to be there for you. Both of you."

"I'm sure."

"I have questions."

I smile. "Go ahead. I talked this out with Kaylee the other day and I've been thinking about nothing else."

"Kaylee knows?"

I nod. "She's the only one."

"When is the baby due?" His gaze drops to my stomach and for the first time, I press a hand there, thinking about the peanut growing inside.

"March. March first."

We talk. We talk about practical things, like maternity leave and childcare and money. We talk about our parents and how they'll react and when to tell them.

"Listen," Brandon leans forward. "I didn't sleep much last night because I was thinking about this."

I nod.

"But here's the thing—we're friends. Right?"

I'm not sure where this is going. "Right."

"We get along okay."

I eye him silently. We get along like gasoline and a match. Okay, that's not the entire picture. We have fun together even when we're not fucking.

"We can co-parent this baby. As friends."

"Uh…" What is he saying?

"Like, shared custody. Shared financial support. Making decisions together. Divorced couples do it, but since we're friends, it should be easy."

Friends. I feel like a stick is poking me in the heart and my stomach grows heavy.

That night before he left, when we shared so much and he stayed all night, I felt my feelings change for him. I felt I could fall in love with him. Only now I realize there was a tiny seed of hope inside me that things weren't over between us just because he'd come here for the summer. That maybe he felt the same.

Clearly not.

"Easy," I manage to say, my throat dry and rough.

"Well, maybe not easy." He grimaces. "I don't know if kids are ever easy? Maybe. But you know what I mean."

"I think so."

I knew Brandon would at least contribute financially. Not that I need money. But I didn't know if he would want to be in the child's life, given his feelings about children and marriage. I'd already considered the very real possibility that if I decided to have the baby, I could be raising them by myself. And yet...

There was that tiny bit of hope again, that he would want more than just being a "co-parent." Maybe...knowing how Brandon stepped up for his team during the playoffs, the leadership role he took on and his commitment to the team...maybe I thought his stance on marriage and children had grown or changed, too.

The heaviness in my belly spreads through me and I swallow my disappointment. It's probably just hormones. "Are you sure?"

"Yes. No. Fuck." He covers his mouth. "I told you about my parents. I saw how a kid can strain a marriage to the point it breaks. I don't want that."

Ouch. I knew this about him, but having a man tell you outright he doesn't want to marry you is a little demoralizing. "I never expected you to marry me," I say acidly, ignoring the sensation of my heart shriveling.

He winces. "I know. I know you don't want that. Look, my schedule during the season is brutal. I'm afraid a lot of parenting will fall to you during that time."

"I understand that." I certainly thought through that. I saw how the playoffs put most of his life on hold.

"I want to be there when I can." He opens his mouth, closes it, then opens it again. "I'll try my best."

"Th-thank you."

25

BRANDON

"What can I do?"

Lola blinks back at me. "About what?"

"To help you. Anything."

She smiles. "I'm fine, Marlon."

I roll my eyes at the nickname, but actually I like it. Yeah, I'm off my game at this news, but as Lola and I talk, I'm settling down.

We made a baby.

"When did it happen?" I rub my chin.

"It had to be that last night before you left."

Huh. That night I'd been wrestling with a bunch of feelings, not wanting to leave her, but not wanting to break my word about the deal we'd made. That night had been…emotional. It was because I was leaving. It was also the night we didn't use condoms. And we made a baby.

Holy shit.

I grin.

"What?" She gives me a squinty-eyed look.

I shrug. "I just like it that we made a baby that night when things felt really…" I stop. "Nice."

"Nice." Her eyebrows shoot up. "Um, okay."

"So what do you need? Should I come back to New York?"

She hesitates, then shakes her head. "No. I'm fine. I don't need anything right now. I'll have doctor appointments, but that's no big deal."

"When can we find out if it's a boy or a girl?"

"I don't know. Do you *want* to find out?"

"Maybe. I just thought of that. We should agree on that, I guess."

"Good point. I'd like to know."

"Me too."

"Okay, if we do another ultrasound and it's far enough along that they can tell us, I'll let you know."

"I want to be there."

"Sure."

"We have to think about names."

"Yes." Her lips twitch. "We have a while."

"Still. It's good to be prepared."

"Absolutely."

"So we're not telling anyone else yet."

Her forehead furrows. "Did you tell James?"

"No! Jesus."

The ridges on her forehead relax. "What about Daniel and Nate? I know they're your friends. You could tell them."

"Okay. I might tell them. I'll see them at the wedding."

"Oh, right. When is that?"

I tell her the date. "So I'll be in the city then, at least. Are you sure you don't want me to come back?"

"There's no need. Life will just go on as normal for a while."

Normal. Ha. "You'll let me know if you need anything, right?"

"Sure."

How the hell am I supposed to just hang out here, painting and gardening, when she's in New York, growing our baby?

Jesus. A hallucinatory feeling passes over me. What is happening here?

"Okay," I finally say, casually.

"Well." She sits forward, hands on her bare knees. Today she's wearing a pair of shorts and a loose T-shirt. "I'll get going."

I frown. "You said you could stay the weekend."

"I know, but…" She doesn't meet my eyes.

"I acted weird last night. I'm sorry."

She shakes her head, lips curving. "It's fine. I don't want to intrude."

"Stay." I pause. That word just burst out of me. "We're friends, right?"

She presses her lips together and gives a tight nod. "Yes."

"Bomber's gone. We can talk more. Process things." Also, I don't want her to leave. Even though I'm flabbergasted by the turn of events, I was happy to see her when she arrived.

But I have to remember we're just friends. That was my idea—we can be friends and co-parents. Neither of us wants marriage. She agreed, so I have to stick to that.

"I guess I can stay."

I nod firmly. "Okay. It can be a mini vacation for you. What do you want to do? Lie on the beach? Swim? Fish? Chop wood?"

Her eyes bug out and I laugh.

"Kidding."

"I don't think I'm into fishing, but the beach sounds nice."

"It's going to be hot today." I rub my hands together. "Did you bring a swimsuit?"

"Yes."

"Perfect. We can have a picnic. Later we can go for a walk along the shore."

I'm giddy with the idea of her relaxing on the beach. She's so driven and focused, taking a day or two off can only be good for her. And for the baby. I'm going to wait on her hand and foot and make sure she has everything she needs while she's here.

When we walk down to the beach, I carry all the stuff—the cooler with food and drinks, lounge chairs, towels, sunscreen. "Sun or shade?" I ask, prepared to move her chair.

"Sun. For now."

"You better not get too hot. That might not be good."

She eyes me like I'm wearing a straitjacket. "I'll be fine."

She takes off her shorts and tank top to reveal a red two-piece suit. A fucking bikini. Moms aren't supposed to wear bikinis. Not tiny ones like that.

I've seen her naked a lot. Even so, my eyes roam over her sweet curves and silky skin as she stretches out and sighs. She doesn't look pregnant. At all. She looks…hot.

Oh Jesus. I'm starting to pitch a tent.

There can be none of that. This is the mother of my child. My friend. I can't be having filthy thoughts about her.

I stretch out on my stomach, painfully trying to adjust my position.

"This is so nice." Lola's voice is soft and relaxed. "Beautiful. I see why you like it here. Your own beach. Nobody around. Water and sun. It's heaven."

I'm glad she likes it. I turn my head so I can see her. "I like the name Remington. For a boy."

She frowns. "Remington? Isn't that the name of a gun?"

"Oh yeah, right. Never mind." I think. "What about Dawson?"

She tilts her head. "That's not bad. I like Xander."

"Xander? With an X?"

"Yes."

"No. You can't give a kid a name that starts with X."

"Why not?"

"I don't know. It just seems wrong."

She laughs. "How about Zeke?"

"With a Z? Huh. That's not so bad."

"I don't know what's wrong with X, if Z is okay."

"What about girl names?"

"I like the name Bexley."

I stare at her. "Seriously?"

"She could be Bex for short. That's cute."

"I don't know…"

"What about Parker?"

"For a girl or a boy?"

"It could be for either."

"Hmmm."

"Don't worry, we have lots of time."

"That's good," I say, a little grumpy.

She smiles, her eyes closed.

I study her again. Her stomach is flat. I admire the swell of her tits in the bikini top. Are they a little bigger? I'd need to hold them to know for sure.

Christ, stop thinking about touching her!

"I'm gonna see how the water is." I jump up and jog over to the lake. The water sloshes cold around my feet and ankles. That's good. I need some shrinkage. I wade out farther.

"How is it?" Lola calls.

"Cold!" I yell back.

"Maybe I'll wait a while before I go for a swim."

I turn to see her rolling over and folding her arms under her head. Great. Now I can see her cute ass cheeks peeking out from beneath the bikini bottoms. I bend my knees and submerge myself in the water.

This might have been a mistake, convincing Lola to stay.

It also might have been a mistake bringing her to the beach with both of us half-naked. It was like slow torture, all goddamn day, being so close to her and not touching her.

I fed her. Offered her drinks. Stayed close to her when she went in the water. Made sure she had sunscreen on and moved her to the shade when things got too hot.

We went for a walk along the beach and her delight at the rocks she found made my chest heat up. By the time we got back, she had a collection of smooth stones she was so enamored of.

I wanted to make her dinner, but she wanted to help, and again her delight in my kitchen made me so fucking happy. So we cooked together and then ate together and then watched a storm roll in over the lake. Thick clouds obscured the sunset, so we moved to the sunroom as the winds picked up, darkness fell, and lightning flashed in the distance.

"This is awesome." She curls her fingers around a mug of hot chocolate. "I love thunderstorms. You really feel part of it here. Yet we're safe inside."

"Yeah." I can't stop watching her. Her cheeks are pink from the sun, her hair windblown, her eyes sparkling. Her features have softened since she arrived last night looking pinched and tired.

The thunder gets louder as the storm nears, and then the rain starts. The scent of it on warm earth and leaves drifts in the screen doors. The trees bend and whip in the fierce winds, and rain pounds down in a short but intense storm. Lightning illuminates the clouds and the trees in bursts and as the storm passes right over, the thunder cracks and rumbles. And Lola laughs.

"This is amazing!"

I grin. "Yeah. It is."

When the storm has passed and it's quiet again except for rain dripping off the tree branches, Lola sighs. "I should go to bed. I get so tired lately."

Alarm heats my blood. "Do you feel okay? Was that walk too much?"

Her lips curve with amusement. "No. It was fine. I'm fine. I just like to sleep a lot."

A tenderness expands in my chest, with more of that need to protect her. "You can do that." I pause. "Are you leaving tomorrow?"

"Yeah. My flight's not until six, though."

"Okay. Sleep in tomorrow then. As long as you want."

"Thanks." She shoots me a quick glance from beneath her eyelashes. "Um. Okay. Goodnight."

"Let me know if you need anything."

"I will." She drifts into the house, taking her mug to the kitchen, then climbing the stairs.

I clamp my teeth down on my bottom lip until it hurts. Sending her off to bed alone is killing me. I think of all the time we spent together in bed—not just the fucking, but the cuddling. I love cuddling with her. Talking. Laughing. Getting horny again.

I groan as blood rushes south yet again.

I can do this. I have to do this. She's made her decision and I'm going to be there for her as a co-parent. And if that's all we are, that's fine. I'll survive.

Maybe.

26

———

LOLA

I haven't told anyone at work that I'm pregnant, and I don't plan to. I'd like to think that pregnancy wouldn't impact their decision making when it comes to the VP position, but I've been around long enough to know it definitely could.

On the other hand, if I get the job, I'll have to tell them at some point, and that's not going to look good. How's that going to work? How am I going to take on a huge challenge like that and almost immediately have a baby?

Maternity leave? Hah. I'll be back at work the day after delivery. It'll be fine. I just need to plan ahead. And I love planning. I'm good at planning.

But wait. How will I be able to go back to work right away? Brandon won't be around to help. His schedule is crazy. The baby's due at the beginning of March and if they make the playoffs again this season, he could be playing intense hockey until June. He could even be traded!

If I'd planned this, I would have done better. That annoys me, but we didn't plan this and so we deal with it. Plan B. Or C. I don't know how my parents are going to react to this, but I'm sure they'll be there for me. And my friends. I have to start looking for a nanny.

Also the doctor suggested prenatal vitamins. I have to pick those up. And I could start looking at baby things now. A crib. Jesus—where am I going to put a crib in my little place?

I freeze up. Yikes. There's barely enough room for me and my plants, never mind a baby, or a child. Do I need to move?

My heart rate speeds up. I press a hand to my chest.

"Are you okay?" Zayn speaks from my doorway.

My head jerks around. I stare at him. "Yes. Fine. Fine."

"Project problem? Anything I can help with?"

"No, no. It's all good." I stretch my mouth into a smile. "What can I do for you?"

"I need to ask you about the questions for the focus group."

He takes the seat on the other side of my desk and we talk through the issue.

I'm still behind on so many things. And yet I'm having trouble focusing. I've heard women talk about pregnancy brain and I rolled my eyes, but maybe there's something to it. Or maybe I just need to try harder to focus on work. My career goals haven't changed.

That evening I meet Kaylee at Central Park to go for a walk. I haven't seen her since I got back from Pelican Beach, and I still haven't sorted out what exactly happened.

I arrive at Columbus Circle and scroll through my phone while I wait for Kaylee. I have a message from Brandon, a picture of the lake near sunset last night. Glorious. I sigh.

"Hi!" Kaylee arrives. Her dark curls bounce and she smiles. "How are you, Hot Mama?"

I roll my eyes as we start walking along the path. "Don't call me that."

She laughs. "Sorry. I'm so excited!"

I did tell her about the decision to have the baby.

"I'm going to be an aunt!" she adds. "I've already started shopping for baby gifts."

I smile. "I've been thinking about baby stuff, too."

"How are you feeling?"

"Still tired. A little moody. And fat."

She lifts an eyebrow. "You don't look any different."

"I've been eating like crazy. Brandon fed me so much food when I was there."

"Okay, tell me all about it."

"Brandon was a little, uh, shocked when I first told him."

"Well, that's to be expected. What else? He calmed down, I take it."

"Yes. The next morning he apologized. But..." I pause and roll my lips inward briefly. "He...we didn't sleep together there."

"Oh."

"He put me in a guest room and left me there like I hadn't showered for days and had a bad case of BO."

She blinks. "Oh."

"And even the next night, after we talked more, he was the same. He didn't touch me or kiss me once after I told him the news."

The corners of her mouth turn down. "Huh."

I look down at the pavement beneath my sneakers. "He talked about us being friends and said we could co-parent the baby."

"Co-parent."

"Which I was happy about! I'm glad he wants to be part of the baby's life. But...what about me?" That sounds pathetic and selfish, and I sink my teeth into my bottom lip as I look up at Kaylee.

"You *are* friends," she says slowly. "Friends with benefits. Remember?"

"Yes, of course. But..."

"Ohhhh." She closes her eyes. "You want more than that."

"No! I just...I mean..." I stop. I'm having a hard time figuring out what I'm feeling, never mind expressing it. I thought I was falling in love with him. Now... "I like Brandon. And I'm attracted to him. That hasn't changed. I thought if we're going to still be friends, we could at least still be bang buddies."

"Sounds like he doesn't want that?"

"What guy doesn't want sex?"

"Solid point. But it's more complicated now."

"I guess." I sigh. "I felt lonely. And…sort of rejected. Even though he was totally nice to me. After he got over the shock, he was so sweet, bringing me drinks and feeding me and making sure I wasn't too hot. But…I wanted him to grab me and throw me up against the wall and…." I glance around and lower my voice. "Bang my brains out."

Kaylee grins. "Pregnancy hormones can make you frisky, I hear."

"It's not the hormones. It's Brandon." I cover my eyes. "Shit."

"Oh no. You're not going to cry, are you?"

"Maybe. I never know these days. It's so annoying." I press my lips together.

"Look. You were adamant you could do this—this bang buddies thing. All you wanted was some hot boinking. Something about being too busy with your career…" She taps her chin. "And a promotion, I think?"

"Yes." I sigh. "You're right. This pregnancy kind of messes things up, though."

"Why? Women have babies and careers."

"I know, I know! But…" I stop. "I guess I'm a little scared."

She softens her tone. "Of what?"

My throat squeezes and I gaze across the open green space. "I'm afraid of not getting the promotion. I'm afraid of *getting* the promotion and then having a baby and pissing management off. I'm afraid of how my parents are going to see this. I wanted to show them how good I am at my job, and now…" I grimace. "This wasn't the plan."

"They're going to love their grandchild."

"I know they will. But they're going to be shocked at first, too."

We take a seat on a bench.

"So. Back to Brandon," Kaylee says. "Do you want him to be more than friends? More than a co-parent?"

"I don't know. I just know I felt so disappointed and hurt. But I should be glad that he's accepted this is his baby and that he'll be there."

"Yikes. Were you worried he'd think it's not his?"

"That's always a possibility. I'm going to get a DNA test done. He never mentioned it, but I want to do that for him."

"Okay." She pauses. "Maybe you should talk to him about your relationship?"

I consider that, tipping my head to one side. "You know, you're right. We talked about boundaries and promised that if things were going to end with us, we'd be up front about it. So it's only fair that I know where he stands on that."

"Yes! You're right. Good." She nods.

My emotions are all over the place. I'm so emotional, and not thinking clearly. "He's coming to New York for a wedding in a couple of weeks, so I'll see him then, probably."

"Perfect."

Brandon arrives in town on Tuesday for the wedding because there's a bachelor party Wednesday evening, so I don't see him until Thursday. I have a doctor appointment Thursday afternoon, so I ask if he wants to come with me and he agrees.

He comes up to my office to meet me. Our receptionist Aaliyah shows him back and he walks into my tiny space. His large presence fills the room with energy and his usual cocky confidence.

"Hey, superwoman," he greets me, his smile melting my panties as usual. Damn. Maybe it is hormones.

Oh God, I missed him. I drink in the sight of his easy smile, his mossy green eyes, his carved jaw. He's wearing white jeans rolled up at the ankle, white sneakers, and an untucked blue and white striped shirt. "Very GQ," I murmur. "Hi. Just let me shut things down here." I use my mouse to close programs and save documents. "I won't come back to the office today."

He makes a shocked face. "What?"

"I know, I know." I'm thinking maybe we'll have dinner or something after the doctor appointment. Or "something." Ha. My vibrator's been getting a lot of action the last couple of weeks. Yesterday, someone bumped into me on the subway and I wanted to tell him "harder."

Kidding.

"Okay." I stand from my desk and grab my suit jacket from the back of my chair. As I put it on, the fabric of my blouse strains over my boobs. They're getting bigger.

I get some satisfaction from the fact that Brandon looks at my boobs.

But then he looks away.

My heart shrinks a little in my chest.

I pull my purse from the cupboard where I keep it and we head out. As Brandon steps into the hall, he nearly runs into Zayn.

"Oh, sorry!" Zayn steps back. "Hey...aren't you Brandon Smith?"

Brandon smiles. "Yeah."

Zayne turns wide eyes to me.

"Brandon, this is my assistant, Zayn. "

Brandon extends a hand. "Nice to meet you, Zayn."

"Whoa. This is wild. I'm a fan of yours."

I watch Brandon deal with this admiration and pose for a picture with Zayn, which I take using his phone.

"We have to get going," I say to Zayn.

"Right, doctor appointment." Then a puzzled furrow appears between his eyebrows.

Uh oh.

"Okay, let's go!" I bolt for the exit. I punch the down button for the elevator and wait. "Why are you looking at me like that?"

"Why did you run out of there?"

I bite my lip. "Zayn knows I'm going to the doctor. He's probably wondering why you're coming with me."

"Ohhhh. Hopefully he doesn't like to start rumors."

We step into the elevator.

"Where's your doctor?" Brandon asks in the elevator.

"Just a few blocks away."

"Okay, good. Should you be wearing heels like that?"

I peer down at my feet. "Why not?"

"Uh…I don't know. Maybe your, uh, center of gravity is changing?"

My eyebrows fly up. "Are you saying I've gained weight?"

"Jesus. No. But I mean, you're supposed to."

"Yes. And I have gained a few pounds. But I think my center of gravity is okay for now." We set out along Madison Avenue. "I need to ask you something."

"What?"

"I want to get a DNA test done."

He frowns. "Why?"

"A paternity test."

His eyes pop open and he stops walking. "What? Why?"

We face each other, standing on the scorching hot sidewalk. "I know you're the father. I want to make sure *you* know."

He stares at me. "I don't doubt it, Lola." His deep voice is serious and even.

I swallow. "I believe you. I just wanted to be sure. I know that pro athletes have to, um, be careful…"

He closes his eyes. "I'm not worried about that." Then he opens his eyes and fixes me with a steady look.

"I know. I just want it to be done. Then there'll never be any doubt."

"What does it involve?"

"You need to have a blood test done. We can do it today at the doctor."

His eyes tighten and he still gazes at me. I hold his gaze.

"Okay," he finally says. "If that's what you want."

"I do want it."

Today the doctor listens to my belly with a Doppler stethoscope. "We should be able to hear it today," she murmurs. "Ah, there it is."

We listen to the swooshing sound.

"That's the baby's heartbeat," she says.

I meet Brandon's eyes. My chest squeezes. He looks like he's going to pass out, but he flashes a cocky grin.

"Heart rate is perfect," Dr. Geller says. "Everything else is fine, but I'd like to do another ultrasound since your first one was quite early."

"Will we be able to tell the gender at that appointment?" Brandon asks, wiping his forehead.

"Possibly. We can usually tell around fourteen weeks, but the baby has to be in the right position, so you never know."

We go to the lab for the blood tests and have the ultrasound appointment scheduled for September. Out on the street in the late afternoon sunshine Brandon grabs my hand, his eyes wild. "This is jacked. We're having a fucking baby!"

27

LOLA

"Calm down, Marlon. It's going to be okay."

"How the hell are we going to do this?" He slaps his forehead. "I thought I was okay with it, but hearing that heartbeat made me realize that I'm in no way capable of taking care of someone who's completely dependent on me."

"Yes, you are. We both are." *I hope.* "Believe me, I've had my doubts, too."

"I need a drink." He glances around and spots an Irish pub. "Come on."

Still holding my hand, he tugs me down the street and into the cool darkness. He heads straight to the long bar. There are a few empty stools and he pulls one out for me.

"Thanks." I hop up.

"You can't drink. I forgot." He rubs his forehead again.

"That's okay. I'll have water." This is good, because I need to talk to him about our shagship and our boundaries.

He sits on the stool next to me. A pretty bartender approaches with an appreciative smile for Brandon.

"I'll have a whiskey," he says. "Straight up. And water for her."

"Are you okay?" I ask.

"Oh yeah. No. I don't know. I'm being an idiot. I'm not even the one who's going through the pregnancy. But I've put on a few pounds." He pats his rock-hard abs.

I stare at him.

He grins sheepishly. "I'll try not to make this all about me."

I lift an eyebrow. "Good."

The bartender sets our drinks down and Brandon picks his up and downs half of it. "Okay," he says. "Sorry. I'm okay."

I nod. I have to admit his emotional rollercoaster ride is amusing. I pat his forearm—his warm, strong, sinewy forearm. I want to run my hand all the way up his arm and under the sleeve of his T-shirt and onto his shoulder and—*stop*. I jerk my hand back.

"Have you told your friends about the baby?"

"No. Not yet. I'm seeing Nate and Bergie tonight. I saw them last night, too, but it wasn't the time to tell them."

"Where was the bachelor party?"

"First we went to the Yankees game. That was cool. We had a suite. Then we went to this club owned by Jay Z. We had a private lounge there, too. We even met him."

"Oh my God. You met Jay Z?"

"Yeah." He grins.

I shake my head.

"It was fun. Great hanging out with the guys. Hellsy's cousins were there, too."

"Well, good."

"So everything is still going fine with the baby," he says. "That's great."

"Yep. I'm fine. Peanut's fine."

His eyes soften and warm. "Yeah. Okay, what else do we need to talk about while I'm here?"

"I need to find a nanny."

"Oh." His forehead puckers and he gulps more whiskey. "That's going to be hard since there is nobody on this planet good enough to look after our child."

I grin at his exaggeration because for once I'm thinking the exact same thing. "I know."

We talk about nanny services and what we're looking for and interviews.

"Someone with a college degree would be good," he says. "Maybe a doctor?"

I choke on my water. "I don't think many doctors become nannies."

"You never know. Let's set the bar high and see what we come up with. I'd feel comfortable with a doctor because then if Peanut gets sick they'll know what to do."

I get this. "Do you want to help interview them?"

"Absofuckinglutely."

My heart warms. "Okay. I guess we could do it in August when you're back?"

"I can come back any time. Maybe I'll cut my summer at the lake short this year."

"You don't have to do that. I know you love it there."

"Yeah, but this is important."

Now my heart is expanding into my throat. I nod. "Thanks," I squeeze out.

We talk more and then Brandon glances at his phone. "Damn. I have to go. I'm meeting Nate and Bergie."

Now my heart shrinks a couple of sizes. "Oh no."

"What?" He pulls out his wallet.

"I wanted to talk about..." I stop. Why am I so hesitant? I give people negative feedback all the time. I initiate difficult conversations all the time. I have no trouble speaking my mind. Speaking it tactfully is sometimes another matter. But this...this is scary. This is Brandon.

"We can get together again." He lays a twenty-dollar bill on the bar to cover his drink.

Shit. "Okay. Tomorrow?"

"Sure."

"Can you come to my place?"

He doesn't look at me. I sense the tension stiffening his shoulders. My breathing goes shallow and my stomach tightens.

"For dinner," I add.

He nods abruptly. "Okay."

We set a time and leave the bar. I stand on the sidewalk and watch him walk away, his long-legged stride athletic and graceful. He catches the eye of more than one woman as he cuts through pedestrian traffic, a head above others, his shoulders wide.

My throat aches and my bottom lip pops out. I roll it in between my teeth and turn the opposite direction.

I walk briskly, ignoring people, blinking back stupid tears. I really hope this emotional crap goes away after the first trimester, which is right fucking now.

I start toward home but change my mind. Why bother? I have tons of work to do. I may as well go back to the office, even though it's six o'clock.

BRANDON

I have to get away from Lola.

Being close to her, inhaling her tropical flowers scent, looking into those amazing Caribbean eyes, just makes my mind immediately go to fucking her. Touching her. Tasting her. Everywhere. She's so goddamn beautiful and strong.

She's pregnant.

My heart pounds in time to my feet as I hoof it down the city sidewalk. I round a corner and walk another block, then slow my pace. Jesus. I'm sweating like a hooker in church.

I'm meeting Nate and Bergie at our favorite burger place, over on Seventh Avenue. I was running late, but practically sprinting here made up for that and we all arrive at the same time.

They eye me askance. "Working out?" Bergie asks.

"No. I thought I was late." I wipe my brow. There are tables outside on the sidewalk with a few people seated at them. "Let's go in. I need AC."

We enter and are seated in a booth. This place is small and not fancy. No beers, just fountain drinks and shakes. The burgers are fantastic. I order my usual with bacon, tomato and ranch dressing, and a pecan pie shake, which is unbelievable.

"I need to stop eating like this," I say, once we've ordered. "No wonder I'm gaining weight."

"Go easy, man," Nate says. "You don't want to show up for training camp all fat and pudgy."

"I know, I know. I've been a little stressed."

"I didn't know you were a stress eater," Bergie says.

"Neither did I." I grimace.

"What are you stressed about? You've been relaxing at your lake-front mansion all summer."

I suck in a breath and lift my chin. "Remember Lola?"

Neither of them has met her. They weren't in Aruba.

"No," Nate says slowly. "Who's that?"

"Oh yeah, you ran into her at Bloomingdale's that day." Bergie nods. "Hot Marilyn Monroe blonde. You were seeing her again that night. Are you still seeing her?"

"Depends what you mean by 'seeing her.'" My stomach gyrates. "We were, uh, bang buddies. Just casual."

"Uh oh. I know where this is going." Nate shakes his head. "She wants to come to the wedding, doesn't she? Chicks always want to go to the wedding."

I squint at him. "No. That's not it. And she wouldn't want that. The agreement was no dating."

"Where can I find someone like that?" Nate blinks. "Does she have a sister?"

"You have enough women." I roll my eyes. The waitress brings my milkshake and I reach for it as eagerly as I did that beer earlier. "The problem is—she's pregnant."

Dense silence plunges over us.

They stare at me, speechless.

"Hooooly shit," Nate says. "Seriously?"

"Yeah."

"Are you sure?" Bergie leans forward. "You have to be careful, man."

"I'm sure. I heard the heartbeat today. Also, we got paternity tests done, even though we don't need to." I suck down more milkshake. "Fuck me."

"Wow." Nate still gapes at me.

"Are you *sure* it's yours?" Bergie asks.

I shoot him an irritated glance. "Yeah. Of course."

"No wonder you're stressed. What the hell are we doing *here*? We need tequila."

"I really do. Let's do that. After this." I slouch on the wooden seat. "She's having the baby. I said I'm okay with it, and I thought I was, and then today I heard the heartbeat, and holy fuck, she's having a *baby*."

"When?"

"March."

"Fuuuuuck." Bergie shakes his head, then blows out a long breath.

"I know. Don't tell anyone else, okay? She's just twelve weeks. We're waiting because our parents are both going to freak the fuck out. Also, she's trying to get a big promotion at work and she's worried they won't give her the job if she's pregnant."

Bergie holds up his hands. "My lips are sealed."

"Same," Nate adds. "So...what? Are you going to marry her?"

"Hell, no." I frown. "Neither of us wants to get married."

"Women always want to get married."

I pick up the note of bitterness in his voice. "Is that what happened to you?"

He lifts one shoulder. "It basically was why we got married, but at the time we both thought it was a good idea. We loved each other and we thought it would work. We were wrong."

"Damn. But that just reinforces that getting married would be a bad idea."

"Depends on the people, I guess," Nate says. "I'm not saying it could *never* work out."

"Huh." I give him a curious look. "Anyway. We both have our reasons for not wanting to get married. So we're going to share custody and co-parent the baby. As friends. We're friends."

"Friends who fuck." Nate nods.

"Not anymore." I throw my hands up. "That is now off the table."

"Hey. Let me share some good news with you." Bergie leans forward. "Women can have sex when they're pregnant. I know this from experience."

I roll my eyes. "I know that." I swipe more sweat off my forehead. "Not from experience," I add. "But she's pregnant. I can't do that to her."

"Do what?" Nate asks, looking baffled.

"I can't treat her like a fuck buddy. She's the mother of my child."

Bergie sits back and crosses his arms. "Hmmm."

"What?"

"You're not attracted to her anymore?" Nate asks, frowning.

"Christ. Are you kidding me? I want to bang her into next week. Oh God. I'm going to hell in gasoline shorts."

"Are you religious? I didn't know you were religious. What is this crap?" Nate asks. "She's not a whore just because she slept with you and you knocked her up."

"Whore?" I gaze at him blankly. "You're calling her a whore?" My hands curl into fists, ready to drive one into his face.

"No! Listen. I said she's *not* a whore. Is that why you think you can't be with her now? Is that how *you* see her?"

"No!"

"I think it's the opposite," Bergie says slowly. "Now he's knocked her up he's lost sexual interest in her."

"No!" Christ, these guys are my friends and they're not getting it. "I just said I want to fuck her senseless. But how can I think about her like that?"

"No, no. Wait." Bergie nods knowingly. "It's not that you're not attracted to her. It's that she's become…hmmm, like a saint to you. You put her on a pedestal because she's pregnant, and worship her as the mother of your child."

I make a disgusted noise. "That's fucked up." *I think…*

Our food arrives so our conversation ceases for a few minutes. Why did I bother talking to these guys? They're both fathers, but they're not getting it. "Okay, just forget the psychoanalysis," I eventually say. "We're friends and we're going to be parents. That's it. I lost my shit at first, but I've accepted it."

"Uh huh." Nate takes a bite of his burger. "Sure."

I give him a narrow-eyed look, then shrug. "Hearing the heartbeat this afternoon just made things seem a little more real. We need a nanny! Where are we going to get a nanny?"

Nate squints. "I only have a teenage babysitter I use once in a while when I have Quinn."

"I'll give you some names," Bergie says. "We ended up only hiring someone part-time but we did some research."

"Okay. Thanks man." Finally, he's actually being helpful.

"I still think she wants to come to the wedding," Nate says.

I lift my middle finger at him. "That would be a date. We don't do dates."

"Riiiiight."

"Seriously, though." Bergie grins. "Congratulations. You're gonna be a dad! Our kids can have play dates. This is gonna be so much fun!"

Nate grins. "Quinn will love a baby to play with."

"I'll need advice from you guys," I say. "I don't know anything about kids."

"Any time! Will you be in the delivery room with Lola?"

I blanche. "Uh. I guess so."

"Okay, I have lots of advice for you there. Like when she yells at you to fuck off and never touch her again...she doesn't really mean that."

"Maybe not applicable here, but I get what you mean."

"Also," Nate says. "Don't ever give any hint that you're tired or want to take a nap. And no complaining about *anything*. With what she's going through, if you say you have a headache, you will lose that head. Also turn off your phone. When she's trying to push that baby out and your phone rings, trust me, it is not a good thing."

I'm making mental notes. "Got it."

"Okay." Bergie stands. "I gotta go."

"What? Why? I thought we were going out for tequila."

"I miss my wife. See you guys at the wedding."

I stare at him as he leaves the restaurant, going home early because he misses his wife.

I want that.

Wait, what?

28

BRANDON

I keep thinking about my conversation with Nate and Bergie. About Lola. About me not wanting to touch her because she's pregnant. That is some seriously messed up shit. I don't like thinking of myself as that messed up. The more I think about it, the more pissed off I get at them.

Because I do want to touch her. More than anything. But not just to bang her. I want to put my hand on her stomach. I want to feel that baby when it moves. I want to rub her back or her feet when they hurt. I want to brush her hair because I know she loves it.

And yeah, I do want to bang her.

So why am I not? I'm going to her place tonight and could easily do it. If she wants. Obviously.

When I said we could co-parent as friends, it didn't seem right to include the "benefits" in that. I mean, we might as well be married if we're going to hang out together, sleep together, and have a kid together. Right?

And neither of us wants that.

Hearing that heartbeat was like a punch in the face. Every time I think I've accepted it, something happens that makes me realize I haven't. I'm an idiot to even think I can be a good dad to a kid. I know how shitty it felt listening to my parents argue all the time, especially about me. I don't want to let my own kid down that way. I'll be responsible for someone else and that scares the hell out of me.

This has really complicated things and I'm annoyed by it all. I'm also fucking terrified.

And now Lola wants to talk more. I want to be there for her, but all these doubts keep crowding into my brain and making me want to run.

Outside her door, I knock and she opens it immediately.

Just seeing her takes my damn knees out. Every time. She's wearing a summery floral dress in shades of blue and green that match her eyes and leave her shoulders and arms bare. Her legs and feet are also bare.

"Hi." She smiles and I read the uncertainty in her eyes.

I'm an asshole.

"Hi." I hand her the bottle of wine I brought.

"Um. Thanks." I see the confusion on her face.

"It's non-alcoholic. The dude at the store said it's actually pretty good."

"Oh. Okay. That's really…nice. Thank you."

She walks into her kitchen and I go around to the side of the counter in the living room. I set my hands flat on the granite counter and watch her pull two wineglasses out of a cupboard.

She looks at me over her shoulder. "Do you want some? Or would you rather have real wine, or a beer?"

"No, I'll have some." I will join her in abstention.

She pours two glasses and sets one in front of me. We both take a sip and look at each other. "Huh. It's not bad."

"Yeah. This is nice."

"It smells good in here."

"Thanks. It's nothing fancy—chicken with lemon and herbs. I had to make something quick since I didn't have much time."

"I could have picked up food."

One corner of her mouth lifts. "I guess. But I like cooking."

"You're a great cook." I discovered that when she came to Pelican Beach.

She sets a bowl of mixed nuts in front of me, and I munch on them and watch her as she finishes preparing dinner.

"How are Bergie and Nate?" she asks. "What did you do last night?"

"We went to Skyline Diner for burgers. And then to the Crown for tequila." I blow out a breath. "I told them you're pregnant."

"Oh."

"They won't tell anyone else. They had advice for me for the delivery room."

"Oh, Jesus." She stares at me.

I laugh. "I know. I'll try not to pass out or something."

We keep the conversation going while we eat. I help her clear up and she opens her freezer to produce a carton of butter pecan ice cream with a questioning expression.

"You're a goddess." I press my palms together. "Thank you. But damn…I better only have a little. I've put on a lot of weight."

She frowns and eyes me. "I don't think so, Marlon."

The nickname is my clue that I'm being dramatic.

I like the way she looks at me. Like I'm hot. And she's hot for me. Goddammit, now I've got a semi.

She scoops ice cream into bowls and we sit again.

I dig my spoon in. "So what did you want to talk about?"

"Oh. Right." She pokes her ice cream with her spoon. "I wanted to talk about our friends with benefits thing."

My gut tightens. "Uh…what about it?"

"When we started this, we agreed on some boundaries."

"Right." Where the hell is this going?

"One of the things we agreed on was that if one of us wanted to end things, we'd be up front with each other about it."

My eyebrows pull down. "Yeah." She's looking at me and I feel compelled to meet her eyes.

"I feel like you're ending things."

My head jerks. "How am I ending things?"

"Seriously? I have to spell this out for you?"

My gaze flickers away from her and back. I think I know what she's getting at, and I don't want to go there. I'm still irritated from talking about it last night.

She goes on. "When I came to see you at the lake, I know I didn't exactly have good news for you. And I know you were freaked out that first night, but I didn't expect you to put me in a guest room and not touch me."

I drop my gaze to my bowl.

"I appreciate that you want to be here for me and for the baby. That you want to co-parent. As friends. And if you don't want the 'benefits' part of it, f-fine. But you need to tell me that."

Tension seizes me, every muscle in my body tightening. My heart slams into an uneven rhythm and I have that sick feeling in my gut like I used to get when I heard my parents' fighting.

When I'm on the ice, I can use my body—sometimes even my fists—to deal with altercations. But off the ice—I'd rather walk away. I shove my spoon into my mouth and let the ice cream melt while I think about how to respond, my gut churning.

"Tell me what you're thinking," she says. "What you're feeling."

I smile at her. "I'm thinking you're cute."

Her eyelashes flutter double-time. "*Brandon.*"

Adrenaline spikes in my veins and the urge to run intensifies. My mind is racing, trying to figure out how to get out of this. "Look, neither of us wanted kids or marriage. Right?"

"Right…"

"We're having a kid. Also which neither of us wanted."

She flinches, barely, nodding slowly.

"So staying friends is the best thing for us, right? So we can be good parents." No fighting in front of the kid. No emotional melt-downs in front of the kid. Just two parents who get along. My insides tighten even more, my stomach now hard as a fucking rock.

She stares at me for a long moment. "Okay. I understand."

"Okay, good." Whew. I set down my ice cream bowl, prepared to make a fast exit.

"I understand you're an idiot."

My head jerks back. "What?"

"What is wrong with you?" Then she closes her eyes. "I'm sorry. That was wrong to say. My emotions are taking over."

I just stare at her.

She meets my eyes and I see her carefully choosing her words. "I feel like you avoid certain topics. You alw—" She stops. "You often make a smartass comment or change the subject. You didn't tell me that you don't want to have sex with me anymore and I felt confused and rejected."

I feel like a fist just punched me in the gut. "I'm sorry."

"I feel like you're not really telling me everything. If we're friends, if we're going to be parents together, we need to be honest with each other."

"Yes." I can't argue with that.

"Arrrgh!" She tips her head back. "You say that, but you won't do it!"

I frown. "Hey. I just did." Okay, yeah, there are things I'm not opening up about. "I'm here, aren't I? I went to the doctor appointment with you. What more do you want?"

She blinks at me. "What more do I want?" She pauses. "I want…" She stops again. "I just want you to be honest with me. When you're not, it's…hurtful. It's selfish. I feel like you don't trust me."

I hold up my hands placatingly. "Hey, I—"

"Don't." She slides off the stool. Her cheeks have reddened and her eyes flash. "Unless you're prepared to be truly honest and tell me what's really going on with you, this isn't going to work."

My eyes fly open. My heart kicks against my sternum. "What do you mean this isn't going to work?"

"This. Us. Co-parenting." She lifts her chin and narrows her eyes at me. "We're not doing this. *I'm* not doing this."

All the air is sucked out of my lungs. I can't breathe. I can't speak. "No. You can't do that."

"How can you be a father? How can you parent? How can you be a *friend*?" The words pour of out her. Each one is like a slap in the face. "If you won't open up, just forget it." She levels an icy look at me. "I can have this baby by myself. I can raise this baby by myself."

My jaw damn near bounces off the floor. "Are you fucking kidding me?"

"No. I'm dead serious." She jerks her head.

I stare at her. This can't be happening. I try to find my voice. Finally, with a caustic edge, I say, "Well that escalated quickly."

And I walk out.

29

BRANDON

"What the hell are you wearing?"

I look down at myself. "What's wrong with this?"

Nate stares at me. "Uh. Nothing, if you're going to a Liberace concert."

I shrug. "I like it." My silver and black velvet jacket looks sharp with my silvery shirt and black dress pants.

"You're not even wearing a tie."

I toss back the rest of the pre-wedding whiskey I'm drinking at Spinning Tap Brewpub. "The wedding is in a beer hall. I didn't think a tie would be required."

He shakes his head and sips his own beer. "Okay. Whatever."

We met here with some of the other guys for a drink before the ceremony starts. I'm not a fan of weddings, but this is a cool place—a beer hall and brew pub in Chelsea, really old, with cobblestones, lots of old brick and wood, and big arched windows.

We finish our beers and head to the room where Hellsy and Sara will say "I do."

Beneath exposed wood beams, wooden benches have been arranged in rows with an aisle between them. The creamy old brick walls glow in the light from sconces, although late afternoon sunshine still brightens the big arched windows. A massive chandelier above us is draped with pink flowers and greenery.

People are already filling the space and we find seats with some of the other guys. Nate and I seem to be the only guys without dates.

Fine with me.

I'm still grumpy from last night. That fight with Lola is eating away at my insides. Two whiskeys haven't softened my mood.

Finally it's time for the ceremony to start. I hope it's quick so I can hit the bar again.

Hellsy appears along with Millsy, Morrie and Hellsy's friend Billy Boyko, who he played with in Dallas, all of them dressed in dark blue suits, Hellsy wearing a pale pink tie, a pale pink rosebud on his lapel, and a huge grin. I shake my head.

Then the music changes and the bridesmaids start down the aisle —first Millsy's girlfriend Lilly, then Morrie's girlfriend Kate, and another woman I don't know with long red hair. They're all wearing pink satin gowns and carrying small bouquets of pink and white flowers.

Finally it's time for the bride. Sara appears at the back of the space. I may not be entirely happy to be here, but hell, she looks gorgeous. I think Hellsy's going to cry.

She glides down the aisle alone. Her dress isn't even white, it's super pale pink, lighter than the bridesmaids, and she must be sewn into it because it fits her snugly all the way down to just below her ass where it flares out into a froth of sheer layers.

Hellsy's all emotional watching her walk toward him as the Goo Goo Dolls sing "Iris."

Something sticks in my throat and I cough.

Oh Christ. All the bridesmaids have tears running down their faces.

I heave a sigh.

We get into the ceremony. I'm not paying much attention when suddenly music starts playing from Hellsy's pocket. As people recognize the song—"Rescue Me" by One Republic—they start laughing. Hellsy gropes around and pulls out his phone which is playing the song. "Who changed my ring tone?" he yells.

The guys up front with him double over laughing, and beside me Nate is silently shaking. I glance at him and see he's holding his phone. He was in on it! I grin.

Hellsy finally silences the song, shoves his phone away, and returns his attention to his bride. "Sorry," he mutters. "Okay. I know a lot about teamwork. In hockey, we're a team because we play together, but also because we respect each other. We trust each other. And we care for each other. And that's how I feel about you. I respect you. I trust you. I love you. You and I…we're a team now." He pauses, his lips twitching. "Also, I wrote a poem for you."

Sara laughs. "Oh no."

Great. Hellsy's a poet? Who knew?

Gazing into Sara's eyes, he says, "Roses are red, violets are blue. Love never crossed my mind until I the day I met you."

Sara's "aaaaw" is echoed by most of the women in the crowd. It's kind of cute. I guess.

Then it's done and Hellsy and Sara melt into each other in a scorcher of a kiss that gets people clapping and cheering. They turn and walk back up the aisle together. You've got to be kidding me—they're leaving to "Young, Dumb, and in Love" by Mat Kearney. I laugh out loud. Finally something I can get on board with.

They're laughing, too, their smiles as bright as a supernova. They sure look happy.

Whatever.

We follow them out to a reception area where there's a bar lined with glasses of champagne. I'll take it. I scoop one up and a bunch of us gather into a conversational group. I get shit about my velvet jacket again. I don't care.

"You're just jealous because you have no sense of style," I tell Dutchy. "I like what you've done with your hair, though. How do you get it to come out your nostrils like that?"

Everyone guffaws. Dutchy rolls his eyes.

"And hey, Murph, I see you polished your crocs for the occasion."

"You're on fire," Nate mutters.

I have to have fun somehow.

We move back into the other room for dinner. Long wooden tables are arranged in rows with lots of candles and pink flowers. There are ice buckets on the tables with bottles of red, white, and pink wine. Rosé, I guess. We listen to speeches, including a hilarious one by Millsy, the best man, which recounts Hellsy and Sara's first date, in which he managed to put her in the hospital. (He fed her something she was allergic to.) He also makes everyone choke up when he talks about the bus accident he, Hellsy, and Morrie were involved in years ago and how lucky they are to be here together celebrating life and love.

Shit. I kind of choke up, too. Those three guys went through hell and now here they are, all happy and successful and in love.

Wait, what am I thinking? Love is fighting and arguing and complaining.

I think.

I've been helping myself to lots of wine throughout the dinner as the efficient serving staff replaces empty bottles right away. No one else at our table seems interested in the pink wine so I drink a lot of it. Everything is pleasantly blurry by the time dinner's done.

Dancing starts beneath the party lights draped above the dance floor. First it's the newlyweds dancing to "Sparks" by Cold Play. Unusual choice. Damn, it's romantic. And sexy. I watch Hellsy and Sara dance, hands clasped between them, gazing into each other's eyes, smiling, and holy hell, the ache in my gut nearly takes me down. What *is* that?

I've been trying not to think of Lola, but images of her crowd into my slightly inebriated brain. We've never danced like that. We've never danced, period. I'd like to dance with her, and not just the mattress mambo.

I rub my forehead. What is happening to me?

I refill my wineglass.

The music picks up tempo. Good. I need to get out of this funk. I need to daaaaaance!

I grab Kate's hand and drag her onto the dance floor. She laughs as we get down to Ed Sheeran singing about bad habits. I find Hellsy's little sister Amy and dance with her, then the maid of honor whose name I now know is Kaylee.

Wait. Kaylee?

"Are you Lola's friend?" I ask her.

She frowns. "Who?"

"Lola. Lola McGrath. She has a best friend named Kaylee."

Still with a faint notch between her brows, she shakes her head. "No. I don't know Lola McGrath."

"Oh. Okay. Coincidence, I guess."

I need to stop thinking about Lola.

I'm busting out my best moves and working up a sweat, so I ditch my jacket and grab Hellsy for the next dance. "Daaaaaance with me, gaijin!" I yell.

"What?" He gives a confused laugh.

But it's a slow song. What the hell. I take his hand like I'm leading and dance him around the dance floor.

"You okay, man?" he asks, smiling.

"Never better! Helluva wedding, Hellsy. Great party."

"Thanks." He gives me a look that tells me he's not convinced I'm fine. I make a move to twirl him and bring him back in, nearly taking both of us to the floor.

Luckily he laughs.

"Hey, take it easy, guys," Sara says. "I don't want my groom injured before the wedding night." She gives me an exaggerated wink.

There are so many Hellers here. It's kind of cool being at a wedding with a hockey legend family. All of Hellsy's uncles and his dad played hockey—Jase, Tag, Logan, and Matt. I manage to not make a fool of myself when talking to them.

Next I dance with Hellsy's mom, Kyla. She's hot for a mom, with long dark hair, wearing a sexy mother of the bride dress that's deep pink lace. I'd dance with her again, but Hellsy's dad Tag is frowning at me and he's bigger than I am. I'm younger, though. Also a little shit-faced. So I let Kyla go and dance by myself as "Wobble Wobble" starts playing.

"Oh yeah!" I punch a fist in the air then set my hands on my thighs, pop my ass out and shake it.

"What the fuck, Brando?" Bergie's next to me, shaking his head, but laughing.

"Twerking." I do it again as the song tells me to shake that ass.

I'm getting lots of attention from the others on the dance floor and I keep dancing and shaking my ass until the song ends.

"Need another drink," I mumble, heading back to our table.

"Here." Bergie slides a big glass of water in front of me.

I shrug and down it, then find my wine glass.

"Easy there, MC Hammer."

"I think it's time for more than wine."

"I think you're good."

"Hey." I frown at him. "I'm having fun. Don't harsh my buzz."

He rolls his lips in. "What is up, man?"

I drop into a chair. "Eh. Had a little argument with Lola last night."

He purses his lips, pulls out a chair, and sits too. "Oh yeah? What about?"

"About the baby." I stare morosely at pink flowers. "I wonder if it's a girl."

"Fifty-fifty chance. Is that what you argued about?"

"No. She doesn't want me to co-parent anymore."

"What?"

I nod, not looking at him. "Yeah." I disgorge a gusty sigh.

"*Why?*"

"I don't know."

"Really?"

I look up to see his skeptical expression, then look away. "I'm kinda confused about it all. I think she's pissed because we're not having sex anymore."

"Uh...."

"I *do* want to have sex with her," I mumble. "Like, a lot. But probably not right this minute." I glance down at my lap. "It's not whiskey dick. I guess rosé dick is a thing."

"Wow."

"But it's better if we don't. It's better if we're just friends. Except now...we're not even friends."

My vision gets blurry. I mean, blurrier.

"Are you crying?" Nate pulls up a chair next to us. "What did you do?"

"He fucked things up with Lola," Bergie says.

"I'm not crying. Jesus. Just had a lil too much to drink."

I catch them exchanging glances.

"It's what we talked about the other night," Bergie tells Nate. To me, he says, "Did you explain it to Lola?"

"Explain what?"

"The no sex thing."

"Of course. I told her what I just said—we should be friends. Sex would complicate that."

Bergie looks like I just told him I enjoy eating shit. "That's it?"

"Yeah. That's it."

"What are you so afraid of?" Bergie asks.

"Nothing. I'm not afraid. Jesus."

"Bullshit. Having a baby is terrifying."

I swallow. "Lola called me a selfish idiot." Aw fuck. I think I am crying. "Goddammit."

Bergie shakes his head. "Good for her."

"Whose side are you on?"

"Your side, buddy. Always." Nate claps a hand on my shoulder. "Which is why we're going to be honest with you. You *are* a selfish idiot."

"Hey!"

"Let's talk tomorrow." Bergie stands. "I don't think you're going to remember much of this conversation."

"Fine." Tomorrow's fine with me. Or maybe never.

They leave me alone at the table.

I fill a wine glass and take a couple of gulps. I'm tired. I'll just sit here for a while.

LOLA

My phone is buzzing. It takes a while to permeate my sleep. I gradually surface and slap my hand out for the phone plugged in on my nightstand. It's the doorman downstairs.

"Hi," I croak, still half asleep.

"You have a visitor, Ms. McGrath."

I squint into the darkness.

"Brandon Smith," he adds.

I sit up, shoving the covers down. "He's here?"

"Yes, ma'am."

What the hell? What is doing here? It's the middle of the night!

I glance at my phone. Okay, it's one in the morning. Still, I've been asleep for hours. Is he okay? What's happening? "Yes, he can come up."

I got angry at him because he wasn't willing to tell me how he was feeling, or what was going on in his head, but I have to admit it was also because I was hurt. He wants to be friends *without* benefits, now. He's right that sex would complicate things. We both agreed we didn't want more than that. So why am I hurt?

I regret what I said about saying I can raise this baby by myself. I mean, I can, but the look on his face nearly destroyed me; he was so dismayed it made my heart hurt.

Even so, how can I have a relationship with this man when he won't trust me enough to be honest with me? Even a relationship that's just friendship.

I slide out of bed. I'm wearing a pair of striped shorts and a tank top. I grab my robe and pull it on, making a quick trip to the bathroom. I hear the knock on the door as I wash my hands.

I let Brandon in and the alcohol fumes precede him. I lift an eyebrow as he lurches in. "Oh my God."

He blinks at me. "Hi."

"Were you at the wedding?"

"Yeah." He sits on my couch, uninvited. "It was only a few blocks from here. I realized that when I left the bar and somehow I ended up walking here."

"Somehow." I sit too, keeping my distance. "What's going on?"

"I'm drunk."

"No! Really?"

My sarcasm is lost on him.

"I fell asleep at the table." He rubs his face. "My asshole friends said they'd take me home, but I escaped."

"Escaped. Huh."

"I can't believe I got drunk on pink fuckin' wine."

I bite back a smile. "Pink wine is the worst drunk."

"I know, right?"

I'm still angry at him, but it's hard to be mad when he's being so adorable. Being drunk isn't funny, but he's…well, it's a little funny.

"I thought I met Kaylee at the wedding. There was a bridesmaid named Kaylee, but she didn't know you."

"Oh. What a coincidence. Probably spelled different." My insides twist, imagining him dancing with this other Kaylee.

"How do you spell Kaylee?"

I spell it out.

"What's her last name?"

"McGrath."

"Hey! Same as you!"

My lips twitch. "She's my cousin, remember?"

"Ohhhhh right." He pauses, then mumbles, "I'm sorry."

I go still. "For what?"

"For fighting. I fucking hate fighting. My parents fought all the time. About me."

My heart bumps hard in my chest. I sink down into a chair, staring at him. They fought about *him*? He told me they fought a lot, but not that it was about him.

"I just like having fun," he says. "Fun is more fun."

"That is true."

"I felt like I was just a big pain in their ass," he continues, not looking at me.

Oh my God.

He's drunk. And unguarded. He always has that cocky smile and vague answers to questions that get too personal, but now…he's being totally open.

Not for long, though.

He leans over and lays his head on a cushion. "Need more sleep."

What do I do? Kick him out? I sigh. I can't do that.

I pull a pillow and blanket from my linen closet. "Lift up." I exchange the decorative cushion for the pillow. "Take off your jacket and shoes." As he struggles out of the jacket, I say, "That's quite the jacket."

"Thanks." He lies down again, stretching out on my couch, and I toss the blanket over him.

His eyes close and I stay there for a minute, watching him.

He felt like he was a nuisance to his parents. Something to fight over. I close my eyes on a wave of anguish. Oh my God, that makes my heart hurt so much. I can't stand that he went through that.

He lets out a soft snore and I have to smile. What an idiot. Reluctant affection warms my chest. Why did he come here?

I'll never understand this man. I'm never getting rid of him, either. He's the father of my baby.

I'm still hurt at his rejection of me. I know I shouldn't care. Our relationship wasn't like that. But it still hurts. And I don't know if I can forgive him for that. Not right now, anyway.

I turn out the lights and go back to bed. I can hear Brandon's breathing as it deepens…and turns into soft snoring. I'm so aware of him, only a few feet away in my tiny apartment. I remember all the time we spent here, in this bed, together. It makes me sad. My chest hurts at the wanting…I want that again. I want *him* again.

But he doesn't want me, and I have to live with that.

A faint groan wakes me up in the morning. Sun beams through the blinds on my big window, creating a soft, hazy light in the apartment. I turn my head and see two big feet hanging over the end of my couch.

Brandon.

His feet are bare. What about the rest of him? He was fully clothed when I left him there last night. He better not be naked. My libido can't handle the test.

I take a few steadying breaths. "Are you awake?" I call softly.

"No. I think I'm dead."

My mouth twists into a smile. "Should I call an ambulance?"

"Maybe."

I hear covers rustling and he sits up. Bare chested.

Gulp.

He lifts his hands to his head and shoves his fingers into his hair. Jesus. His biceps bulge, his triceps flex, his chest and abs tighten. I take in the dark tufts of hair under his arms and the smattering of hair across his chest that tapers down into a fine trail disappearing beneath the blanket.

Heat slides through my veins. I can't breathe.

"I might need some Advil," he says, his voice jagged.

"I have some." I slide out of bed, pull on my robe, and head past him to the bathroom. I find the painkillers and return to him with a glass of water to wash them down.

"Thanks." He swallows them, draining the glass which he hands back to me. He falls to his back again on the couch. "I'm sorry for showing up here drunk."

"It's okay. At least you made it somewhere safe to sleep it off."

"Yeah."

He falls silent and I don't know what to say. I cross over to grab some clothes and scoot into the bathroom to dress in a pair of cropped leggings and loose T-shirt. I brush my hair and check my reflection in the mirror. I don't know why.

He's still lying there, eyes closed, when I return. Is he asleep again?

I move to my kitchen to make myself a cup of coffee.

"Is that coffee?" he rasps.

"Yes. Do you want some?"

"God, yes."

Then he appears across the counter from me, dressed only in a pair of snug black boxer briefs. I swallow my tongue and jerk my attention away from him to the Keurig.

"Damn." He sits on a stool and scrubs both hands over his face. "I *am* an idiot."

"Did you at least have fun?"

"Not really. I tried."

His phone is buzzing furiously and he goes to retrieve it, thankfully stepping into his pants, but he doesn't do them up, just peers at his phone while he slowly moves back toward me. That area beneath his navel is so, so attractive…

He scowls at his phone. "Ah, hell."

"What?"

"They took video last night." He closes his eyes. "This better not be public somewhere."

"Uh oh. What did you do?"

He turns his phone toward me and I watch him twerking on a dimly-lit dance floor.

"Oh boy."

"Yeah." He swipes at the screen and shows me another image, him asleep with his head on the table. "I'll have their balls if they post this shit."

"At least you're a good dancer."

He snorts.

I hand him the coffee.

"Thanks." He takes a sip, then another. "I think I came here to apologize."

I regard him over the edge of my own mug. "Last night you said you were sorry. For fighting."

"Uh, yeah."

"We were having a discussion," I say evenly. "Not fighting."

He frowns.

"I'm sorry I made you angry. That wasn't my intention. I wanted to know what you were thinking and feeling but I know I pushed you."

He nods. "I'm sorry too for making you mad."

"Do you even know why I was mad?" I ask.

"Uh, because of the no sex thing?"

My eyebrows shoot up. I blink a few times. I almost want to laugh. Or maybe cry. Finally I say, "Yes. That's it. I'm sexually frustrated." Once again, my sarcasm is not apparent to him. Of course, he's seriously hungover, so his brain cells might not all be firing today.

This is better than telling him how hurt and disappointed I am. Except—I'm not being honest about my feelings...just like him. Protecting my heart, that jab of hurt inside me goading me on, I continue. "It's okay, though. I realized I can have sex with anyone."

"What?" His head jerks around and he winces. "What the fuck?"

I shrug. "I'm also sorry about saying I can raise the baby by myself. I'm sure we can work things out."

He stares at me. "Fuck, Lola." Then he shakes his head. "Yeah. I'm sure we can."

"So don't worry. We'll figure it out." I glance at the clock on my stove. "I have to get going. I'm meeting Kaylee for brunch."

"Oh. Damn. Sorry." He stands, still holding his cup. He looks around, spies his shirt and heads toward it. In a moment he's dressed again, socks and shoes on, as well as the ridiculous jacket. "Sorry again for barging in like that."

I smile. "No worries. Go home and nurse your hangover. I hear Gatorade is good."

"I have that."

"I thought you might." I follow him to the door. "Are you going back to the lake?"

"Yeah. This afternoon. You'll keep me posted about how things are going, yeah?"

"If I think you need to know, sure."

His eyes are red-rimmed and shadowed. The dark circles beneath them give him a gaunt look and his jaw tightens. He looks utterly miserable.

My heart squeezes but I keep my chin up and shoulders back.

The air around us throbs. I feel it inside me and on my skin. I feel it in the ache at the back of my throat. I want to stretch my hands out to him, emotion welling up inside me.

"Okay. Thanks. Bye."

I close the door and sag. I suck in a shuddering gasp of air as a hot knife of pain slashes through me. My throat aches and I squeeze my eyes closed. Why does this hurt so much? And how am I going to deal with this, since he's the father of my baby?

I don't have brunch plans with Kaylee.

I just needed to get him out of here.

Being around him is too hard. It hurts too much. It makes me so sad and full of disappointment.

It's better if I only see him when I have to, for the baby.

BRANDON

I manage to avoid seeing the guys. I text them back and tell them I'm heading out and I'll see them when they come visit. They're having a hoot making fun of me, but I don't want to tell them I went to see Lola and maybe made things worse.

When I get to Grand Rapids, I pick up my vehicle at the airport and head to Dad's place to pick up Martha. He's been spoiling her while I've been gone.

It's late Sunday afternoon and Dad's neighborhood is quiet, lawns neatly mowed, flowers blooming in yards. I park in his driveway and find him in the backyard pressure washing his deck. His place is immaculate; he enjoys taking care of it. I guess that's where I get it from, because I like working around my house, too.

"Hey!" He looks up with a grin and turns off the power washer. "You're here."

Martha uncurls herself where she's chilling under a tree and lopes toward me, tail waving in the air. I bend to greet her, hugging and rubbing her. "Hey, girl. How are you? I missed you, too." I straighten. "Looks good out here." The lawn is lush and even. Dad doesn't have a lot of flowers, but the trees and shrubs are all neatly trimmed.

"Thanks. Have a seat." He gestures to the outdoor chairs at the other end of the deck. "Want a beer?"

I wince. "No, thanks. I'm driving. Obviously." Also brutally hungover.

"I need some water, how about that?"

"Sure."

He goes inside and I relax into one of the comfortable wicker chairs at the other end of the deck, in the shade from the heat of the day. Martha sets her paws on my knees, demanding more attention.

Dad returns and hands me a cold bottle of water.

"Thanks."

"How was the wedding?" He takes a seat, too.

"Great. Fun."

So far, none of my shenanigans have showed up on social media. I hope it stays that way.

"When does training camp start?"

"September twelfth." Lola's birthday.

"The day after your birthday," Dad remarks.

"Yeah. We don't have the exact schedule yet, but that's when the medical testing will start."

He nods. "Have you been working out?"

"Yeah, some." Has he noticed the weight I've gained? I better get back into my workouts.

"Good, good. When are you going back to the city?"

"I don't know." I guzzle down some water. I've been thinking about that. I feel I should be closer to Lola. Except she clearly doesn't want me there. I gave myself a headache, thinking about all that on the plane. Or maybe the Advil wore off and it's the hangover.

"I can't believe tomorrow's August. Already." He shakes his head.

I nod absently as Dad talks. I keep thinking about Lola saying she's sexually frustrated but she can sleep with anyone. What the fuck?

The more I ponder it, the more I think—hope?—she was being sarcastic. Is she really going to see other guys?

I guess there's no reason she can't.

What if…what if she ends up meeting someone? She says no relationships, she's focused on work. But it could happen. That guy…he'd have to be okay with her having a baby. My baby. What if he was? What if she found someone like that? Where would that leave me?

In a fucking snowbank in Siberia, that's where.

"What is wrong with you?" Dad says.

I focus on his frowning face. "What?"

"You haven't heard a word I said."

I give a guilty grimace. "Sorry."

"What's going on?" His gaze sweeps over me. "You look like shit."

"Gee, thanks, Dad." I rub my forehead. "I drank a little too much at the wedding last night."

"Huh." His forehead remains furrowed. "Is that why you're lost in thought?"

I sigh inwardly. "I was thinking about something." I pause, then blurt out, "I got a girl pregnant."

Dad's eyebrows shoot up to where his hairline used to be. "Jesus Christ."

"I know." I didn't intend to tell him that. Lola and I both agreed we'd wait to tell our parents and other people.

One corner of his mouth lifts. "I worried about hearing that when you were a teenager."

"We were safe," I say. "Took precautions. It was a freak thing."

He nods, lips pursed. "Who is she?"

"Her name is Lola. Lola McGrath."

He tips his head. "Obviously not planned…but are you okay with this?"

"I have to be."

"That doesn't sound very positive."

"I'm kind of mixed up about it, to be honest." I gaze out over the lawn.

"I get that. Even though your mom and I planned for you, I had mixed feelings. Fear. The weight of responsibility. Happiness. Pride." He pauses. "That never goes away."

"Jesus. Thanks a lot." I peer at him. "Really?"

"Sure." He lifts one shoulder. "All of it. Forever." He smiles. "But it's all worth it."

I stare at him. "I never felt like I was worth it."

His smile fades and his eyebrows slope down. "What?"

"You and Mom argued all the time. A lot of it was about me. That didn't exactly make me feel like you thought I was worth it all."

His jaw goes slack and his eyes shadow. He slowly moves his head from side to side. "We love you."

"Yeah, I know." I drop my gaze and pick a piece of thread off my jeans. I shouldn't have started this conversation.

"Brandon." His voice is dry and rusty. "We love you. We've always loved you."

"I said I know." I jerk my head. "Just forget it. Anyway, she's having the baby. She's due in March. I'm going to be part of the kid's life, but Lola and I aren't together."

"Ah. Damn."

"No, it's good. We both agree on that." I swallow. "She's very career focused and doesn't want to get married. We're both on the same page about that. I don't want a relationship like…" I stop.

"Like your parents?" he asks quietly.

I grimace.

"I get that, I guess. But marriage doesn't have to be like that. If you find the right person. Is that…" He narrows his eyes. "Is that why you're not married?"

"Well." I scratch the back of my neck. "Partly. Yeah."

He blows out a breath. "I guess we weren't very good examples for you."

"I'm afraid…" Once again I stop myself.

"Say it. Just tell me." Frustration hardens his voice.

I shift in the chair and tug at the neckline of my T-shirt. The nape of my neck itches and heat pours over me. "That's okay."

"Did you feel like we didn't love you?"

Oh Christ. I study a tree in the yard, then the fence between Dad's yard and the neighbor's. "Did you just paint the fence? It looks good."

"Brandon."

I close my eyes briefly, then gulp some water, draining the bottle. "I should get going."

"*Brandon.*"

"What?" I meet Dad's eyes with difficulty.

"You always do this."

"Do what?"

"You're not comfortable talking about your feelings. Hell." He rubs his eyes. "Neither am I. But come on. I can't let this go."

I grin and jump to my feet. "Sure you can."

"Sure, sure. Make a joke out of it. Listen. Our marriage wasn't exactly happy, and I'm sorry that all our conflict made you feel like we didn't care about you. But we absolutely did. Jesus." He stands too, moving right in front of me. "Tell me what you're so afraid of."

Pressure rises inside me. I curl my hands into fists, my arms stiff at my sides. "I'm afraid of doing the same thing to my kid."

Ah hell. I really said that out loud. To my dad.

His mouth tightens and he nods. "There it is."

"I'm sorry." I push past him. "I really have to go."

"Wait. Just listen to me. *I'm* sorry. I'm sorry you feel you can't talk to me. I'm sorry that you keep all this bottled up inside you. You need to talk to someone about it. Maybe that's not me, but come on, son."

I meet his eyes. "I'll...think about it."

On the drive to my place, my head is full of everything Dad said. And everything Lola said. When I pull into the driveway at home, I don't even know how I got there. I don't remember a minute of the drive. Maybe I went through some red lights, I don't even know. Thank God for the cruise control. Fuck.

LOLA

"I really think you should meet this young man."

I frown, listening to my mom in my earbuds as I walk down Madison Avenue. "Oh, Mom. I've told you—I'm not interested in dating right now."

"But why not?"

"I'm super busy at work and…and…"

"That promotion you didn't tell us about," she says.

"Well, yes." I haven't told her about the pregnancy. "It's just not a good time."

On top of all that, I'm not even a little interested in any other man. I've got Brandon imprinted in my brain. I dream about him all the time, sometimes hot sexy dreams that have me waking up wet and aroused, sometimes dreams where I'm chasing him or looking for him and I can't find him, and I wake up frustrated and sad.

I've thrown myself into my work the last couple of weeks since he was here for the wedding. I have to stop thinking about him, because it hurts so much, and work is a good distraction. Also, I'm behind on so many things. Learning I was pregnant, trying to decide what to do, then everything that happened with Brandon took my attention away from business. I can't let that continue, especially right now.

"Oh, Lola." Mom sighs. "You're going to regret this when you're old and alone."

For the first time, I wonder if she's right.

Ah, what am I thinking? I won't be alone. I'll have a child. And all my friends. I'll be fine. I need to worry about my life right *now*.

"I'll be fine whatever happens, Mom. My life is full and busy."

I know Mom just wants the best for me, and wants me to be happy, but she can't pick my dates for me. I've told her this so many times in the past but as I say it, it doesn't feel quite as true. Because it feels like there's a big hole where Brandon used to be.

Even though we were "just friends." Somehow he became a substantial presence in my life.

I guess that's to be expected since he's the father of my baby.

"Roger is a gastroenterologist," Mom says. "He's good looking, smart, ready to settle down."

"Those are all wonderful qualities."

"Right? He'd be perfect for you."

I'm tired. I can't do this. "I'm sorry, Mom. Maybe we can talk about it some other time. I'm at the office, so I have to go."

We end the call. I know she's disappointed. Wait till she finds out I'm pregnant.

When Keith calls me into his office a couple of hours later, I don't think anything of it at first. Then I remember this is the week they're supposed to announce who our new vice president will be.

Excitement grips me. My pulse speeds up and my mouth goes dry. I bounce in my chair, then try to sit still. *Calm down. Calm down.*

This is it. This is everything I've been working for. It will finally be a permanent job, with stability and security. And now, not just for me, but for my child.

Whoa. I press a hand to my stomach where there's a tiny baby bulge.

This is for you, Peanut.

Peanut's not peanut-size anymore, but I still think of him or her that way.

It will also prove that I can accomplish things all by myself. I've been trying to prove that since college. My parents will be proud of me. My coworkers and friends will respect me. And I'll be proud of myself.

My heart bumps unevenly in my chest as I make my way to Keith's office. "Door open or closed?" I ask with a smile.

"You can close it."

I do so. Keith moves from his desk to the round meeting table in the corner of the office near the big windows. The city skyline is sharply outlined against a clear blue sky. I pull out a chair, sit, and cross my legs.

Keith sets his coffee cup on the table and sits, too. He looks at me across the table. "We've made a decision on who the new VP will be," he says.

I keep my smile under control. "Oh, good." I wait.

"They've offered the job to an external candidate, and he's accepted."

The words beat against my ear drums. Did I hear him right? Heat floods through me as the reality sinks in.

I didn't get the job.

My stomach clenches hard, to the point of pain. I resist the urge to lay my hand over my baby. I school my expression to keep my disappointment from showing. "Oh," I say. "Who is it?"

He tells me his name and a bit of his background. I nod along, smiling faintly, but my mind is spinning.

"Obviously, I'm disappointed," I say.

"I know. It was a really difficult decision. We had a lot of excellent candidates and you were one of them. You bring a lot to the position —your experience, your communication skills, your accomplishments."

I swallow and nod.

"Honestly, for me it was down to you and Chris," he continues. "You two are very equal in almost every way."

"I would have thought hiring someone from within the organization would have been an advantage." I think I manage to sound objective and unemotional.

"Yes," he agrees. "If I can give you some feedback, the thing that made the difference was delegation."

Now I frown. "Delegation."

"This is something for you to work on. The examples you shared in the interview process were acceptable, but not strong, and I've seen this in your day-to-day work. You take on too much yourself."

"Because I can do it better than anyone else." I smile.

"That is probably true." He smiles, too. "But just because you can, doesn't mean you should. You can't do everything. No manager can. As a manager, you need to use the expertise of others to accomplish goals. You tend to be a perfectionist, and while perfection is a noble goal, it's not always possible. It serves you well in that you're always looking for ways to make things better. That's a definite strength. You set high standards for yourself and for others."

His complimentary words are nice, but they don't completely allay my crushing disappointment.

"For example, when you missed that deadline on the Comtech project," he goes on. "I think you could have met the deadline if you had asked for help. If you had delegated more of the work."

I let that sink in. I want to argue with him, but I don't want to come across as defensive. So I nod and say, "Thank you for the feedback."

"You put in long hours and work hard. We see that and appreciate that. But give some thought to whether you could accomplish the same work by using other resources differently. Including your staff."

I nibble my bottom lip briefly. "I will. Thank you." I stand. I don't know if he's done, but I am. I need a quick trip to the bathroom for a mini meltdown.

I lock myself in a stall and sit. Quiet weighs in on me as my emotions bubble and swirl.

I'm a failure again.

I wrap my arms around my middle, leaning forward, trying not to cry. My heart feels like a walnut in my chest. My lips push out and I swallow through a constricted throat. Damn.

I can't believe this happened. I thought I had such a good chance at this job.

Maybe I should just quit. Goddammit, my loyalty to this company isn't being rewarded. I've been a contract employee here for eight goddamn years. I deserve better. What's the point of working my ass off and being loyal to the organization when they don't appreciate me?

Well, Keith did say they appreciate me. But that doesn't mean a thing. Talk is cheap.

I leave the bathroom while I'm angry, returning to my office. Nobody else knows yet so I don't have to face sympathy. Or maybe glee. Maybe there are people who didn't want me to get the job. Fuck them.

It's nearly lunch time so I grab my purse and leave the office. I'm not hungry but I start walking. When I get to Bryant Park, I find a small table and chair and sit in the shade of the big trees. I pull out my phone. This isn't the news I wanted to share. I tap in a text message to Kaylee that I didn't get the job.

Oh no! Her response comes quickly, complete with a horrified face emoji. *I'm so sorry.*

Me too.

They made a stupid decision, obviously.

I smile. I love her support. *Thanks.*

Want to talk about it?

Not right now. Maybe later.

Want me to come over tonight?

Okay.

I sit longer, not looking at my phone, not even really seeing all the office workers enjoying lunch in the park on this bright summer day, the pretty flowers, the green lawn. I feel heavy and tired.

What should I do? Should I seriously consider looking for something else? Right now that's top of my mind, but I also know this isn't a decision to be made on impulse. I'm not going to walk into Keith's office this afternoon and hand him my resignation letter. Much as I'd like to.

That would be satisfying. But stupid.

I'm due in March. This isn't a great time to look for a new job.

I haven't told them I'm pregnant. Should I? My contract is up in November. We always renew it, but they could choose not to. Or I could.

A niggle of fear twists inside me. It's not just about me, now. It's also about Peanut. I have to do what's best for my baby.

Well, I don't have to decide this minute. I stand and slowly walk back to Fifth Avenue. I pass by the lions in front of the library then cross and continue on to Madison Avenue to go back to work.

I'm a failure. A disappointment. Who did I think I was, trying to be a vice president? This is such a blow to my confidence and self-image after working so hard. I feel like just giving up.

But I can't. Because I have a baby to take care of.

33

BRANDON

I've been back at the lake for a week after the wedding. I love it here. But I've never been more miserable.

Bergie, Mandy, and baby Benjamin come for a few days. He's three months old now, and I'm still kind of scared of him, but he's actually really good. He doesn't even cry that much.

"He sleeps all night now," Mandy says. "It took a while, but we're finally there."

We're sitting on the deck and Benjamin is lying on a folded up blanket Mandy spread out. Damn. He's cute, smiling, laughing a bit, making little noises, and kicking his pudgy feet.

"Tummy time," Mandy says, tuning Benjamin over. She lays beside him and he lifts his head, pushing himself up on his arms. "Look how strong you are!"

She pats his little diapered butt. "Uh oh. I think he needs a change."

Bergie swoops in and picks him up. "I'll do it. Unless Brando here wants to. You should get some practice, man."

"Christ," I mutter. "I don't know how to change a diaper."

"Come watch."

Reluctantly, I follow him into the house. He changes Benjamin on the living room floor, pulling a diaper out of a bag.

"You gotta be careful with boys," he tells me, holding the diaper over the guy's little penis. "He's already peed on me twice."

I choke on a laugh. "Good to know."

I watch him efficiently perform the undertaking then tightly roll up the used diaper. He stands to go toss it in the trash, leaving me alone with Benjamin. Panic flares in my gut.

I stare at the little dude and he gives me a big smile. "Okay, yeah, you're a handsome guy." I reach out and he grabs my hand and sticks my finger in his mouth.

"Pick him up," Bergie says, returning.

"Uh. That's okay."

"You gotta learn, man."

I break out in a sweat and lift the baby. He makes those cute little noises again. "Is that right?" I say. "Tell me more."

Bergie grins. "So, have you talked to Lola?"

I frown. "Uh, no. Not since the wedding."

"You were in rough shape that night."

"Yeah." I sigh and awkwardly jiggle the baby. "I went to her place that night to apologize, but I think I made things worse."

"Shit." He pauses. "You know, I was thinking about the reasons you don't want to fuck her anymore."

"You're going to have to learn to watch your language around your son."

"Don't change the subject. You always do that. I think the reason you don't want to fuck her anymore is because you're in love with her."

I jerk back. "What? That doesn't make sense."

"Like you made sense that night? Ha. You admit you *want* to fuck her."

I'm silent. It's true, and I did say that.

"And you like her and want to be co-parents with her."

"Yeah."

"You respect her too much to treat her like a fuck buddy."

"Yeah."

"Because you love her."

"Oh, Jesus Christ."

"Language, man." Bergie smirks.

I roll my eyes.

"Seriously. Think about it."

We go back outside and I carefully return Benny to the blanket on his tummy.

"You ready for training camp?" Bergie asks.

"Yeah. I need to get back on the ice. I've been running and working out with the equipment I have here, but it's not the same."

After Bergie and his family leave, I sink into a funk. Seeing their little family and how happy they are just emphasized the fact that I'm alone and the mother of my child is eight hundred miles away. It shouldn't be like that.

Also, I'm thinking about what Bergie said. About being in love with Lola.

I fucking miss her.

The days are getting a little shorter and even though it's still warm, it's starting to feel like fall. Which to me always feels like hockey season. I love it. Except not right now. In my head I'll be happy to get back to hockey. In my heart, I don't feel happy. I don't feel anything.

The only good thing about going back to New York is that I'll be closer to Lola. Only, she doesn't need me. Or want me.

Today is the annual Pelican River Clean Up. I've participated and loaned my name to the cause for the last few years, which hopefully gets more people out. I'll get in there and do my part to remove garbage from the Pelican River, but I'll also be spending time signing autographs and talking to the public. This is a good way to take my mind off my own problems. Keeping our water clean is important. Pollution impacts plants, wildlife, drinking water, and the natural beauty of the area.

People in the area are happy to see me, talking hockey, and I tell kids about why we need to keep our rivers and lakes clean and other ways we can keep from polluting the water. "Do you wash your car at home?" I ask one boy as I sign a jersey. Babies scare me, but I like kids.

"Yeah. I help my Dad."

"One thing we can do is wash our cars on the grass instead of the street or the driveway. That way the soap doesn't wash into the storm drains and end up in the river. It gets absorbed into the grass."

"Okay! That's cool. I'll tell my dad."

I talk to a couple about capturing rainwater with rain barrels and using mulch to keep soil from washing away. "Keeping leaves and grass away from the curbs helps, too," I say.

I tell kids about some of the crap I've found on my beach and how I pick up the trash I find. I tell kids about going fishing when I was their age and how some of the fish I caught are hard to find now. And I have some laughs as I get into the water and get wet picking up garbage, showing them I'm not just talk, that I really believe this stuff.

When I get back to my place around four o'clock, I blink at seeing a car in my driveway. Is that Mom's car?

It is.

She's sitting in the screened-in porch, which isn't locked. She stands on hearing my truck and comes to the door.

I park and walk toward her. "Mom. Hi."

"Hi."

I jump up the steps. She opens the screen door and I walk in. "What are you doing here?"

She scowls at me. "I'm here to talk to you."

My eyes widen. Uh oh. Then...*uh oh*. "Dad talked to you."

"Oh yes, he did." She smacks my shoulder. "You got a girl pregnant!"

I flinch. She's a foot shorter than me, but she's my mom. "It's not like that. It took two of us."

She rolls her eyes. "Don't you smart mouth me, young man. Get in here and sit down."

"Uh, could I go shower and change? I've been in the river cleaning crap out of it."

She huffs. "Fine. Go. I'll be waiting."

I unlock the door and lead the way inside. "Help yourself to something to drink if you want."

She marches into the kitchen and I jog upstairs. Yikes. Mom seems pissed.

I'm almost thirty years old. Not a sixteen-year-old in trouble. It's not like that. Lola and I are both adults, we're both dealing with this in a mature, responsible way.

I wince as I turn on the tap of my shower. Lola's being mature and responsible. Except for that crack about raising the baby by herself. And sleeping with anyone she wants.

Man, I'm still pissed about that.

I step under the spray, scrub clean and shampoo my hair. After drying off, I pull on a pair of worn jeans and a T-shirt, run a brush through my damp hair, and go back downstairs.

Mom's back sitting in the porch, this time with a glass of iced tea. She looks up as I walk in and lifts her eyebrows. I feel like I'm a kid, the time I melted the family room carpet trying to make a grilled cheese sandwich with the clothes iron. Mom was pissed! I was terrified. Similar to now. I managed to charm myself out of a spanking that time. I don't know if I can now.

I sit stiffly on one of the chairs and attempt a smile. "Good to see you, Mom."

"Huh." She clears her throat. "Who's the girl?"

"Didn't Dad tell you all this?"

"Your father's a terrible historian. *You* tell me."

I swallow a sigh. "Her name is Lola."

She rolls her eyes. "Your dad said Lulu. Go on."

"Lola McGrath. She's one day younger than me. She works at Synoptic Global Services as a change manager and she's probably going to be a vice president there. Any day now." I pause. Will she tell me when she finds out? Probably not. Fuck. "She's intelligent, and funny, and a little bossy. She loves to cook and she's really good at planning. She's a little weird, because she names her plants and talks to them." I pause. "Actually, that's kind of cute. And she's really beautiful."

By the time I'm done, Mom's mouth has softened and she's staring at me. "Oh." She lifts a hand to one eye.

Christ. Is she crying?

She swallows. "The pregnancy wasn't planned, I gather."

"No. Her, uh, birth control, uh…"

Mom levels a stare on me.

Sweat breaks out on my forehead and the back of my neck. Fuck, I'd rather circumcise myself than talk about birth control with my mom. "She had an IUD and it slipped. We'd agreed not to use condoms because we were exclusive."

"But your dad says you're not a couple."

"No." My mouth tightens. "Neither of us intends to get married or have children."

"So much for that plan."

I grimace. "True."

"So you're not marrying her."

"She doesn't want that."

"Did you offer?"

"No!" I stare at her.

Her stare could cut glass.

I remember telling her bluntly I'm not going to marry her. I feel a shriveling sensation inside me. "She doesn't want that," I repeat slowly.

I don't either. Or do I?

"Oh, Brandon." She sighs.

"Mom! Getting married because of an unplanned pregnancy is never a good idea."

She tilts her head. "I suppose you're right. But the way you talk about her…I think you have more feelings for her than you're letting on. Or that you even realize yourself."

I stare at her. Now her too?

"And what is this bullshit your father said about you thinking I didn't want you?"

"Oh, man." I close my eyes. "That's not what I said."

"What did you say?"

"I said…hell, I don't remember. Dad said that having a kid is worth all the worry, and I said I never felt like I was worth it, because you two were always arguing about me. About how much new skates cost and how much the registration fees were and how you didn't have time to take me to practices."

Mom falls silent. I glance at her and her face has completely changed. She's not bossy pissed, she's… sad and hurt.

"Mom…"

She holds up a hand. "Wow. Is that what you heard?"

I hesitate, then say, "Yeah."

She bows her head. She doesn't speak.

"Maybe I heard wrong," I finally say.

She shakes her head. "It doesn't matter. It's what you thought you heard." She sighs. "The truth is, we probably did argue about that stuff. There were times I got frustrated. But it wasn't about you." She lifts her head and meets my eyes. "It was *us*, pushing each other's buttons and trying to make each other mad."

My throat pinches up. "Why?"

"It's how we communicate." Her mouth slips into a rueful smile. "It's not healthy. We both know it. That's why we're divorced."

It wasn't about you. "I thought you divorced because of me."

"Oh my God. No." Mom's eyes widen. "It was never because of you. *Never.*"

"I figured I was the one that put the strain in your relationship." My throat is tight so my voice is low.

"No, no, no. I mean, sure, kids can add stress to a relationship. But our breakup was never because of you."

It wasn't about you.

I don't know if I can believe that.

"We still fight all the time." Mom leans forward. "So it's obviously not about you."

I swallow hard. Whoa. "That is true," I croak. "Mom…do you still love Dad?"

She's silent for a moment. "Yes. I always will."

And yet…they're divorced. That's…so fucking sad.

"When is the baby due?" she asks in a softer tone.

"Early March."

Her eyes brighten. "I'm going to be a grandma!"

"Yeah." My chest inflates. "Lola hasn't told her parents yet. She's worried about how they're going to react."

"Oh. Well, I don't even know them, so I can't spill the beans. But I won't tell anyone else until you say it's okay."

"Thanks."

"Why are you here when she's in New York and pregnant?"

"She doesn't need me." Oh Christ. That came out sounding pathetic.

"Oh no. She needs you." Mom gives a dry laugh

"She can do anything," I explain. "I call her superwoman."

She smiles. "I'm sure she is super, but believe me, a new mom needs all the help she can get."

"I don't know." My mouth twists. "She's not entirely happy with me right now."

Mom tilts her head and regards me thought fully for a long moment. "That bothers you."

"I'm fucking losing my mind!" I burst out. Then I contort my face. "Shit."

"Oh, honey." She shakes her head. "What's she angry with you about?"

"I'm not sure." I'm not going to tell Mom about the sex agreement. And my cancelling it.

"Well, you better find out." Her laser stare returns. "Your father and I weren't good at communicating. Don't be like us. Just ask her."

"You make it sound easy."

"It's not easy. But you have to. You can't have any kind of relationship unless you can be honest with each other."

Actually, deep down inside I know why Lola's angry. It's not just because of the sex. I tried to make it about that but, it's not. It's because I wouldn't tell her how I was really feeling.

"We don't have a relationship," I reply glumly.

"But I think you want to."

My head snaps up. "What?"

"Look at you. You're all dejected. You clearly have feelings for her."

I frown.

"Whether you and Lola have a relationship is up to you," she adds. "But I do think you two need to talk. And be honest with each other. She's going to be the mother of your child."

I lift my chin and meet Mom's eyes.

"You need to tell her how you feel. It may not be easy. But a real man has nothing to hide. A real man is honest. And if you're honest with *her*, she'll trust you enough to be honest with *you*."

I so badly want to make a joke and laugh all this off. But fuck… she's right.

I also so badly want Lola to be happy. "Thanks, Mom."

"Now. Make me dinner before I drive back to town."

I smile and stand. As I walk to the kitchen, I pause. "Wait." I turn to face her.

"What?"

"Could you…" I stop. "I hate it when you and Dad complain to me about each other. It makes me feel…" I pause again. Yeah, this is hard. "I love you both and I don't like being put in the middle."

Her face falls. Shit.

"Could you stop calling me with all your issues with him? And I'll ask Dad, too. Maybe you two should try some counseling." That's probably dumb. They've probably done that. But I feel I should suggest something other than bitching to me.

After a heavy pause, Mom nods. "You're right. I'm sorry I've done that to you. And…" She meets my eyes. "Thank you for telling me how you feel." One corner of her mouth lifts.

Warmth hits my chest. I swallow. "Yeah." I nod, then head to the kitchen.

I did it.

Pain changes people. It makes you shut others out. When I was a kid, I learned to keep a smile on my face and to keep a joke at hand to change the subject when things got uncomfortable. When I was sick inside about my parents fighting, I pretended nothing was wrong. But that meant hiding a lot of shit I didn't want people to see.

Sitting on a rock at the beach, I stare at the lake. Low clouds obscure the sky and the lake is a rough, dull gray, choppy with white-caps. I've spent a lot of time thinking about the things Mom said. And the things Dad said. But mostly what Mom said about Lola. *You clearly have feelings for her.*

Dammit, Bergie said the same thing. *I think the reason you don't want to fuck her anymore is because you're in love with her.*

I know I miss Lola. I miss her so fucking much. I've never been in love before, so I'm not sure if that's what I'm feeling. But I do know that I like her a lot. I care about her. I feel like shit without her.

I feel like shit that I hurt her.

So what am I going to do about it? Besides hide out here at the lake.

It does kind of feel like I'm hiding. Which in a way I've been doing my whole life. And now I realize that's what made Lola angry at me.

She's seen more of the real me than anyone. But I was just too damn scared to let her all the way in. And now I've lost her. Fuck.

I tilt my head back and stare up at the pale sky. Mom said I need to talk to her. Obviously, I will talk to her; we're having a baby. But she meant, *really* talk to her. And I'm seized with a sense of urgency—like, if I don't do it right this minute, it'll be too late. I actually jump to my feet. Curling my fingers into my palms, I stare at the water again.

Hold on, hold on. I need to do things right. I don't want to screw up again. I made some mistakes with Lola. I don't want to repeat them. She deserves better. Maybe better isn't me. But I have to give it a shot.

34

LOLA

It's so much fun going to a bar when you're pregnant. Ha.

Not only can I not drink, this place is kind of a pickup bar and I'm not even a little interested in picking up a guy.

I sigh inwardly. Oh well. My friends wanted to come here tonight, so here I am. I take a sip of my club soda with lime and smile at the girls.

"Check out that guy over there," Isla says with a subtle jerk of her head. "In the blue shirt. You should go say hi, Lola."

I sigh. "It *has* been a while since I had sex." Like, thirteen weeks and two days. But who's counting? "Once, I didn't wear pierced earrings for a long time and the holes closed up. Now I'm worried about my vagina." And there's a baby that needs to come out in a while.

They all convulse with laughter.

"This is probably a good time to tell you my news," I say to Isla and Sadie. They're going to be hurt if I keep it from them much longer, now I'm past the first trimester.

"What news?" Isla asks.

They smile, looking at me expectantly, holding their cocktails.

"Did they change their mind about the job?" Sadie asks.

"No." I make a face. "I don't think that's going to happen."

"They offered you a different promotion?" Isla says.

"No." I shake my head. "This is going to blow your minds. I'm pregnant."

"Whaaaat!"

They stare at me.

"You're kidding!"

"Nope." I grin and pat my belly. "This is why I'm drinking club soda."

"Oh my God!"

Of course they're full of questions, which I answer, trying not to be too sad about the fact that Brandon and I aren't together anymore. We're co-parents. Bleh.

Kaylee listens and adds comments here and there, but her eyes are darting around the bar.

"Have you spotted him yet?" I ask dryly.

"What?" She jumps and stares at me. "Who?"

"The guy you want to pick up tonight." Clearly she's checking the place out. And she's single again now, so why not?

"Oh! Hahaha. No."

I'm reminded of that night in Aruba when I spotted Brandon and pointed him out to Kaylee. *Him. The good looking one. The guy in the crazy shirt.*

Sadness swamps me briefly, but I shake it off and focus on Isla and Sadie's incredulous questions. But they're happy for me and promise to support me any way they can.

"Thank you." I get emotional and blink back tears. "I know I need to get better at asking for help."

"And accepting help," Isla points out gently.

I frown.

"I need to use the ladies' room," Kaylee suddenly says. "Back in a few!"

"I need a drink," Isla says. "Anyone else?"

"I'm good," I answer.

"I'll come with you!" Sadie jumps up and the two of them disappear into the crowd.

I sit at the small table by myself, sipping my drink, watching people on the dance floor. Then someone takes Kaylee's chair next to me.

I turn and open my mouth to tell him the seat is taken and see Brandon.

I blink rapidly a few times. What is he doing here?

"Hi." He smiles tentatively. "What does it feel like to be the most gorgeous girl in the room?"

I stare at him.

"Not working, huh? How about this…I don't mean to intrude, but you owe me a drink…because when I saw you, I dropped mine."

"Are you seriously using cheesy pickup lines on me?"

"Yeah. Like you did with me. The night we met."

"I was just thinking about that night," I say slowly, staring at him. His face…so handsome, all tanned and shadowed with dark stubble, his eyes now a deep forest green. He's wearing the same ridiculous shirt he had on the night we met.

"Do you fish?" he asks.

He knows I don't. My forehead pinches.

"Because you have me hooked."

"Oh my God." What is he doing? My heart flutters wildly in my chest.

"Do you happen to have a Band-Aid? 'Cause I scraped my knees falling for you."

That one makes me laugh out loud. I've never heard it before.

He grins, although his eyes are serious.

"What are you doing here?" I ask.

"Trying to pick you up. Isn't it obvious? Fuck, I'm bad at this. How about you try to pick me up instead?"

I laugh again. "I don't believe you're bad at flirting. You're a flirt master. A thirst trap. A chick magnet."

He rolls his eyes. "The only chick I want to…attract…is you. Remember?" He holds my gaze. "You told me I reminded you of a magnet because I was attracting you to me."

Something insides me goes all soft and quivery like jelly. "You were."

His slow grin is light and warmth and comfort and temptation.

"Did the sun come out or did you just smile at me?" I say.

His eyelids lower slightly. "Good one. How about this: I'm learning about important dates in history. Wanna be one of them?"

My own smile fades as I search his face, taking in the earnest expression. "A…date?"

He reaches for my hand and curls his fingers around mine. "Yeah. I want to take you on a date."

My breath hitches. "Brandon…?"

"Yeah?" He lifts my hand and kisses my knuckles.

"What are you doing? What is happening?"

"I've never taken you on a date." He kisses my hand again. "I've never danced with you. And…" He meets my eyes. "I've never been totally honest with you."

My eyes widen and I lean forward as if I'm being drawn into his spell. "I know."

A shadow flickers on his face. "I'm sorry."

"O-okay."

"So you'll go on a date with me?"

What is happening? He wants to go on a date. My insides tremble. I don't know what this means. But, as always…I can never resist him. I swallow. "Yes."

"Good. Tomorrow night." He brushes his lips over my hand again and glances to the side.

I follow his gaze and see my friends watching us from across the room, big grins on their faces. Wide-eyed I turn back to Brandon. "Did you…how…?"

He gives me that sexy smirk. "I have my ways. I'll pick you up at seven tomorrow night."

He stands, gestures at the girls that they can have their chairs back, and leaves.

I stare after him, mouth agape.

Kaylee, Sadie, and Isla all rush to the table and scramble into their seats, leaning toward me. "Okay, what happened?" Kaylee asks.

"You don't know?" I turn to her with a reproachful look.

She gives me a toothy grin. "All I know is he wanted to talk to you and he promised it would be good. He tracked me down on Instagram and DMed me."

Slowly I move my head from side to side, still a little dazed. "He asked me out on a date."

She stares at me, as do Isla and Sadie. But Kaylee knows the meaning of this.

She squeals. "Oh. My. God!" She claps her hands together, beaming.

I can't stop my own smile.

"Did you say yes?" Isla asks eagerly.

"Yes."

"Oh, Lo." Kaylee reaches for me and gives me a shoulder hug. "He was right. This is good."

"Is it?" I bite my lip. "I'm not sure."

"You've been miserable since he left. You know you care about him."

My lips try to push out and I firm them and swallow past the wedge in my throat. "I do."

"What are dates for?" she asks softly. "For getting to know someone better...right?"

"Right." I try to inflate my lungs with air, but it's hard. "Right."

"So, go." She pats my shoulder. "Have fun. Get to know each other better."

Isla and Sadie watch us intently. "Sounds like a good plan," Isla says. "He is absolutely gorgeous. And sweet."

"I agree." Sadie lifts her glass. "Definitely worth one date."

I'm ready at seven, like Brandon said. Actually, I'm ready before seven because I'm so anxious I'm buzzing with energy. I feel like a teenager going on her first date ever. I stood in front of my closet agonizing over what to wear. I took extra care with my makeup. I even did a wax touch up and shaved my legs.

I finally decided on a casual dress in a bright fuchsia shade, a short-sleeved tunic style that's forgiving of my thicker waist but still shows off my legs. I add flat sandals and a bright pink lipstick that tones with the dress.

My head swirling with questions, I pace my apartment, plucking a couple of yellow leaves off Ivy, checking the soil of Jake the Snake plant, then padding to the bathroom to inspect my teeth and make sure there's no food stuck in them.

Finally, the doorman calls up to let me know Brandon's here.

My belly flutters. I fluff my hair one more time and grab my purse.

When I open the door to him, he's standing there, his face hidden behind an enormous plant.

He peers around it. "Hi."

"Hi." I step back uncertainly to let him in.

"This is for you."

Eyes wide, I take it from him. It's in a galvanized pot, a vine with glossy green leaves and tiny white star-shaped flowers, shaped into a circle. "Is it…jasmine?"

"Yes. Smell it."

I lower my nose to a cluster of blooms. "Oh wow. Heavenly."

"I think it smells like you."

"You have a good nose. The perfume I wear does have jasmine in it."

"I knew it." He smiles. He's so handsome and big, wearing a pair of dark jeans, a navy shirt with a tiny white dot pattern and a fitted charcoal blazer. He always dresses well, sometimes a little quirky, but I admire his choices today.

"I'll name her Jasmine." I carry her over to my plant table and set her down. "She's beautiful."

"You're beautiful."

I look up at him. He's watching me with an intent expression. My heart flutters.

"Thank you. You look so nice too." I move closer and smooth a hand over a lapel.

"Thanks. Should we go?"

"I'm ready."

He sets a hand on the small of my back to lead me out.

Outside, it's warm and humid. The day started out bright and sunny, but clouds gathered through the day, creating a muggy feel.

"We can walk to the restaurant," he says. "Our reservation's at seven-thirty, so we have lots of time."

"Okay." We fall into step together. "Where are we going?"

"It's called Etienne."

"I've heard of it but I've never been there." I think it's super pricey. I seem to remember seeing a picture of Julianna Margulies dining there.

"French," he says. "I haven't been there either."

We go up to the High Line and make small talk as walk to the restaurant on Ninth Avenue in an old renovated meat packing building. Brandon leads me to the elevator and we ride to the rooftop. I gaze around in awe as we exit into a glass-walled roof-top terrace. The seating is all dove gray velvet and opulent crystal chandeliers hang above the tables. Greenery lines the walls, and potted trees spread their leafy branches overhead.

Almost every table the hostess leads us past is full. She stops at a small round table in front of a curved banquette where we both sit, not quite side by side but not opposite each other either. It's very intimate.

"This is lovely." I'm still taking in all the details—how the chandeliers are reflected over and over in the glass walls, enclosing is in a glittering cocoon, a fountain softly splashing nearby, the fluffy square cushion I can tuck behind my back.

Brandon looks around, too. "It is nice." He turns back to me, the corners of his mouth quirked. "Acceptable for a first date?"

I melt. "More than acceptable. When are you going to tell me what this is all about?"

"Let's order, and then we can talk."

"Okay."

We study the menu. I order a citrus fizz mocktail, which comes in a lovely champagne flute, and Brandon decides to have the same.

"It looks appropriately fancy," he says.

Eventually we order our meals, too, and with the menus whisked away, we settle into the comfortable cushions with our fizzy drinks and a platter of artisanal prosciutto, cheeses, fruit, and a delicious warm baguette to nibble on.

"I have a lot to say," Brandon starts in a low voice. "I hope you'll hear me out."

I nod, my heart jumping around in my chest, into my throat. I have no idea what to think, no idea what he's going to say.

"I'm just not sure where to start." He rubs the back of his neck and blows out a breath.

I can see his struggle. I reach out a hand and lay it on his forearm and gently squeeze. "Just talk to me. Tell me what this is all about."

"Okay. I just have to be honest with you. I don't want to be co-parents with you."

My insides freeze.

"I don't want to be friends. Or even friends with benefits. I want everything with you. I want to be your friend. Your lover. Your partner. We're having a baby and we didn't plan it but I want that, too, now. But...we've never even gone on a date. I want to do things the right way...in the right order."

Oh my God. My insides thaw and expand, my heart swelling into my throat. Brandon meets my eyes and I see his doubts but also his determination. "Really?" I whisper. "That's not what you said that night."

"I know. And I'm sorry. I owe you a huge apology. I showed up fucking hammered after the wedding and passed out on your couch. I'm sorry. It was a dick move. I just...couldn't stay away from you."

I relate to that. I find it hard to stay away from him, too. "You said you came to apologize that night, too."

"Right."

"I don't think you really knew what you were apologizing for."

"I did." He meets my eyes. "I just couldn't admit it."

One corner of my mouth lifts and I sip my drink. "Can you now?"

His throat works. "I'm sorry that I've been a mess about this baby. And about you. I tried to talk to my friends about it and they just pissed me off. They didn't get what I was feeling. But I had to figure it out myself." His lips press together briefly. "Well, Bergie helped me figure it out. And my mom."

"Oh."

"I'm sorry I wasn't honest with you about how I was feeling. I should have told you. After you told me you were pregnant, I was terrified."

"I know."

"Not really." He grimaces. "I wasn't totally honest with you. Or myself. The reason I wanted to just stay friends and be co-parents was because I was so fucking scared of bringing a kid into a relationship like my parents. I'm not cut out to be a parent. Or a husband." He closes his eyes briefly. "I thought I wasn't, anyway. That's why I acted like that. The truth is...I wanted you. I wanted all of you. But I was terrified."

His sincere, somber expression has my heart thumping in painful beats He's not joking around, evading things. He's telling me he was afraid.

"I'm sorry that I hurt you," he continues in that low, husky voice. "I never meant to hurt you and I feel like shit about it. I did then, too.

You told me I was being selfish. And you were right. I was trying to protect myself instead of thinking about you and how you were feeling."

My throat squeezes. I take another fizzy sip. "I'm sorry I got upset that night."

He shakes his head. "It's okay. It triggered me a bit, because I hated listening to my parents argue—which I'll tell you more about—and I didn't react well. But you were right. We weren't fighting. You were trying to communicate, and I wasn't."

Wow.

"I've thought a lot about what you said—how can I be a father if I won't communicate? And that's exactly what I was afraid of. I was afraid I can't be a good father. I was afraid I'll be like my parents. I don't want that for our child. I never—" His voice cracks and he clears his throat. "I never want my child to feel like I did growing up."

My nose stings and my eyes water. "I get it, Brandon."

"I talked to my parents. Separately. My mom drove up to the cottage and gave me shit."

"They know...?"

"Yeah. I had to tell them. They tried to talk some sense into me, and I've been giving it a lot of thought, and I'm still not convinced that I believe them. But they both told me that their arguments were never about me. It was about them and how they communicated. Or didn't." He shakes his head.

"You thought it was because of you." He made that drunken comment that night, tugging at my heart, and now I feel it even more. He grew up blaming himself for his parents' dysfunction and divorce. He grew up feeling like they didn't care about him. No wonder he doesn't want kids of his own. But does he really think he can't be a good father?

"Yeah." He bows his head, then looks up at me. "And...I've been torturing myself about what you said—that you could have sex with anyone." His face draws into lines of anguish. "That fucking killed me, thinking about you with someone else. Maybe having a relationship with someone else. It made me so fucking mad…and…jealous."

Heat spreads through my chest. My throat is so constricted I don't think I can speak.

"Do you want that?" he asks in a low voice. "Do you want to sleep with someone else?"

35

BRANDON

I'm staring into Lola's wide eyes, that Caribbean blue I could drown in, every muscle in my body rigid as I wait for her reply.

And our dinners arrive.

I sit back and let the server place my meal in front of me. I don't even remember what I ordered and my heart is hammering so hard that's all I can hear and feel. Our water glasses are refilled. Lola declines another mocktail. The server looks at me. I don't even know why, but I shake my head.

Then we're alone again.

The air around us is thick, the noise of the restaurant muted into the background. I study her beautiful face, the smooth curve of her cheeks, her long eyelashes and shadowy eyes, her plump bottom lip. It's been so hard to keep my hands off her all this time.

She picks up her knife and fork and looks at me.

I'm begging her with my eyes.

The corners of her mouth hook up and she says, "No."

I nearly sag with relief. I swallow. "I don't either. Just you."

"Oh my God, my vagina is closing up from a lack of sex."

"What?" I stare.

"Never mind. A bad joke." She waves a hand. "I'm sorry. You're being so open and that was stupid."

I can't resist my smile. "You want sex with me, don't you?"

She bites her lip and drops her gaze to her plate. "You're back to being your cocky self, I see."

I laugh softly. I feel like I could float away. Good thing this outdoor terrace has a glass roof or I'd be soaring among the New York skyscrapers like a helium balloon.

"I shouldn't have said that," she adds quietly. "I never meant it. I was being a sarcastic bitch because I was hurt. I thought you didn't want me."

Anguish tugs my eyebrows down. "Fuck. I am so sorry, Lola. That was never the case."

She swallows and gives a tiny nod. "Okay."

Finally I drag my attention back to my meal. "What is this?" I mutter.

"You ordered the braised chopped beef."

"Right." I pick up a fork.

Lola takes a bite of her coq au vin. "Amazing."

"I have more to say." I pick up some of the beef. "But let's eat."

"Okay." She smiles at me and something expands in my chest.

"What's happening with your promotion? Have they made a decision?"

She goes still, her fork partway to her mouth. "Oh. Yeah. They made a decision." She lowers her hand. "I didn't get the job."

My head jerks up. "What?"

She gives a weak smile. "My boss met with me and gave me some feedback about my interview and my performance. I don't delegate enough."

"That's bullshit!"

She smiles. "I think so, too." She shrugs. "But the decision's made. Now I have to decide what I want to do going forward."

"What do you mean?"

"I don't know if I want to stay at Synoptic. After all these years, they still haven't given me a permanent position. I don't think they deserve my loyalty."

"Oh. Wow. I'm sure you could find something else. You're so smart and hard working."

"Thanks. I had a call from a headhunter the other day, actually. It made me feel a little better. They'd heard that I didn't get the promotion and have a client who's interested in me."

"That's fantastic! Who is it?"

"I don't know. If I'm interested, they'll do a preliminary interview. I said I wasn't sure right now. I don't want to make a rash decision."

"Okay, I get that. What about…the baby?"

"That's a complicating thing for sure." She purses her lips ruefully. "I still haven't told my boss, or anyone at work."

"I'm sorry."

"It's not the best timing, but it is what it is." She lifts her chin. "I got this."

"Of course you do." Then I frown. "When did you find this out?"

"About a week ago."

Anger flares in my gut. "Why didn't you tell me?"

She gazes at me. "I…I didn't think you'd care. I said I'd keep you posted about the baby."

"Fuck." I close my eyes. "I deserve that. But…I do care, Lo."

She nods, her chin puckered, then quickly takes another bite of chicken.

"You must have been disappointed."

"Oh yeah. But I'm okay."

"I wish I could have been there for you," I say quietly. "I can't make it better, but I could have been there for you to talk to."

Her chin puckers even more as she nods. "I find I'm not quite as devoted to my job lately. Not getting that promotion took the wind out of my sails a bit."

"Maybe that's a good thing. You were killing yourself with the long hours you worked there."

"Yeah." She lays her hand over her stomach and my heart explodes into a rapid beat. "And now I have Peanut to worry about."

"Can you feel the baby move?" I stare at her hand with wonder.

"No, not yet. Apparently around eighteen or twenty weeks." She rubs her belly.

I want to rub her belly. I want to press my face there. Kiss her there. Talk to our baby.

Christ. I'm a goner.

"Well." I refocus. "They fucked up by not promoting you and if they lose you because of it, it serves them right."

Her smile is wide and warm and she leans over to press her forehead briefly against my shoulder. "Thank you."

We share dessert, an amazing crème brulée. As we eat rain starts to fall, pattering on the glass above us. The reflections in the windows turn to blurry gold and white, and a crack of thunder startles everyone in the restaurant into nervous laughter.

"Guess we're not walking home," I say.

"I like walking in the rain."

"Yeah?"

"Unless it's a downpour." She opens her purse and pulls out a tiny umbrella. "Voila."

I grin. "I don't think that's going to shelter me much."

"It's bigger than it looks."

"A grower not a shower."

She collapses into laughter. "Oh my God. Brandon."

I grin. "I can't help it."

I take care of the bill. Out on the street, the rain has let up, with just a few sprinkles falling, although the streets are wet. The High Line is closed so we start walking up 10th Avenue. I open the umbrella and hold it above us, sliding my other hand into hers. She flicks me a quick smile.

Traffic passes us, swishing tires on wet pavement, shimmering lights reflecting on the shiny surfaces. The temperature has dropped but it's still comfortable as we stroll past Chelsea Park, then the shopping mall. All the way, tension builds inside me, anticipating arriving at Lola's apartment. I want her so fucking much I hurt.

The way she listened to me at dinner—no judging. Accepting. Understanding.

I've never told anyone but my parents the things I told her. I've never felt like this with anyone, a closeness that makes me feel safe. It sounds weird, but my whole life I've been protecting myself...but with her I don't feel like I have to. I feel safe with her.

"I always thought love was mean and hurtful," I tell Lola as we walk. "But when Bergie and Mandy and the baby came to stay with me, I watched them. I saw how they laugh together and support each other and, yeah cry together when things go wrong, like with Benjamin being born too soon."

"Is he doing okay now?"

"Yeah, he's totally fine. He's a cute little guy." I squeeze her hand. "I thought about what my mom said. She said a real man has nothing to hide. A real man is honest. I wasn't being honest with you. Ha. I wasn't even being honest with *myself*. I was fucking terrified and didn't want to admit it."

She stops walking and I turn to face her. "What?"

"I'm terrified, too," she whispers. "I don't know if I can be a good mother."

"We'll do it together." I touch her cheek. "When Hellsy got married, he wrote his own vows. And he told Sara that they're a team now. That they respect each other, and trust each other. That's what I want. I want us to be a team."

"Is it...just because of the baby?"

"No." I shake my head. "It took me a while to figure it out, but I was falling for you before you got pregnant. That last night, knowing I had to leave the next day and not see you for weeks, or months...it was wrecking me. But I couldn't admit it. We had our deal."

She gazes up at me with clear sea-green eyes, listening intently.

"Being a father scares me," I go on. "But I was destroyed by losing *you*. And I was afraid to tell you that, too." I squeeze my eyes shut, then open them determinedly. "I sat on the beach after Mom left. I didn't know what to do. I felt desperate. Hopeless. Like I'd fucked things up so badly I could never fix it. But Mom said I had to talk to you. And she was right."

She curls her hand around my wrist and leans her cheek into my hand. Rain taps softly on the umbrella above us. "I felt you didn't trust me enough to open up."

"I had to figure it out. I realized I do trust you. I've been trying to protect myself, ever since I was a kid. I couldn't show how hurt I was. I turned into a joker. A flirt."

Her lips pucker.

"I realized I had to get past that. And show you the real me. I decided that if I have to try harder to be a better man, to deserve you, that's what I'll do. I won't hide things from you. I'll be honest with you." I pause. "Do you trust me?"

She doesn't answer right away and my muscles tense. I wouldn't blame her if she said no. Finally, she says, "I do."

I'm glad that she thought about it. "Thank you." I turn my hand to catch hers and bring it to my mouth. I press my lips there, my gaze fastened on hers. My heart feels full. "I won't let you down. I never want to hurt you."

We start walking again.

I hold the door of her building for her and close the umbrella before following her inside. My body vibrates with longing and nerves. She turns to me in the lobby. We observe each other for a long, wordless moment, heat building between us, the air electrified.

"Are you coming up?" she asks softly.

I move closer and set my hands on her waist. "It's only our first date...remember?"

Her mouth pinches on a laugh. "Right."

Then we both grin, our eyes meeting, and it's like something breaks open and flows between us, something sparkling and warm and beautiful.

"Let me just be clear." I lean closer to her ear. "I want you. I want you every way I can have you. I want to fuck you until you're hoarse from screaming."

"Oh." She shivers.

"But not tonight. Because it's our first date and I respect you."

She gazes at me, her eyes bright. "I want you, too."

"I know."

She chokes out a laugh. "Jerk."

I grin and rub my nose alongside hers. "Yeah. I definitely can be."

Our mouths touch and cling together. I lift mine from hers, then kiss her again, softly, carefully. I'm terrified and shaking inside but I need to kiss her.

She kisses me back, going on her toes, opening gently, her mouth silky and sweet. For a moment, I'm lost in it. My eager dick thickens but I ignore it and slowly ease back to stare into Lola's eyes. "I'm not coming up because I want a second date."

"Oh." Her eyes shine back at me.

"I'll call you tomorrow, okay?"

She nods and smiles. "Okay."

LOLA

"How was your date? Tell me everything."

Kaylee and I just met up in the South Village to go maternity wear shopping.

"We went to Etienne for dinner. It was amazing. The food, the décor—gorgeous."

"Okay, good, but that's not what I want to know."

"I know. I'm still not sure what's happening." I share some of the details about our conversation and the things he said. "He shared a lot with me. He apologized for how he was acting and…" My smile slips. "He told me more about his childhood and why he never wanted to be a dad."

"Oh."

"I always knew there was something more beneath the charisma and smile. And because he hid it, I knew it was something painful. But he talked to his parents about it, so I'm glad. I just hope he believes them. I hope he believes in himself."

"Oh." Kaylee's forehead creases. "You don't have to tell me those details."

I smile. "Thanks. But he's working on some stuff and trying to talk more about his true feelings instead of just making a joke."

"And you?"

"And me what?"

"Are you going to let him be part of the baby's life?"

I frown. "Of course."

"I mean, *really*."

I slant her a glance. "I don't know what you mean."

"I mean…you always try to do things on your own."

I blink. "Yeah…"

"And I understand why. And I admire you for that. For how you worked so hard to prove you could do things on your own. But that's not always a good thing, Lo. Look what happened with that VP job."

I frown. "What do you mean?"

"Your boss said you don't delegate enough."

"Yeah, but I do."

"Do you, though? You work such long hours and take on so much yourself."

That is true. I think about that as we walk. I wanted to deny what Keith said, but…maybe there's some truth to it. "When Keith told me I don't delegate enough, I told him I can do it better than anyone else," I say slowly.

Kaylee chuckles softly and bumps my shoulder with hers as we arrive at Bambino. "I'm sure that's true. But think about this—if you're going to keep working, you're going to have to hand over total care of your baby to someone else."

Obviously, I know that. But…I get what she's saying. "That *is* kind of scary."

"I'm betting that nobody can change a diaper as well as you can," she teases. "I bet you want this baby to be your best project."

My mouth falls open. "What? A baby's not a project!"

"I know that." Her tone is gentle. "I'm kidding. But I also know you. You don't have to do this by yourself."

Just because you can, doesn't mean you should.

I stare at my best friend.

"Don't be mad. I'm being honest with you because I love you. That's important, right?"

"Right," I mutter. I can't argue that after what happened with Brandon. "I won't treat the baby like a project."

She squeezes my hand. "We're all here for you—me, Isla, Sadie. You have to let us in, though."

Suddenly I want to cry. Damn, I thought the hormonal stuff was done. With my throat thick, I nod. "I will."

She nods solemnly. "Remember your parents, doting on you, protecting you?"

"I don't want to be like that," I say slowly. "You're right. Now I'm having a baby, I have to recognize that it's not fair to the baby either to try to do it all on my own."

"I don't want to have to beg you to let me babysit."

I smile. "You won't!"

"And what about Brandon?"

I nod again. "Of course. He's the baby's father."

"He's really trying to open up about things."

"Yes."

"And you care about him." She lowers her chin to peer up at me warily. "Don't you."

It hurts when I swallow. "Yes."

We walk into the store. I keep thinking about our conversation as we explore racks of dresses and suits for work, jeans and tops for casual wear. This store has nice things—more stylish than I expected for maternity clothes. I try on a bunch of things and end up with an enormous shopping bag full of pretty clothes.

"When are you seeing Brandon again?" Kaylee asks as we leave the store.

"I don't know. He said he'd call today." I pull out my phone. "Damn! I missed his call."

"Call him back."

"There's a text, too. He wants to take me to a movie tonight." I grin and look up. "Another date."

"I love that he's doing that."

My heart swells. "Me too." I pause. "I'm sorry I was annoyed earlier. I think...you're right. I'm going to have to let go of some things."

She smiles. "You can do it."

37

LOLA

Brandon takes me to a movie and out for ice cream. We go to a Yankees game. We go to Coney Island.

Tonight, we listened to Broadway show tunes in Bryant Park. Brandon brought me home and this time he comes in with me. He's been taking his time and I'm getting impatient. I feel achy and needy as I turn to face him.

He slides his arms around me. I touch my lips to the skin of his jaw, and a shudder runs through him. His arms tighten. That heat and ache low down in my belly blossoms and spreads. It always does around Brandon, but it's been so long. Pressed to his body with his arms around me, this time it feels more intense, layered with complex emotions that go so deep inside me.

I shift in his arms and tip my face back, and he immediately claims my mouth with his, sliding his tongue into my mouth, and I touch my own tongue to it. He groans, softly bites my lower lip, then kisses me again. Longing floods my body, my breasts growing heavy. He hardens against me, flames licking over us as the kiss goes on and on. Need for him builds, sweet and powerful and compelling.

My hands roam over him, eager and greedy, over his big, strong shoulders, the soft skin at the nape of his neck, his silky hair. I can't get close enough, melting into the solid heat and power of his body, and I moan into his mouth. "Brandon…oh God. Brandon."

"Mmmm." His mouth burns a trail down the side of my neck and over my shoulder, pushing aside the neckline of my dress, then his hand slides down to curve over my breast. Sweet heat flows through me, and I press into his palm. "You feel amazing, Lola. Soft. Strong. But…I want to be careful with you."

"It's okay. I want you to do this. So much."

He cups my face with his palm so tenderly and kisses my mouth, then moves me toward the bed. Beside it, he takes my face in both hands and kisses me again, a gentle kiss of such devotion, tears spring to my eyes. I lay my palms on his chest, feeling his heartbeat thudding beneath one, and give myself up to his endless, sensual kiss.

"You are so beautiful," he murmurs. "So strong and beautiful."

"Oh Brandon." I love how he makes me feel—like superwoman.

He finds the zipper at the back of my dress and lowers it. I let it fall and step out of it, standing before him in a pink lace bra and panties, and his eyes darken with appreciation as they move over me. He makes me feel strong but also safe. And beautiful.

His hands move over my body, touching me everywhere, leaving trails of sparks in their wake, and his gaze follows his hands, heating me even more. When his hands come to rest on my shoulders, he turns me to face away from him. I close my eyes as he draws my hair to one side and kisses the back of my neck. Shivers cascade down my spine.

He opens his mouth and gently grazes his teeth over my flesh. Fire flashes through me and a soft sound rises to my lips. He flicks open the fastener of my bra and pushes the straps down my arms, then whisks my panties down and off. Crouching behind me, he pauses for a moment to kiss the small of my back, his tongue lingering there. Then he pats my butt and says gruffly, "Get on the bed."

I climb on and lay down, moving languorously like I'm in a dream. I roll to my side to watch him as he unbuttons his shirt and shrugs out of it. The whole time his gaze is fastened on me in a sizzling connection. My skin burns everywhere.

When he kicks his jeans aside, my gaze tracks down over his muscled chest and abs to his erection, so bold and beautiful. My lips part hungrily.

"Christ, Lola." He groans, taking the two steps to reach the bed where he joins me, sliding his big, hot body against mine.

I let out a soft cry at the bliss of his skin against mine. "Oh God, I missed you."

"Missed you too." He rolls me to my back and moves over me, kissing me again. His weight on me a delicious pressure, I hold on to him, parting my legs so he fits between them, so perfectly, and I kiss him back with everything I have.

Emotion swells in my chest, huge and sweet and scary.

"Brandon."

"Yeah?" He kisses my neck, then my chest.

"I think...I'm falling in love with you."

He goes very still, then lifts his head. His eyes glitter. "Good. Because I'm falling in love with you, too."

Joy bursts inside me and I hold on tighter. "I was falling in love with you before...and I thought...I hoped maybe you were too. And then..."

"Fuck. We wasted so fucking much time because I'm an idiot."

"We're here now."

He kisses his way down my neck, my chest, then he closes his mouth over a nipple and tugs at it. Pleasure streams straight to my womb, and I arch into his mouth with a soft cry. He closes his hand over my other breast in a gentle squeeze. "Mmm."

My eyes fall closed, and I give myself over to his touch. With his hands and his mouth, he creates a cocoon of intimacy around us, the scent of jasmine floating faintly in the air. It's love and light and magic.

He moves his mouth to my other breast, catches the wet nipple between his fingers and pulls, and the sensation on both nipples has my body twitching hard beneath him. My hips lift into his, aching with need for him. "Please." I slide my hands into his hair. "Please, Brandon. I need you."

"Say it again." He lifts his head, and I open my eyes to see his gaze fixed on me intently.

"I need you." It feels so good, so liberating and giving, I say it again. "I need you, Brandon, so much."

His eyes warm and his lips curve into a tender smile. "Thank you."

Oh God. He undoes me.

He moves up on me, his knees pushing my thighs wide, and I watch as he fists his cock. When he pushes into me, it's blissful... euphoric. He fills me, so deep inside me, touching nerve endings that thrill me and saturate me with aching pleasure, so deep he touches my heart, touches my soul.

He pauses. "Okay?"

I slide my fingers through his hair. "Yes. So good."

I watch his face, entranced, as his eyes fall closed, his long eyelashes resting on his cheeks, and then he falls over me, taking his weight on his elbows, his arms sliding around my head, one hand coming to my forehead in a possessive, protective gesture that softens my heart and makes me go liquid around him.

My body tightens, pulling him in, and I wrap my arms around his back and my legs around his waist as he moves against me. Our bodies push together, seeking more, finding a rhythm that matches the beating of our hearts. His breath rushes hot over the skin of my neck.

"Lola, God Lola...I need you too."

"I'm here. Always." Sensation spirals inside me, a taut coil of pleasure and heat, everything inside me tightening, pulling hard, up and up. "Yes," I urge him. "Yes, yes...oh *God*."

He rises up again onto his knees, spread wide between my thighs. He cups my breasts, thumbs my nipples, then slides his hands down my rib cage to close around my waist, holding me as he thrusts into me. Once more our eyes meet, his blazing at me with fecks of gold, full of worship and devotion. God! I am so lucky, so grateful to have this man in my life and I want to give him so much—anything. Everything.

Emotion swells and rushes through me. He reaches for my hands and holds them, and I tighten my fingers around his, still holding his gaze. I never want to let him go, never want him to let me go, and I grip his hands as my climax bursts upon me, an explosion of sparks and heat, pleasure sliding outward from my core, lovely and warm and sweet.

With our clasped hands at my chest, his eyes fall closed, and his body tenses and goes still for long, pulsing moments. A long, low groan vibrates in his chest, and then once again he stretches out over me and presses his mouth to mine.

"I'm not falling," he groans. "I've already fallen. I love you."

My heart lurches. I pull in a shaky breath. "I love you, too."

38

BRANDON

I roll over and look at Lola. I'm still wasted from a brain-destroying orgasm. My muscles are gelatinous and my lungs are finally expanding enough to get air into them.

"I want to dance with you." I stroke my fingers over Lola's collarbone.

"Right now?"

I smile. "Not that kind of dance."

"Oh, twerking."

I choke on a laugh. "Not that either. I want to slow dance with you to a romantic song. I wished you were at that wedding with me."

"Was that why you got drunk?"

"Yeah. Probably. I was hurting. Thinking you didn't want me to be part of your life, the baby's life. And that is was my own damn fault that you didn't."

"I'm sorry. I was hurt, too."

"I never want to hurt you again."

"Same."

"We're having a baby and we didn't plan it but I want that, too, now. I want you to be my family. Both of you."

"Oh, Brandon." Her eyes shine in the dim light. "I want that, too."

"You know what my first reaction was when you told me you were pregnant? I was excited. Ecstatic."

"Really?"

"Then I was pissed at myself. Why was I so happy, when I know how much conflict kids can cause? How much pain."

"Oh."

"I'm still scared. I don't know if I can be a good father."

"You will be. You care about your friends. You care about Martha. You even care about that plant I gave you. I saw it at the lake."

"I love that plant."

Her smile trembles. "You know love. We can figure stuff out, but love is the most important thing."

"Right. Okay. And you'll be a great mother."

Her lips droop. "I felt like such a failure when I didn't get that job."

"Jesus. Lola. Stop. You are not a failure. Look at what you've accomplished."

"I know. It's just hard not to think I should have tried harder. I should have been better."

"Perfect."

"Yes."

"Nobody's perfect, beautiful. Not even a superwoman."

She lets out a strangled little laugh.

"You don't have to be perfect. I love you. All of you. As you are."

"Oh. Thank you. I love you too."

"And I'm sure as hell not perfect." Our eyes meet in the dimness of her apartment. I touch her cheek, softly, reverently. "Thank you."

"For what?"

"For listening to me. And still being here."

Her eyelashes drop, then lift again. "I'll always be here. For you." She pushes my hair back off my forehead and lets her fingers trail over my cheek and jaw.

The tenderness of the gesture makes my heart squeeze. "And I'll always be here for you." I pause. "This wasn't the first time we slept together, but it almost felt like it was."

Her lips curve. "Yes. It did."

I slide my body lower on the bed and pull the covers down. I lay my hand on her stomach, protectively, questioningly. I look up at her to see her gentle smile. Then I turn my face and press my mouth to her soft skin there, closing my eyes. "I'm sorry to you too, Peanut," I whisper. "I promise you will never hear your mom and me argue."

"Oh, come on." Lola pokes my shoulder. "We're going to argue."

"But we're going to do it respectfully. And Peanut doesn't need to hear it. Okay?"

"Okay."

"I promise you'll always feel wanted," I continue. "I promise to try to be the best father I can. You're not even born yet, and you're the best thing that ever happened to me."

Lola's fingers slide tenderly into my hair.

"Other than your mom, of course," I add. "But you...becoming a father...made me have to step up. Grow up. I can't be selfish anymore."

Lola makes a small sound.

I flash her a smile. "You were right. It was selfish to hold myself back. I'm going to do better. Punch me if I don't."

"You might regret saying that."

I shake my head and press my cheek to her belly. I stay there for a few minutes, then slide back up to kiss her. I slide my tongue into her mouth and she tastes so sweet, her tongue against mine making me hard again. Fire lights up every nerve ending in my body and I lift my mouth from hers and kiss her bare shoulder, lick her skin. Her soft moan inflames my senses even more.

I kiss her throat and lick my way down between her breasts. Her head falls back and I take my time sucking at her tight little nipples, loving the sweetness, the feel of them fitting to my tongue, the soft resilient flesh pressed to my lips.

I slide my other hand down her back and cup one smooth cheek. She trembles and I move over her. Her hands reach for me and her soft murmurs have liquid pleasure running through my veins. Her body ripples under my hands as she gives herself up to me, and I get lost in it, in the sensation, in the heat, in the unbearable sweetness and erotic pleasure, but also in the emotion of it, swelling inside me, powerful and huge.

We roll and twist together, mouths fused in long, endless kisses, hands all over each other, sliding into a hazy, erotic dream. She bites my shoulder softly, licks my skin, makes me burn. I worship her with my mouth, my tongue, my hands, everywhere, slip my hand between her legs, find her soft, wet center, and rub my thumb over her clit until she vibrates.

I fall over her and bury my face in the side of her neck, breathing in the familiar jasmine scent of her. Something clenches in my chest. Struggling to breathe, I lever myself up above her.

Gazing up at me, her lips part, and she presses her hands to my chest. Our gazes hold for a long moment while heat builds and shimmers around us. My heart beats in a slow, heavy rhythm against my ribs at the raw emotion on her face, her shining eyes, soft mouth.

I lift her thigh, push into her body, and the overwhelming intimacy of it makes me feel like I'm flying up to heaven, lost, completely lost. I slide in and out of her silky heat as she squeezes around me, her hands pressed to my chest.

"Brandon."

I gaze down at her, riveted by the sight of her, feeling her lift into me as I thrust deeper, harder. I watch her eyelids drift closed, her mouth open, drink in her hot little whimpers and soft sighs that build to a climax of pleasure, her fingernails digging into my pecs in sweet bites of pain. I've never seen anything as beautiful as watching her come, her body tightening, her pussy rippling around me, and it undoes me, the surge of emotion and sensation inside me almost unbearable.

This is what I want. What I need. What I want to give. This is everything. It's sex. It's life. It's love.

My thighs quaking, my balls tight, the tension at the base of my spine sizzles painfully. My vision darkens, electricity sparking up my spine, searing my brain, singeing every nerve ending in my body. I drop my head between her breasts and I come, my cock jerking with every wrenching pulse inside her, so hard and violently, I'm afraid I'll completely lose my mind. And my heart. Forever.

Forever's not long enough, with Lola.

39

LOLA

"I'm coming with you."

"No, you're not."

Brandon frowns.

We're standing in my apartment and I'm about to leave to go to my parents' place. The time has come to tell them they're going to be grandparents.

"You don't need to come with me," I tell him. "I don't know how they're going to react. You don't need to be there for that."

"I'm coming." His voice is gentle but firm. "We're a team now, remember?"

I open my mouth to protest again. *I can do this by myself.*

But I don't have to.

I want Brandon to be part of my life. I want to do better at letting people in, at asking for help, at accepting help. Brandon is working to change how he deals with his past and his expectations for himself, trying to be a better team member, a better leader. A good father.

I have to work on things, too.

I smile at him. "Okay. Thank you."

His eyes soften and warm. "I want to take care of you. Even if you think you don't need it. I want to be there for you, no matter what."

I nod vigorously, swiping at my eyes. I know how he feels, because I want that too—to be there for him no matter what. It might be hard, but I have to let him. "Let's go."

He drives us to my family home in White Plains, parking on the street in front of the house. It's a Sunday afternoon in late August. The neighborhood is at the height of summer with lush flowers in flowerbeds and pots, the lawns neat.

I ring the bell but walk right in. Mom appears from the kitchen with a dish towel. "Hi, honey!" She spots Brandon behind me and her head tips.

"Hi, Mom. You remember Brandon?"

"Yes…of course. Come on in, both of you."

"Nice to see you again, Dr. McGrath."

"You too Brandon. I didn't expect to see you. And please call me Carrie." Her gaze flicks back and forth between us curiously. "Dad's out on the patio, go on out and join him."

I lead Brandon through the living room and dining room, and out sliding doors onto a patio.

Dad does a double take on seeing Brandon and jumps to his feet. "Oh hey," he says. "Brandon Smith."

Brandon smiles and shakes his hand. "Hello, sir. Good to see you again."

He's turning on his charm and both my parents are falling under its spell. I understand completely.

Dad fusses around offering us seats and drinks. Brandon takes a beer and I tell him I'll go get some water or something. I step into the kitchen and open the fridge.

"What do you need, honey?" Mom asks, stirring up something in a bowl.

"Mmm. Something to drink. Is this lemonade?"

"Yes."

I lift out the pitcher and set it on the counter while I find a glass.

"Why is Brandon here?" Mom asks in a low voice.

"He's…" I stop. It's still kind of new and kind of weird, but… "He's my boyfriend." I pour lemonade into the glass.

"I didn't know you were seeing him! Since that night we met him at the restaurant?"

"Um, before that." Sort of.

"You never said anything!" She stares at me with wounded eyes. "Why? Why did you lie to us?"

"I didn't lie!"

"I tried to get you to go out with so many nice men. You could have just said you were already seeing someone!"

I suck in a breath. "It's a little complicated, Mom."

She gazes at me sadly. "Why don't you talk to us? You didn't tell us about that promotion, either."

"Which I didn't get." I've already given them the disappointing news. I scrunch my face up. "I'm sorry, Mom. I didn't want to tell you because I knew you'd feel sorry for me if I didn't get it."

"Sorry for you?" She stares at me. "I wouldn't put it that way. We'd be *disappointed* for you. Because you wanted that. But we wouldn't…*pity* you."

"Really? Because I've always felt that. Every time I let you down—by not getting into med school. Or even law school. I felt like you pitied me because I wasn't good enough."

"Oh, Lola." Mom grabs my hands. "We've never pitied you. We only wanted the best for you."

My insides quiver and my breath quickens. "I know that."

"There is nothing to pity you for. You're a beautiful, intelligent, hard-working young woman with all kinds of determination and focus." She pauses. "Did you ever really want to be a doctor?"

I swallow past the lump lodged in my throat. "N-no. Not really."

She tilts her head, her eyes soft. "There you go. If you'd wanted that—*really* wanted that—you would have found a way to do it."

I stare back at her. "I felt like a failure."

"You were finding your way. Every failure is a lesson. Every challenge makes you stronger. And look at you. You're a successful businesswoman, recognized in your field. Maybe you didn't get this promotion, but you'll learn from it and you'll get the next one."

The pressure behind my eyes and cheekbones is painful. I fight back tears, my heart full. "Thank you, Mom."

She pulls me in for a long hug. I get control of my emotions, then step back and pick up my lemonade.

"You go outside. I'll just finish making this dip."

"Okay." I walk back out to the patio where Dad and Brandon are talking baseball.

Brandon lifts an eyebrow as I sit. I give him a shaky smile.

I sip my drink and listen to them, then Mom comes out with a big chip and dip bowl that she sets on the table.

"So this is obviously your big news," she says, taking the chair next to Dad. She turns to him. "Brandon and Lola are dating."

Dad beams. "I wondered. That's great."

"That's not all the news," I say. After my conversation with Mom, this feels a little easier. "I...we also wanted to tell you that...I'm pregnant."

It feels like a cone of silence descends on the patio.

I smile at Mom, her face drooping, her jaw slack, then Dad, who is blinking rapidly.

"Um...what?" Mom gapes.

"I'm pregnant. Having a baby. In March. Brandon's the father."

"I...I..."

"Wow," Dad says. "Uh...wow."

"It wasn't planned," I add. "So it was a surprise for us, too. We're happy about it now."

Brandon reaches out for my hand, and I love the feel of his big, strong fingers curled around mine. "And a little terrified," he adds with a smile. "Apparently that's normal for first time parents."

"Oh. Yes." Mom still hasn't got her shit together, her gaze bouncing around. "We always wanted more babies..."

Now it's my turn to blink. "You did?"

Mom's still flustered and blurts out stuff I've never heard. "Yes. Everyone in our families has lots of children. Big families."

"That's true," I murmur.

"We wanted lots of kids, too," she says. "But we couldn't…" An expression of pain flickers over her face.

"Oh." I stare at her. "I never knew that, Mom."

She shakes her head. "Well. We didn't talk about it. "

I exchange a glance with Brandon, a knot of concern between his brows. He squeezes my hand.

Now I'm thinking of my mom at my age, trying and wanting to get pregnant and have more babies and she couldn't. How heartbreaking and devastating that must have been. I always figured I was babied my whole life because I was an only child, but I never realized it was more than that.

"This is…wonderful," Mom says, still looking a little dazed. "Are you going to get married?"

Whoa. There's a loaded question. We know we want to be a family, but neither of us has mentioned married. We just started dating!

Brandon meets my eyes and smiles. "We haven't talked about that yet," he says easily.

Yet. What?

"I guess that doesn't really matter." Mom presses her hands to her cheeks. "I'm going to be a grandma!"

Dad laughs. "We didn't think this would ever happen."

I suck on my bottom lip. Obviously, they're surprised but they don't seem to be horrified.

Mom starts bombarding me with medical questions and seems almost excited at this news. This is going better than expected. I mean, I'm still not convinced they're not going to take over the baby's care and sign them up for med school. But if they do, I feel like I can handle it.

Brandon and I can handle it. We're a team now.

EPILOGUE

Lola

"Do you know if you're having boy or girl?"

I smile at Nadia Barbashev. "Not yet. We have an ultrasound appointment in a couple of weeks, and we might be able to find out."

We're at the Barbashev home for a pre-training camp party. Next week, training camp starts for the Bears. Also, it's my and Brandon's birthdays next week, so we're celebrating those a little early. Not a wild celebration since I can't drink and Brandon doesn't want to. The first part of training camp is medical testing and he's paranoid that he's put on weight over the summer, so he's given up alcohol like me and is eating a lot of vegetables and lean protein. I made him step on the scale and he's put on a whole two pounds compared to the weight he was listed at last year.

"Hey, did you guys see this?" Nate walks into the party and holds up his phone.

"What?" Igor Barbashev, Nadia's husband, asks.

"This article on the Hockey Times. About the Bears."

"What does it say?" Brandon asks.

Everyone's focused on Nate as he reads from his phone. "Citing losses of $42 million over the last two seasons and an inability to negotiate a more favorable lease at the Apex Center, owner of the New York Bears Vince D'Agostino has filed for reorganization under Chapter 11 of the Federal Bankruptcy Code."

"Holy shit." Brandon glances at me.

Whoa.

"What the hell," Owen Cooke mutters. He turns to his girlfriend, Emerie. She bites her lip.

Oh yeah…Brandon told me that the owner of the Bears is her stepfather.

"Did you know about this?" Owen asks her.

She shakes her head slowly. "No."

"What else does it say?" Brandon asks.

Nate reads more. "'This will have absolutely no effect on Bears games, on our payroll, on the club's playing schedule, or any of our hockey operations,' D'Agostino said in a statement. 'The team, our season-ticket holders and our corporate sponsors will be protected during this reorganization.'"

"Huh." Brandon frowns.

Nate keeps reading. "'This is no doubt disappointing,' NHL commissioner Thomas Yang said. 'But the team ownership has committed to work to resolve their financial issues and we are optimistic that the franchise will be financially and competitively successful in New York. There are rumors that former team star Johnny Risley is planning to sue the team over deferred payments still owed to him, but this has not been confirmed at this time.'"

"Risley's suing them?" Josh Heller says. "Wow."

"Planning to sue them," Brandon corrects. "But yeah, wow."

Emerie looks troubled by this. If her stepfather is in financial trouble, what does that mean for her? I have no idea. I don't know her at all; I'm meeting a lot of these people for the first time tonight.

"So…he says it doesn't change anything," Nate says.

"We still get paid," Igor jokes. "I hope."

"Hell, yeah." Hunter Morrissette nods.

"Hopefully they can work things out," Brandon says. "It sucks that we had to hear like this."

"True. Maybe they'll call a meeting tomorrow."

"We should buy the team," Easton Millar says with a grin. He looks at Josh and Owen. "Remember, we talked about that?"

"Ha. I remember talking about the fact that we don't have enough money to do that."

"Maybe we can get a good deal if Mr. D'Agostino is having cash flow problems."

"I wonder if he *will* sell it," Brandon muses. "A change in ownership might shake things up."

"And trade your ass away," Nate jokes.

I bite down hard on my bottom lip. Brandon and I just had a conversation about that the other day. His agent is talking to the team about a new contract for Brandon. He wanted to make sure I know what I'm getting into. If we're going to be together and he ends up playing for another team, I won't have a choice about quitting my job.

That doesn't freak me out the way it used to. But Brandon wants to stay here, so I really hope his agent can negotiate a new contract with the Bears.

Yesterday, I got a call from my friend Wendy. She and another colleague are leaving their jobs to start a consulting business. She asked if I'd be interested in joining forces with them because they want someone experienced in change management.

I was taken aback. I've never thought of starting my own business. At first, I was a definite no, but as we talked I started to warm up to the idea. Being my own boss has definite appeal. I really like and respect Wendy. And when I told her in the interests of full disclosure that I'm pregnant, she was fine with that. So we're going to meet for lunch next week, all three of us, to talk about it more.

Brandon and Nate have moved apart from the crowd a bit, closer to me.

"How's the knee?" Brandon asks Nate.

He scowls. "Fuck. I'm gonna fail the physical."

"Seriously?"

"Yeah. It's not getting better."

"You need to have that surgery."

Nate heaves a sigh. "I thought it would get better with time off over the summer. I've been doing rehab."

"You shouldn't have been playing during the playoffs."

Nate grimaces. "Probably not. Don't give me shit about it. You'd have done the same."

Brandon lifts a shoulder. "Yeah, probably. You should have had the surgery months ago."

"The doctors said conservative treatment and rest might be enough. I don't want to have fucking surgery if I can avoid it."

"Okay, I get that."

"I know." Nate shoves a hand into his longish dark hair. "I'm talking to the doctors again next week."

"You'll miss training camp."

"Yep."

"We could be without you for months if you have surgery."

"You'll survive." Nate flashes a wry smile. "We learned that last season, right?"

Brandon shakes his head. "Yeah."

I hate that Nate's hurt, but I also love watching him and Brandon talk. Seeing Brandon with his teammates and friends is new for me and I have to say the camaraderie and respect (which is obvious beneath all the trash talking) is fascinating. Also entertaining. And wonderful. These people care about Brandon, and I can see he cares about them. I love it.

"What's wrong with your knee?" I ask Nate.

"Meniscus tear." He makes a face.

My parents are both doctors, but I know nothing about knee injuries. "They can fix it with surgery?"

"Yeah."

"Then you should do it."

Nate grins. "Thank you, Dr. McGrath."

"Gah. Sorry. None of my business." Luckily he didn't take offense at my comment. I like Nate. He seems like an easygoing guy, though I've seen his intensity on the ice.

"No, no, it's fine. You're right. It makes total sense."

Nate's a key player for the Bears. They'll definitely miss him if he's out.

"Well, look on the bright side," he says. "Wait…what *is* the bright side?"

"You'll have time to work out and be in top physical shape by the time you come back," Brandon says, nudging him with an elbow.

"Or my career could be over," Nate says.

"Oh my God! He's just like you!" Eyes wide, I turn to Brandon.

"I am not!" Nate eyes bulge.

Brandan and I both laugh. "It's the superstitious thing," he says. "Imagine the worst. But your career isn't going to end because of a torn meniscus. Gunner had that surgery, too, and he's fine. And he's a goalie."

"Right." Nate's unconvinced. "Okay. I got this."

"You do," I tell Brandon's friend firmly. "You're a hockey player! You're brave. Courage is doing it even if you know it might hurt."

"So is stupidity," Nate says dryly.

Brandon chokes on a laugh.

I purse my lips and tilt my head. "Hmmm. True. Well, I guess that's why life is so hard!"

Brandon leans closer and murmurs, "You like it hard."

Now it's my turn to choke. "Brandon!"

Nate rolls his eyes. "Always gotta make it about sex."

"Sorry," Brandon says easily. "Okay, not sorry. We should go, huh?" He uses his big body to ease me toward the door.

Laughing, I look back over his shoulder. "Bye, Nate."

He grins. "Bye, kids. Have fun."

Thank you so much for reading Good Hands!

Bears Hockey continues with...

Scoring Big

And read on for an excerpt!

EXCERPT - SCORING BIG

Nate

"There's one more thing we can try."

My ears perk up like a puppy being offered a treat. "I'm up for anything. What is it?"

"PRP Therapy."

No, I'm not talking to a woman about bedroom activities, sadly.

I look blankly at the doctor.

"Platelet-rich plasma therapy is a new procedure for treating knee injuries. We get a small sample of your blood from your arm, process the blood in a centrifuge, and then inject the concentrated platelets directly into your knee."

"Jesus."

"It uses your body's own healing blood cells, the platelets, to stim-ulate the natural repair process."

I purse my lips, nodding. "Okay."

"We're using it on a lot of professional athletes," Dr. Perez says. "I think it's worth trying before we go to surgery."

Dr. Perez is a specialist who I've been seeing about my knee. It's been bugging me for months, since last season. During the playoffs it got worse, but I was determined to play as far as we could go. The team doctors weren't happy about that, but hey, I'm a hockey player; we play with broken bones and fresh stitches.

At the end of last season, they told me rest and rehab might help, so I've been doing everything I'm told. I've been at the gym faithfully four times a week, doing the exercises they tell me to do, strengthening my quads, avoiding squatting and pivoting, definitely not running. I've been swimming a few times a week. I ice my knee when I do too much, rest it, take the anti-inflammatories they tell me to, but I worry about taking them too much.

The bad news is, my meniscus tear isn't healing.

"Yeah, I'd rather not have surgery."

"Right. This is minimally invasive, with a faster recovery period than surgery. There's low risk of infection. That said, it doesn't work for everyone."

"Oh."

He gives me more details including some stats, but he doesn't have to convince me. It doesn't sound like there are big risks, only that it might not work. "What's the recovery time?"

"It takes about two to three weeks before healing."

"That's nothing."

He nods. "You'll need to restrict yourself to light activities after the injection, then we'll gradually work back up to exercise. Usually physical therapy along with PRP will have a better result."

"I can do that. Okay. I'm in. Let's do it."

He smiles. "We'll schedule another appointment for it."

"I need this fast. I need to be in shape for training camp in September."

"I think we can squeeze you in next week."

I don't even want to wait a few days, but I guess I can if I have to. "Okay. Perfect."

I zip from the doctor's office over to my ex-wife's place in Lincoln Square to pick up my daughter.

Quinn is the best thing in my life. My ex and I have a deal that she keeps Quinn during the season when I'm playing hockey and traveling, and I take her when I'm off for the summer. Right now, we're sharing custody until school ends.

"Daddy's here!" Brielle calls to Quinn when I walk into her apartment. "How was the appointment? Good news?"

"No."

"Oh. I'm sorry." She eyes me sympathetically.

We're on reasonably good terms. When I started playing for the New York Bears, I got caught up in the big city, pro-athlete lifestyle and dating a gorgeous actress made me feel like I'd really made it. She got pregnant and we got married. Then she fell for someone else—a billionaire who finances Broadway shows.

I met the guy a couple of times. He's everything I'm not—educated, polished, sophisticated. She talked about him all the time, and it bugged me, so when she told me they'd fallen in love I wasn't completely surprised. It still fucking hurt, though. But we both love Quinn more than anything and that's enough motivation for us to work together and make sure her life is everything it should be.

"Daddy!" Quinn bounces down the hall from her room. "Can we go to the beach this afternoon?"

"Hmm. It's kinda late today. How about we go to Central Park on the way home?"

"Can I ride the carousel?"

"Sure."

"Yay!"

I grin. "Okay. Let's go, pop tart."

I smile at Brielle as she bends to hug Quinn.

"See you tomorrow night," Brielle tells our daughter. "I'm off."

I nod, remembering the schedule. Brielle has a role in a Broadway play that's doing really well. Yes, financed by her husband.

I take Quinn's hand and she skips along beside me as we enter the park. Trees provide green shade from the heat of the sun and it's so pleasant and peaceful here in this oasis in the middle of the big city, the skyscrapers rising up at the edge of the park a reminder of the world outside the green space.

Quinn attempts to chase a squirrel across the grass, then we ride the carousel not once but twice, followed up by ice cream. My knee is aching and I need a rest so we find a bench to sit on.

There's a woman sitting on a bench next to us. She has a notebook and pen in her hand, but she's staring into space. Long golden-brown hair in messy waves is held back by a headband with a pink bow on it, showing off big eyes and high cheekbones. Her lips are full and rosy, a mouth made for kissing and sucking and…well, the rest of her looks incredible too, although her outfit is…interesting. A short flouncy pink skirt shows off a long length of fantastic leg, and a tight black tank top hugs her top curves. Chunky black boots complete the ensemble.

The woman turns and her eyes meet mine as I complete my once over. Jesus. Is she crying?

I frown, resisting the urge to jump up, stride over to her, and demand, *who hurt you?*

The woman's gaze lands on Quinn next to me. She takes in Quinn's red and silver face mask and bright red cape. And she smiles. Wow. That smile illuminates her face even more, lighting up her green eyes, something so attractive about her my breath stalls in my chest.

"Are you done your ice cream?" I ask Quinn.

"Yeah."

I clean her up with some paper napkins then walk to the trash bin, which means walking past the woman next to us. I drop our garbage into the bin but as I turn back, I forget to not pivot my knee. It locks. I stumble and hit the grass. "Shit!"

Oops. Language.

The woman jumps up. "Are you okay?"

Great. So impressive, sprawled on the ground in front of a beautiful woman. Heat runs up my neck into my face. Even my ears feel hot. "I think so." I try to gather my composure and get my legs under me to stand.

She extends a hand. Christ. I take it and try to save face. "Do you have a Band-Aid?"

Her eyebrows slope together, her gaze moving over me searching for blood. "Are you hurt?"

"I think I scraped my knee falling for you."

After a startled beat, she bursts out laughing. I grin sheepishly.

Quinn turns to look back and sees me sitting on the ground holding the woman's hand. I let her help me up, putting my weight on my good leg, and dust off my jeans as Quinn skips back to us.

"Your beauty must have made my knees weak," I add to the joke.

"Oh, that's bad," she says, but she's smiling.

"Daddy, what happened?" Quinn asks. "Is it your knee?"

"Yeah. I'm okay." I meet the woman's eyes. "Minor injury."

She gazes at me with concern. "Do you need any help?"

"No, I'm good."

"Hi," Quinn says to the woman.

"Hi." The woman's gaze softens into an almost wistful expression. I have no idea what that's about, but the fact that she likes kids...*my* kid...is hugely attractive. "I like your cape."

"Thanks. I'm Clover. From Harmonia."

I doubt this woman has a clue what she's talking about.

"Clover is my favorite," she replies seriously.

My bad. She does know. Harmonia is a comic book series about girl superheroes that's become hugely popular and is now turning into a whole universe.

"Me, too! And we went on the carousel. Twice!"

"Did you?" the woman replies. "Lucky you. I love the carousel."

"Me too. My favorite horse is the white one."

"Because Clover has a white horse."

"Yes!" Quinn jumps up and down.

"Hmmm. I don't have a favorite. It's been a long time since I was there."

"You should go," Quinn says. "Then we got ice cream. Strawberry shortcake."

"Oooh, I love those. You really *are* lucky." She shoots a smile my way. "Now I want ice cream."

"You can get one right over there." Quinn points.

Damn. This would be the perfect time to say, *I'll go get you one*, but I'm here with my daughter, not trying to pick up chicks.

I love my daughter. But she's a bit of a cock blocker.

Ugh. *Sorry, Quinn.*

That sounds like I'm on the prowl, but I'm really not. I mean, not anymore. When the season ended, I went on a sex bender. Actually, I've been doing that for years, but this year it didn't feel right. Maybe I'm getting old, but I want something more than hookups. Something real. And this woman is hot, but doesn't exactly give off "long term relationship" vibes.

"What's *your* favorite kind of ice cream?" Quinn asks the woman.

"Hmm. I do love strawberry. I used to go to a place that had strawberry cheesecake ice cream. It was amazing. I don't know if they're still around."

"I love strawberry, too. That sounds good."

Great, my daughter has so much in common with this woman. And all I want to do is get rid of her.

Kidding.

I repress a sigh. "We better get home, pop tart. You need dinner before bed."

"Daaaad. It's summer."

"I know. But I also know how you like to stall at bedtime and we need to start early if I want you asleep by midnight." I send Quinn's new friend a wry glance.

She smiles back. "A bedtime staller, huh."

"Daddy says I'm a kickass staller."

My face heats. "Quinn." We've talked about her language, but I take full responsibility for the extent of her profane vocabulary. I'm working on it.

"I don't know if that's something to brag about," I add, although I do sometimes admire her creativity. "Okay, let's go."

Quinn ignores me. "I love your headband."

"Thanks." The woman touches the pink bow. "I like bows."

"It's really pretty." Quinn eyes it covetously. "Daddy doesn't know how to do pretty hairstyles."

I grimace. It's true. Styling hair is definitely not one of my strengths.

"A headband is easy peasy," the woman says. She pulls it off, and motions Quinn closer. She slips the band over Quinn's head and uses her hand to smooth Quinn's blond hair back. "See?"

Quinn shoots me a longing glance.

"We can buy you a headband sometime," I say.

"Keep this one," the woman says gently. "It looks good on you."

"Really?" Quinn fingers the bow.

"Sure." The woman smiles at her.

"You don't have to do that," I say.

She lifts one delicate shoulder. "I know. It's fine."

"What do you say, Quinn?"

"Thank you!" She twirls. "Thank you, thank you, forever and ever!"

"Okay, let's go," I try again.

"Can you make it home okay?" the woman asks with a glance down at my knee.

I take a few steps. "I think I can." I hope. "Thanks, though."

"Okay. If you're sure."

If only I was alone. I'd be milking this for everything I could. The good thing is, I appear to have distracted her from whatever she was sad about.

Quinn takes my hand. "I'll help you walk, Daddy."

The woman smiles. "Hold onto him."

"I will."

We turn away from her, me limping. Dammit.

By the time we get home, my knee is hurting like a bitch. I'm going to have to ice it after all that walking. I can't even keep up with a fucking seven-year-old. I've had enough of this shit. That niggling worry about my knee is always there in the back of my mind. Because if I can't play hockey, I don't have much else going for me. Well, besides Quinn, obviously. She's the best part of my life.

AUTHOR NOTE

This is only the second time I've written an accidental pregnancy story and it was so much fun. I also loved mixing it up with the one night stand and friends with benefits tropes. Good Hands came together so easily for me, like a sweet puzzle that fit together perfectly. At least I thought it did, but after edits there were a lot of pieces that didn't quite work as well as I thought! Luckily Kristi Yanta is an expert at finding those things and suggesting fixes, and in the end, the story is so much better. So huge thanks, as always, to Kristi.

Thank you to my assistant Stacey Price, publicist Heather Roberts, and because I'm writing this at tax time, BIG thanks to my daughter who does my books, my accountant sister who gives me great money advice, and my accountant Sherrisse at MNP! I *hate* numbers, so you all make my life so much easier!

And always, always thanks to *you*, for buying my books, reading them, and sharing the love. I appreciate you so much!

OTHER BOOKS BY KELLY JAMIESON

Heller Brothers Hockey

Breakaway

Faceoff

One Man Advantage

Hat Trick

Offside

Power Series

Power Struggle

Taming Tara

Power Shift

Rule of Three Series

Rule of Three

Rhythm of Three

Reward of Three

San Amaro Singles

With Strings Attached

How to Love

Slammed

Windy City Kink

Sweet Obsession

All Messed Up

Playing Dirty

Brew Crew

Limited Time Offer

No Obligation Required

Aces Hockey

Major Misconduct

Off Limits

Icing

Top Shelf

Back Check

Slap Shot

Playing Hurt

Big Stick

Game On

Last Shot

Body Shot

Hot Shot

Long Shot

Bayard Hockey

Shut Out

Cross Check

Wynn Hockey

Play to Win

In It To Win It

Win Big

For the Win

Game Changer

Bears Hockey

Must Love Dogs…and Hockey

You Had Me at Hockey

Talk Hockey to Me

Bears Hockey II

The O Zone

Good Hands

Scoring Big

Stand Alone

Three of Hearts

Loving Maddie from A to Z

Dancing in the Rain

Love Me

Love Me More

Friends with Benefits

2 Hot 2 Handle

Lost and Found

One Wicked Night

Sweet Deal

Hot Ride

Crazy Ever After

All I Want for Christmas

Sexpresso Night

Irish Sex Fairy

Conference Call

Rigger

You Really Got Me

ABOUT THE AUTHOR

Kelly Jamieson is a best-selling author of over forty romance novels and novellas. Her writing has been described as "emotionally complex", "sweet and satisfying" and "blisteringly sexy." She likes coffee (black), wine (mostly white), shoes (high heels) and hockey!

Subscribe to her newsletter for updates about her new books and what's coming up.

Find out what's new...
www.kellyjamieson.com

Contact Kelly
info@kellyjamieson.com